IN DEFENSE OF CHARLOTTE

JOE CARGILE

Severn River Publishing
www.SevernRiverBooks.com

This is a work of fiction. Names, characters, businesses, places, events and incidents are either the products of the author's imagination or used in a fictitious manner. Any resemblance to actual persons, living or dead, or actual events is purely coincidental.

ISBN: 978-1-64875-356-5 (Paperback)

ALSO BY JOE CARGILE

Blake County Legal Thrillers

Legacy on Trial

In Defense of Charlotte

The Wiregrass Witness

To find out more about Joe Cargile and his books, visit

severnriverbooks.com/authors/joe-cargile

1

Lawton Crane walked through the door to his classroom at ten minutes after eleven—late by his standards. The entrance of the first-year law professor stifled the hum of conversation in the room. He made his way to the lectern and offered a nod to the roughly seventy-five students seated before him. Most waited with their laptops open, looking down on him from one of the six elevated rows. He stepped to the center of the room.

"My apologies for being late this morning."

The mass of young faces stared back at him, silent. They only knew the Crane of the present—the fraud of circumstance.

"I am going to allow myself to remain in the classroom on this one occasion. After all, it is the last day of the course."

A grin crept into Lawton Crane's face as his comment spurred a few laughs throughout the room. Jokes were a rarity in the rookie professor's classroom, and he appreciated the charitable reaction to his lame attempt at humor. He was a forty-one-year-old, recently divorced attorney that was still recovering from a hard-charging career in private practice. Though Crane had yet to cement his reputation among the students of Georgetown, he understood funny was not the odds-on favorite for his defining character trait. A fact that would have disappointed a younger, more carefree version of himself.

The practice of law changed people, though, and Crane was no exception. After fifteen years of grappling with demanding partners, judges, and opposing counsel, the business of suing others had created a machine of a man. One that worshipped a harsh, big-law environment ruled by the clock. A world where only the most dogged and determined survived. For that reason, when Crane made his foray into academia, he decided to bring with him a rigorous attendance policy. One intended to prepare his young students for the world that awaited them. On the first day of the course, he announced his policy proudly. It was simple. Arrive early or do not come at all.

As Crane looked down at the watch on his wrist, he almost chuckled to himself. He'd honored his inflexible attendance policy throughout the entire semester, sometimes kicking students out of his classroom when they arrived only seconds late through the door. The first offenders attempted to justify their tardiness, but Crane refused to hear argument on the subject. Now, as Crane stood at the head of the class, he knew exactly what the twentysomethings seated before him were thinking: *There will always be someone above the law.*

"We have a guest speaker that will be joining us in a few minutes," he said, after a short pause. "I expect you will find his message to be intriguing, maybe even inspiring. We shall see."

The professor's announcement changed the plan for the day and brought on whispers throughout the classroom. A young man with the last name Gilroy raised his hand. Crane pointed in the direction of his student.

"What about the review for the final exam?" Gilroy asked, eager to take the first arrows for his classmates. "The syllabus specifically outlined today's lecture as the final exam review day."

Crane nodded as he listened. He'd expected at least one dissenter in the group.

"The material for the final review will be posted on the student portal," Crane replied. "It will be accessible to you all this afternoon. If you have attended my classes, like we all know you have, Mr. Gilroy, then you'll have all the information that may appear on my final exam."

Crane scanned the surprised faces of his students for any other questions. Though he'd never tell them, he too had been surprised that morning when the phone call came in from the guest speaker's office. Gilroy's hand rose again.

"The syllabus stated that we would have an in-person review of the course before the end of the semester. My study schedule is centered around today's review."

All watched as the professor stepped out from behind the lectern. He ran a hand through his thick hair in a disarming manner, slowly walking along the front row of the class as if it were the edge of a jury box. Lawton Crane had once been a talented litigator with a firm of heavy hitters on Louisiana Avenue. He'd spent fifteen years there as a mercenary, ripping witnesses and opposing parties to pieces for a handsome rate per hour. The muscle memory developed through countless depositions, hearings, and trials had not left him. Though he missed little about his prior life, he did miss the occasional scrap of fresh meat.

"Mr. Gilroy, as you know, this is—"

"Professor Crane?" interrupted a familiar voice, its timbre slicing the tension in the room with ease. "I'm sure Stephen here just forgot that the syllabus also allows for changes to be made to the course schedule without notice. With finals starting next week, he is probably just really stressed out like the rest of us."

The comment brought on nervous laughter from the onlookers. The professor kept his eyes on Gilroy as he thought about a response. In the law school ecosystem, Stephen Gilroy was what was known as a gunner. A know-it-all, for lack of a better term. Quick to raise a hand and offer shallow input. Crane loathed the gunners in his courses and relished the opportunity to humble them. There was little time for that today, though. Instead, the professor shifted his gaze to his favorite student. A young woman from Blakeston, Georgia—Charlotte Acker.

"I can certainly understand, Ms. Acker," Crane replied, allowing a hint of sarcasm to enter his voice. "I was a law student myself some years ago."

"I would certainly hope so. This school is charging me an arm and a leg to take classes here."

More laughter ensued. Crane ignored the playful comment.

"That is why I am sending out a video review for the class to watch this evening. Any questions can be emailed to me or addressed in office hours tomorrow afternoon. Is that acceptable to you, Ms. Acker?"

She smiled. "Perfectly acceptable, Professor Crane."

Crane surveyed the room for any other challengers. He saw none. "Anything else?"

Charlotte placed her elbows on the desk in front of her and leaned forward.

"Who is the guest speaker?"

Crane held Charlotte's gaze and felt a tinge of guilt as he considered his response. Charlotte sat three rows up, almost at the center of the room. A fitting spot for her, as she was something of a celebrity among her classmates. Dark hair framed her face and fell just to her shoulders. A yellow quarter-zip fit easily on her athletic frame. Crane knew the young law student had been a two-time National Women's Track Athlete of the Year at the University of Oregon. He knew she'd also been recognized as an Academic All-American each year she ran for the Ducks. She was impressive, to say the least. Still, Charlotte Acker's athletic career had not provided the foundation for her notoriety. She had the trial of her late father to thank for that.

Charlotte's legal father—Lee Acker—had been the accused in a murder trial that took place five years earlier in her small hometown in Georgia. The case received national attention as the victim—Jake Collins—had been the local district attorney and only son of a US senator. The murder rocked Charlotte's small Southern town, sending shock waves that stretched from southern Mexico to the halls of the Capitol. The trial ended without a verdict when Charlotte's father was killed by the matriarch of the victim's family. Lee's killer—Lucy Collins—went on to be indicted and tried as well. After an artful presentation of self-defense, Lucy Collins received a resounding "not guilty" from a jury of her peers. A jury that many still believed had been bought and paid for by some of the oldest money in Blake County, Georgia.

Several documentaries tried to explain the collections of wild theories that still surrounded the deaths of Jake Collins and Lee Acker. Theories that included cartel hit men, secret love affairs, and political scheming originating from some of the most prominent offices in the nation's capital.

Crane had watched a couple of the documentaries and did not know what to believe. No one could tell the whole story. The remaining Ackers and Collinses had feuded through interviews and other means over the last five or six years, each trying to rewrite the story. Charlotte Acker was the only one that refused to join the fray. She was the only one that refused to tell her story.

"Professor Crane?" Charlotte said again, breaking the professor's train of thought. "You have us all on the edge of our seats."

Crane looked away from Charlotte, unsure how the surprise guest's appearance that morning would affect her. The speaker's decision to choose this day to drop in on Crane's classroom had all the makings of an ambush. One that Crane felt complicit in. He looked toward the door of the classroom and saw a man with a crew cut peering into the room. Crane knew the look. A bulky frame squeezed into a single-breasted suit, off the rack. The man motioned his thick arm at Crane.

"Excuse me," Crane said as he walked to the door, turning his back to Charlotte and the rest of the class. "I shouldn't be long."

Crane made his way out into the hallway. When he returned, three men followed in tow.

"It is my pleasure to introduce you to our guest speaker this morning," Crane announced as he arrived at his post. "Please give a warm welcome to an esteemed member of our 117th United States Congress, duly elected United States Senator from Georgia, William H. Collins."

A man in a navy suit stepped to the center of the room. He wore a green tie that ignited the color in his eyes. A politician by trade, he smiled at the group and shook hands with a few students seated on the front row. At sixty-five years old, he remained trim, only showing his age in the wrinkles near his eyes and gray flecks that textured his hair. He needed no introduction. Still, he looked out on the group of students and started in a smooth South Georgia drawl.

"Please, call me Bill."

2

Anger flashed in Charlotte as she considered her options. She could get up and leave. No one would blame her. Bill Collins had been there that night —the night her father was murdered. As she looked on at the politician standing at the front of the room, she could still hear the crack of gunshots. She could still hear the words her father said as she left him that night. Charlotte started packing her bag to make her exit, making no effort to conceal her movements.

"I'm not here to take up a lot of your time," Bill said, comfortable standing at the center of attention. "My office only spoke with Professor Crane this morning, but we wanted to get this little presentation scheduled before your summer break. I understand you're all very busy getting ready for your final exams, so thank you for your patience with me."

Charlotte looked up from her packed bag and realized the senator's eyes were on her.

"I don't want anyone to leave without hearing what I have to say, though."

Charlotte locked eyes with the politician just as she was about to lift out of her seat. She held his gaze, challenging him to look away. He stared back with a softness that surprised her. The last time she'd seen him in person was in a courtroom back home some years ago. They were seated on different sides of the aisle that day—they still were.

"Raise your hand if you have any interest in going into politics," Bill said as his attention returned to the rest of the room. He moved intentionally as he spoke. "Any level of politics."

Charlotte watched the senator as he worked the room. She thought back to the way he looked at the last trial in the Blake County Courthouse. During his testimony, he'd explained to the jury that he believed Charlotte's putative father—her *real* father—had been his late son, Jake. He'd called her his granddaughter several times throughout his testimony. She'd refused to acknowledge him in hers. A decision she didn't regret.

"Come on now, don't be shy," the senator said, prodding the group. "I know this room is full of smart, hungry, and ambitious young minds that plan to make big changes in this world. I don't just want to know who wants to run for office, though I know some of you do. I'm also talking about working in politics. Policy advisers, consultants, lobbyists, and so on."

Hands went up throughout the room.

"Here we go, I see a few now. Thank you."

Bill paused and shoved both hands in his pockets. He looked down at his feet as if thinking hard about his next question.

"Those of you that don't have a hand up, why are you reluctant to work in the political arena?" The senator let the question hang in the air. He scratched the back of his neck as he appeared to ponder the question himself. "Shouldn't every one of us want to use our talents to improve this great nation? Shouldn't we serve our fellow citizens?"

One of Charlotte's favorite classmates raised a hand. As if on cue, the senator looked up from his Oxfords and pointed in her direction.

"I don't see politics as the place to start if I want to improve things, Senator Collins."

The comment didn't appear to surprise the politician.

"Just call me Bill," he replied. "Tell me more, if you will."

"Okay, Bill. Well, many of us want to improve our communities. I imagine some of us even aspire to improve the entire country, maybe the entire world. For me, though, that is not what politics is about."

The senator nodded as she spoke. He did a masterful job in conveying to the room that he was, in fact, listening.

"Politics is about power, Bill. It's about influence. It's about the Party. Politicians serve only those that voted for them and contributed to their campaigns."

"There is power that comes with the responsibilities of elected office," Bill replied in a convincing tone. "That power—that influence, as you say— that is what gives one the ability to implement change, right?"

"Maybe it does," she replied, pushing back. "But that is not what you, or your colleagues for that matter, choose to do with your power. Instead, you mount attacks on the opposition for political gain. You take unreasonable positions on everyday issues. You obstruct until the next election cycle comes around. A few get what they want, but nothing of real substance ends up getting done for the rest of us."

Bill bobbed his eyebrows, accepting the response. The seasoned politician was no stranger to criticism. Those that kept tabs on his career knew he played defense better than most.

"So, come work for me, then," he replied. "Help me change things."

Silence blanketed the room.

"I'm serious," Bill continued as he took a few steps closer to his target. "I agree with a lot of what you just said about politics in Washington. I want to change that. I need smart people on my team that are not afraid to speak up. That are not afraid to remind me of my role in the process."

More silence. He waited for her response.

"I'm sorry, Senator—I mean, Bill," she said after a long pause. "The world of politics just isn't for me."

Charlotte tried to gauge the senator's reaction. To see if he'd expected the response. He proved difficult to read. A skill she knew served him well in his work.

"Is politics for anyone, really?" Bill said with a wink, bringing on some laughter from the students.

The mood lifted again in the room, and a few more hands went up. The senator acknowledged each one with his eyes without inviting input. He continued.

"Every single one of my colleagues in Congress is just a person like you and me. They come from big cities and small towns. They went to fancy schools and public universities. They are not special, nor are they perfect. The legislative process is not perfect, and it never will be because it is a human endeavor from start to finish."

The senator had the full attention of his audience.

"Some of the best candidates for political office are the ones who would never consider running. Those are the people we need in politics, and the kind of interns we need in my office this summer."

Charlotte looked down the row of desks. A number of her classmates appeared enamored with the proposition.

"I'm not looking for students hungry for schemes, backroom deals, or mudslinging. You need not apply if that's the kind of experience you want on Capitol Hill."

Bill folded his hands in front of him and looked up at Charlotte.

"If you disagree with my agenda, fine. If you disagree with me, even better. I want you to know that I am pivoting in my career. The candidates that win out in the interview process will help in the transformation of my agenda while interning this summer."

The senator turned to one of his security types standing at the back of the room. He pointed to a red folder swallowed under the man's massive arm. The senator took the folder and turned back to the classroom. He held the folder up for all to see.

"I have in hand a stack of applications with the information about the time and place for interviews with my office. Fill out an application and send it to my office. I intend to interview every student that applies."

His eyes found Charlotte one more time as he placed the folder on a desk at the front of the room.

"I hope to see you there."

3

Jimmy Benson sat alone at a table by the diner's back window. He ate lunch and watched a heavy rain beat down on the parking lot outside, a sloppy rain that washed over the Alabama landscape. He'd driven all morning in the stuff and still had five hours to go.

"More coffee?" a voice asked over his shoulder, taking his attention away from the window.

"Yes, ma'am," Jimmy said, slowly turning in his seat to look at the waitress, his belly pressing against the table fixed to the floor beneath the booth. Earlier that morning, he'd strung together three or four hours of sleep after stumbling in from a bar in Jackson, Mississippi. It had been restless sleep, though. He'd been running on caffeine and some Yellow Jacket knockoffs since rolling out of bed. "Let me get that coffee in a to-go cup. I need to be getting on down the road."

"You bet," the woman said. "I'll get you the check, too."

Jimmy nodded at the waitress as she turned away from him. When driving a route, he liked to stop at familiar places. It helped him feel at home on the road. He'd been driving trucks for seventeen years now, and there were few places along the highways he didn't recognize. He certainly recognized the waitress fetching his coffee. Knew her from his last few trips through Dothan. He liked the way she always flirted with him.

"You been driving all day in this rain?" the woman asked as she returned with the bill and a Styrofoam cup.

"Oh yeah," Jimmy said as he stretched his arms behind him. "Worn out, too. Been trying to push it on down the road, but it seems like amateur hour is every hour today. All these people turn their flashers on as soon as a good rain starts coming down. Drives me crazy."

The woman smiled at Jimmy, encouraging him to continue.

"I've been driving Peterbilts over these roads for the last couple of decades," Jimmy explained, pointing to a rig parked at the fuel station next door. The outline of the truck was barely visible through the sheets of rain. "I could drive that thing from here to Jacksonville with my eyes closed."

"I know that's right," replied the waitress. "Not too many old-school professional drivers like you on the roads anymore. It's a damn shame."

Jimmy smiled. "It sure is. See, that's why I plan to start my own company. I'll show these new drivers how trucking should be done. All these federal regulations and digital crap keep pushing the experienced drivers off the roads. These young guys need to know how it's supposed to be done."

"I'd love to hear more about that sometime," the waitress said as she started toward her next table. She looked back at him one more time. "I see you in here every now and then. Make sure and ask for me next time."

Jimmy watched her as she walked away, then struggled out of the booth. He made his way out of the restaurant and back into the pouring rain. The noise from the raindrops beating the pavement took over, and Jimmy pulled the bill of his cap low, trudging toward his rig through the puddles in the parking lot. He heaved at the door to the truck and climbed inside the cab. Shaking the rainwater off his cap, he started the engine and cranked the air. He popped the cap to a small bottle and flipped a pill into his mouth, washing it down with a swig of coffee. He smacked his lips and shifted the truck into gear.

Thirty minutes later, at one forty-five that afternoon, Jimmy crossed the Alabama-Georgia line on Highway 84. He rode in the left lane at seventy-four miles per hour as his Peterbilt crossed the Chattahoochee River into Blake County, Georgia.

Ever since she was a small girl, Maya Jones's grandfather had been telling the story of the Valentine's Day tornadoes. The story had evolved over the years, but it always began the same way. *He was standing on the front porch of his old house on Spare Street, and he could hear it coming—it sounded like a train.*

Maya thought of her grandfather as she stared out the window of the car. She rode in the front passenger seat. Her brother and his best friend, Alvin, sat in the back. Maya looked over at her mother. She sat rigid in the driver's seat, gripping the steering wheel with both hands. Her mother hated to drive in bad weather and had already thoroughly shushed everyone in the car. With the radio off, all Maya could hear was the sound of the rain on the roof of their little Corolla and the clipping of the blinkers fixed to the emergency setting.

"I said be quiet, you two!" her mother shouted over the sound of the rain. "I can barely see out the window. Y'all cutting up back there sure isn't helping."

Maya's brother laughed harder. "Mom, us not talking won't help your eyes see any better!"

"Son, how about you say, 'yes, ma'am'? Now, quiet down. I shouldn't have to ask you twice."

"Yes, ma'am," came the humbled reply. "Why don't you just pull over if it's that bad, Mom?"

No response was given to the question. Maya glanced over at the driver's seat and saw her mother's driving stance remained unchanged. Eyes still fixed on the road ahead.

"It looks like it might be slowing up," her mother said as she eased the car into the left lane. They were crossing the bridge from Alabama into Georgia. "These storm fronts always slow down before they cross the river."

"You sound just like Grandaddy."

The rain slackened a bit, and the sound of the wipers rubbing on the windshield grew louder. Her mother reached over to turn the emergency flashers off, and the speed of the wipers slowed.

"Worse things have been said about me," her mother replied, glancing away from the road for a moment to smile at her daughter. "Your grandaddy is right, though. The storms—especially the ones with tornadoes in them—they slow down before they jump the river."

"I know," Maya said. "He says that's why they do all their destruction over here in Blake County."

"Maybe so."

The rain started to pick up again as they passed a car that rode slowly in the right lane. The boys were cutting up again in the back seat, so her mother turned around and leveled a stare to quiet them down. As she did, the car wiggled on the road, sliding slightly to the left. Her mother mashed the brake pedal and the car slowed, pulling them half into the right lane. Maya looked over at her mother and saw her working to turn the steering wheel, trying to correct the vehicle.

She heard the sound first—*smash!*—then felt the violent jerking of the car. The Corolla swung back around to the left, spinning into the fast lane. She could see the tall wiregrass in the median, thick and green. They seemed to be heading toward the grass, but then Maya felt the car stop, still in the roadway. The boys screamed in the back seat, as did her mother. Maya's heart seemed to push against her chest as it tried to right itself from the unexpected tailspin.

That's when she heard it—*it sounded like a train.*

The state trooper pulled his rain slicker from the trunk of his car. As he slipped it on over his uniform, he eyed the emergency vehicles that were already on scene. Four road deputies from the Blake County Sheriff's Office. A truck from one of the nearby volunteer fire departments. An ambulance, probably from the hospital over in Dothan.

"Where's the driver of that semi?" he yelled to the closest deputy, a young buck directing traffic.

The deputy pointed an orange traffic wand toward the ambulance. "In there. He's still getting checked out."

"He injured?"

"Nah," he replied, shaking his head. "He made out better than anyone."

The trooper's eyes drifted over to the mangled Toyota resting upside

7

Lawton Crane sat five blocks from Lafayette Square at the newest tapas restaurant in the District. He wore the casual attire of a law professor, jeans and a button-down. Sipping a Spanish beer, he watched the after-work crowd crawl in from the surrounding buildings. Most looked tired, thirsty. The trendy menu attracted the movers and shakers of the city—all plotting their next conquest. Not far removed from that life, Crane remembered the feeling of climbing onto a barstool after a long day in the office. Though he missed the excitement of celebrating battles won in the long campaign, he didn't miss the hours grinding in the trenches. That sacrifice had proved too costly.

Glancing around the restaurant, Crane noticed a familiar face from his old law firm a few tables over. A hungry young lawyer he and his former partners poached from the Department of Justice's Antitrust Division a few years back. The mid-level associate nodded in Crane's direction as he also made the connection. Crane tried to discern whether there was a sliver of envy in the old colleague's face as he nodded back. He hoped so.

From the patio door entered a blond-haired man wearing a charcoal suit. He started toward Crane's table with the confident stride of an operator. Crane had seen the man in documentaries. A mention here. An interview there. Not a main character, but one content in the shadow of a great family. He looked every bit the part of a man with many faces. As he neared, a hand was extended.

"Mr. Crane, I appreciate you meeting with me," the man said. He wiped sweat from his brow with a small handkerchief as he took his seat. "Spent my years as a kid growing up in the Deep South. This heat shouldn't get to me the way it does."

Crane nodded in response to the comment. He knew a fair amount about the man's history. As much as one could dig up over the course of a few days. Born and raised in Atlanta, Georgia. College at a private school in Macon. A member of the political underbelly since stepping foot inside the Beltway some twenty years ago.

"In all the years I've lived in Washington, I can't remember a spring as hot as this one," Crane replied, lifting a bottle of sparkling water from the center of the table. He offered it to the man.

"I'm going to need a stronger drink," the man said with a wink as he accepted the water being poured in his glass. "What are you having, Professor?"

"This is a beer out of Galicia. The server recommended it. And just call me Lawton."

"That's fine, Lawton."

With a small wave of the hand, Crane caught the attention of their server. The men ordered drinks and added a set of small plates from the menu.

"Now, tell me what you know about the girl," the man said once the server stepped away from the table. He crossed his legs and leaned back in his chair as if preparing for a long story. "What do you know about her life now?"

Crane felt uncomfortable with the man's eyes on him. He'd sat through plenty of depositions and meetings with the unscrupulous. The type never bothered him. There was something unnatural about this political operative, though. Something personal in the way he approached the matter at hand.

"You mean Charlotte Acker," Crane replied, waiting for some reaction on the man's face.

The man shrugged and leaned forward. He tapped a small flower vase near the table's edge as if it were a microphone and said: "Of course, Lawton. Is this thing on? We are here to talk about the senator's grand-daughter. Who else would I be asking about?"

Crane ignored the comment, pausing as two fresh beers appeared on the table. He eyed the glass placed in front of him as he thought about his response. Tiny bubbles in the golden liquid ping-ponged about as they raced to the surface. He followed the eager spheres with his eyes as they made their journey to destruction. A few held tight to the walls of the glass. Only breaking free when the pressure became too much to bear. Their fate at the top of the liquid was inevitable.

Crane picked the beer up from the table. The glass felt cool in his hand. He'd stopped with the liquor last fall. Not beer, though. Not yet. Though he missed bourbon, and gin, and vodka, too, Crane refused to set aside the beer. He'd been blessed with immense willpower, and he stuck with his self-imposed rule each day.

"She is a remarkable young woman," Crane said, returning to the conversation. He took a measured pull from his glass and returned it to the table. "I have some bright, hardworking students in all my classes. She is head and shoulders above all of them. No question."

The man nodded, listening.

"If your boss plans to bring her into his office, he needs to be sure he can trust her. She sees the whole board, if you know what I mean. When talking about real-world legal issues in a lecture, she offers real-world solu-tions. Most of these students she is sitting next to in class won't make that leap until they are first-year associates holed away in some big-law bullpen."

"So, she is smart?" the man replied. "I get it."

"Smart as a whip, resourceful, motivated," Crane said with a shrug of the shoulders. "I could go on. She is the real deal."

"And nice to look at," the man replied with a smirk. "Just like her mother."

There it is again, Crane thought. That look. It's personal to this man. "Has she applied for—"

"Lawton," the man said, interrupting. "You should have seen her mother when she was eighteen, nineteen. Fine little fox. I *mean* fine."

The man leaned forward in his chair, animated by the memory.

"I grew up in Cobb County, but I'd run down to South Georgia to see family during the summers. A cousin of mine ran with her on occasion, and I remember a time when we all went out on the lake together. That girl wore nothing but a small blue bikini all day. I couldn't stop looking. No one could. I still think about that bikini."

Crane tried to think of something to say.

The man winked at him as he took a sip of his beer, then added: "She was something else, Professor."

"I bet," Crane replied, then redirected the conversation to more comfortable territory. "Has Charlotte applied for the internship?"

The man nodded. "I believe she applied this afternoon. I'm sure Bill will want to meet with her on Monday morning."

"How do you know she'll accept the position?"

"She will."

Crane and the man leaned back away from the table as the server returned with two small plates. The smell of *gambas al ajillo* and *croquetas de jamón* wafted in between them.

"You are pretty confident she will take the internship," Crane said as he picked a fork up from the table. He pierced one of the thicker pieces of garlic shrimp on the plate and brought it to his mouth. "You seem to have gotten lucky the last time you tangled with the Ackers. You really want to press that luck again?"

"You say I got lucky, huh?"

Crane nodded, chewing the shrimp—enjoying the moment. He took another sip of his beer. He wanted another.

"Seems like it very well could have been you on trial down there in South Georgia. It's a good thing your boss had half of law enforcement in his pocket, because *State of Georgia v. John Deese* may not have received that same careful attention from the jurors. Probably wouldn't have warranted the same investment, either."

The man—John Deese—narrowed his eyes at Crane. Their server hovered nearby, and Deese waved him over. He looked across the table at Crane and back to the server.

"Bring us two shots of bourbon and the check."

"Both of those can be for you," Crane quickly said as the server walked away. "I'm fine with what I have here."

"We both know that isn't your last beer of the night, Lawton. Have a taste of Kentucky nectar with me. It works on you quicker. Then you can go back to your beer."

Crane sat quiet for a moment, surprised by the comment. How could he know? No one knew about his self-imposed rule. Not his ex-wife, therapist, trainer. No one.

"My job is to know things, Lawton," Deese said with a smile. "I do my job well."

"As do I, John."

Two shot glasses appeared between the men, along with the bill. Deese picked the small glass up and nodded at the one in front of Crane.

"We will see how good you are at your job."

Deese threw his back, while Crane avoided eye contact with his own shot of brown.

"Do your job, Professor," Deese said as he stood from the table. "Then we'll see if you turn out to be as lucky as me."

Deese patted Crane on the shoulder and made his way toward the front door of the restaurant. Crane didn't acknowledge the man as he left. Pulling a credit card from his wallet, Crane placed it with the check and waited. He stared down at the small glass in front of him.

Harmless, he thought.

Crane picked up the glass and felt the familiar weight in his hand. He held it for a moment, considering what new lies he would tell himself tomorrow. What new argument he would craft to justify his actions. He could already feel a persuasive opening statement percolating within him. One that he would make to himself in the morning to stave off the self-loathing. That could wait, though. He'd be a better man tomorrow.

Crane threw the shot back. His decision had been made. It was Charlotte that would be forced to make hers.

8

Maggie pressed the button for the seventh floor and waited as the metal doors slid to a close. She stood alone in the hospital elevator with a small arrangement of flowers in one hand, her folio in the other. The elevator hummed as it began its ascent, then slowed to a stop two floors below her destination. The doors opened, and a man wearing a white coat stepped into the elevator. He nodded at Maggie in a professional manner, noticing the fluorescent orange visitor's badge clipped to her blouse. He returned to reviewing records on a tablet before the doors closed again. From the corner of her eye, Maggie read the name stitched on his coat—Dr. Jay R. Prakash.

The elevator arrived at the seventh floor, and the doors opened to a hallway that looked no different than those below it. Eli Jones leaned against the wall opposite the elevator doors, a cell phone cradled in his hand, waiting.

"Just the people I need to see," Eli said as Maggie stepped into the hallway. He pushed off the wall to stand up straight and started walking toward the bank of elevators. "Dr. Jay, can we all talk a minute about my little sister?"

Maggie turned and glanced again at the doctor exiting behind her. The tablet was now tucked under an arm, and his eyes were on Eli.

"Of course," the doctor replied, his tone void of any agitation. "Can we talk when I come by her room to look in on her? I'll make her the last stop on my rounds."

"This won't take long. She is still pretty shaken up, and I think you both need to hear this."

The doctor glanced again at Maggie. He'd obviously picked up on Eli's use of the word "we" in the request. Maggie knew the rules around discussing private medical information with third parties. Rules that often prevented doctors from discussing a patient's treatment without the patient's consent.

"I'm Dr. Jay Prakash," the doctor said, now turning to Maggie. He didn't offer a hand, a social custom he'd probably abandoned during the recent pandemic. "I'm an internist here with the hospital. Most of my patients call me Dr. Jay."

Maggie nodded to the doctor and tried to place the accent. She guessed it had been cured somewhere out on the West Coast.

"You should have gone into delivering babies," Maggie said with a smile. "'Rock the Baby with Dr. J' would have been a killer marketing campaign for your medical group."

The doctor's face reported some surprise with the vintage reference to the old Sixers' great.

"See, I'm a Laker fan, that wouldn't work for me," he replied, offering his own smile.

"A California boy?"

The doctor nodded, considering the visitor's disarming approach. All kinds joined his patients at their bedside, and he was no stranger to meeting with concerned visitors. It also wasn't unheard of to find an opportunist in the halls of a hospital.

"I'm Maggie, by the way," she added. "Born and raised a Heat girl."

"I can respect that. Are you a friend of the Jones family?"

Maggie nodded again. No sense in hiding her intentions. "And their lawyer."

"Ah, nice to meet you, then."

Eli inserted himself into the exchange with a confidence that surprised Maggie.

"Look, I just want you to both be aware of a couple of things. Maya is starting to remember everything that happened during the wreck. At first, she couldn't tell me how she got out of the car, or even where she was when the paramedics got there."

"There can be memory loss after a traumatic event," the doctor said. "It won't be uncommon if it takes her time to organize her thoughts around what happened. In fact, she may piece together a memory of what happened based on other sources, or she may never remember everything. In memory reconstruction, there can be any number of combinations."

"I get that," Eli replied. "But now she is acting like the moment before the wreck happened couldn't be clearer in her memory. She won't stop talking about it. I just had to step out of the room to get some air earlier because I couldn't keep rehashing everything with her."

In Maggie's prior work as a criminal defense lawyer, she'd been forced to face off against eyewitnesses to crimes her clients *allegedly* committed. Oftentimes those witnesses were close to a traumatic event, sometimes even the victim of violence. It had been explained to her more than once that it was a common misconception that people could remember events more clearly after experiencing a high-stress situation. A fallacy she had exposed and educated jurors about during the course of previous trials. In fact, Maggie knew what the body of research around the issue suggested. Acute stress could have the opposite effect on one's memory. It could critically impact a person's recollection of an event.

"What is she saying she remembers?"

"My mother screaming, for one. She remembers my mother yelling about the steering wheel not working. She says my mother tried to avoid hitting the car in the lane beside them but that my mother's car wouldn't turn."

Maggie couldn't help but offer a solution on the spot. "The crash report notes that it was raining heavily before the wreck. Maybe they were hydroplaning."

Eli shook his head.

"No, I asked her that. She remembers my mother jerking the wheel from right to left, trying to get the car to move. She thinks the steering wheel quit working or something. At least, that's what she remembers."

"I imagine that—"

"She also remembers getting out of the car now," Eli continued, not letting anyone take control of the conversation. "I know she is going to mention it to both of you. She remembers the glass everywhere, and the fire starting to spread from the front of the car. She told me she tried to pull my little brother from the back seat. She remembers the blood everywhere. She remembers it all."

"It's a traumatic event, Eli," the doctor said in a calm voice. "She is physically bruised and cut up from the wreck, but the emotional harm may be where the real treatment is focused once she is released. That's not my specialty, but she will receive the attention she needs. I'll make sure of it."

Eli nodded. "I just wanted you to both be prepared to hear about it."

Maggie's mind had already started running through young Maya Jones's options. She'd not only have to drill down on the damages that could be claimed in a lawsuit, but also on the parties that should have to open their pocketbooks to pay the victims and their families. Maggie's team was already working to gather as much information as they could about Jimmy Benson—the driver of the eighteen-wheeler. By the end of next week, Maggie would know about every traffic violation committed by Benson since first obtaining a driver's license. She would know how many times Benson had been divorced, filed for bankruptcy, or been arrested. She and Tim would find everything in the public record on Benson—then leverage it.

"It sounds like we may need to look at a products liability claim, Eli."

"Look, this is outside my area of expertise," the doctor said, the first hint of irritation in his voice. He was a busy doctor that no doubt avoided lawyers whenever feasible. "I need to see a few patients, and I'll—"

"Hold on, Dr. Jay," Eli said, still looking over at Maggie. "What makes you say that, Maggie?"

"If the power steering went out in your mother's car, there may be someone else at fault there. I'll need to check out the steering manufacturer and see if there have been any complaints. Any other cases like this one."

Eli nodded, then looked over at the California native.

"What would you do, Doc?"

The doctor paused as he appeared to consider the question.

"I'm here to treat your sister for the cuts, and bruises, and burns—maybe even her mental state. I'm not the person to tell—"

"If it was your sister in one of these hospital beds," Eli said, halting the doctor's attempt at a soft-shoe response. "Would you want to go after everyone responsible?"

"There is no question," the doctor replied. "I have three younger sisters, Eli. If I were in your position, I would want everyone who is responsible to be held accountable."

"Then, it's settled," Eli replied.

Maggie nodded in agreement. She'd taken on exactly two products liability claims in her career as a civil litigator. They both sat unresolved on a shelf that she tried to avoid. Cases involving defective products could be time-consuming, expensive, and defended by corporations with plenty at stake. A death case aimed at a major auto manufacturer would be met with the highest level of resistance.

"I'll be by your sister's room shortly," the doctor said as he stepped away from the conversation. "Maggie, nice to meet you."

"And you as well," she replied.

Eli turned to Maggie and gave her a tired smile.

"Let's go see her."

9

Tim Dawson pulled the screen door back and knocked on the front door of the house. The spring to the door creaked as it expanded, announcing his arrival moments before the rap of his knuckles. He stepped back from the old wooden door and surveyed the front porch. At one end sat a well-used weight bench with a barbell at the ready. On the other stood two rocking chairs, one claimed by a fat calico that eyed him with suspicion.

The front door opened, and a tall woman appeared in the doorway. She looked Tim over in a manner much like the cat curled in the rocker. As a Black man working as a private investigator in the South, he could spot the neighborhoods he needed to be careful in. He'd beat the streets for witnesses in countless cities during the past five years. Doors in the hood stayed closed to him as often as those perched on porches behind white picket fences.

Tim pulled a business card from his pocket and offered it to the woman. "Good afternoon," he said, his tone warm and casual. "Sorry to be bothering you like this."

The woman looked at the card being offered to her, no doubt considering whether to accept it. Tim continued.

"My name is Tim Dawson. I'm an investigator with a law firm out of

Florida. I'd like to talk to you a moment about the wreck your son was in yesterday."

"You people sure do work fast," the woman said, taking the card. "I just met with the other man this morning. He said it might be some days before the investigator would be by. Come on in, though."

"The other man?" Tim asked as he stepped inside the house. "Was he with the Georgia State Patrol?"

"Not the trooper," she replied. "It was one of the men from the law firm. I called that number from one of those commercials last night. They sent him right over this morning."

Tim shook his head, amazed at the speed of the competition. *How could Maggie compete with the budget some of these ambulance-chasers had to throw at advertising?*

"A television commercial?"

The woman nodded and looked back down at the card in her hand. "You're from a different firm," she said, staring now at the purple logo of Reynolds Law. "I've never heard of this law firm before."

"Did they have you sign anything?" Tim asked. "A contract, maybe?"

"Did you say you were a lawyer, too?"

"I'm no lawyer," Tim replied with a laugh. "But, yes, ma'am, I do work for a different law firm than the one you apparently met with this morning. I feel a little silly being here now."

The woman offered no argument.

"Well, I hope the lawyers you work for are good men."

"I work for a good woman," Tim said, smiling. "It's her law firm."

The woman paused, considering the information. "Is she a good lawyer?"

"The best," Tim said with a quick nod. "Can I still sit and talk with you a moment?"

The woman motioned to two aging brown recliners. "I don't see why not."

Tim sat and let his eyes take in the room. He noticed a simple frame hung at the center of the opposite wall. The photograph was that of a boy in a football uniform, kneeling in a well-manicured end zone. Tim's own mother had one that was similar. It hung somewhere in his family's home back in Fort Morgan.

"Is this your son?" Tim asked, pointing to the photo.

"That's Alvin," the woman replied without glancing at the frame. She said the name again. "Sweet Alvin."

"A handsome boy."

"That he was," she said with a sigh. "All the other boys on the football team were serious on picture day. Not my Al, though. He was always cutting up about something—always smiling."

Tim tried to muster a smile of his own to honor the boy's memory. He knew anything he offered would fall well short of the mark. Alvin Montavious Hughes simply died too young. Nothing he could do, or say, would fix that.

"I don't want to take up a lot of your time, ma'am. I just want to ask you a few questions about your son and the wreck yesterday."

"Okay, go ahead."

In Tim's last years with the GBI, he worked his fair share of homicide cases. Those investigations brought him into the living rooms of grieving family members for tough conversations. Though he never mastered the art of comforting those hurt by the violence, he came to know investigators and prosecutors that were true practitioners of the art form. He'd learned that patience in the silence could be a powerful tool when interviewing the grieving, allowing them to share their story on their own terms.

"Tell me what you know about the wreck."

The woman looked over at the front doorway. She stared at it for a moment, thinking before she began.

"Alvin went over to Dothan yesterday morning with the Jones boy. Al and Jason had been friends since they were little kids. They planned to go to the mall, then eat lunch somewhere after that. Alvin had sixty dollars left over from his birthday, and he wanted to buy a new hat. My Al always wore a Braves hat wherever he went. Told me he wanted a new one."

Tim nodded, not wanting to interrupt the woman's narrative.

"I had to work yesterday, so I left the house at my normal time. I remember it was raining hard here during the morning, and I thought about my boy being out on the roads in it. I remember thinking how glad I was that he wouldn't get his driver's license until next year."

The woman paused a moment as she picked up a glass of water from the small end table to the right of her recliner. She took a sip and continued.

"I didn't hear from Al all morning, but I wasn't worried. Like I said, Jason and Alvin had been friends since they were small boys. I'd known Shondra—Jason's momma—since well before then. She'd been wild back in those days, but we all were. Time and children just slowed us down. I knew she was driving, so I didn't think anything of it. I figured my boy would be safe."

Tim nodded again.

"And, I didn't know at the time, but Jason's little sister was with them, too."

"That's right," Tim said. "Maya Jones."

"She is in the hospital, from what I hear," the woman added. "Do you know if she is doing better?"

"I think so," he replied. "My wife is with her today."

"Such a sweet little girl. Lost her mother and brother on the same day—Lord, I just don't understand why."

Tim thought the woman might begin praying.

"As far as the wreck, I don't know much. The state trooper is who you need to talk to. He is going to know much more. That's who my lawyers spoke to."

"I understand," Tim said. "Tell me what you know, though. It may help everyone."

"All I know is no one was being careful yesterday," the woman said, a forcefulness growing in her voice. "And from what I hear, nobody was looking out for my boy."

"Who told you that?"

The woman turned and rummaged through a stack of paperwork on her end table. She handed a card to Tim.

"This man," she said. "He told me that tractor-trailer was running too fast in the rain. That Shondra Jones probably was, too."

Tim turned the card over. He studied the familiar logo from the law firm of Husto & Husto before handing it back to the woman.

"I'm glad little Maya is okay," the woman said, shaking her head. "But her momma's recklessness got my boy killed. How stupid do you have to be to be speeding in the rain with a car full of children?"

"I don't think that's the case," Tim replied in a calm tone. "That's not what I've heard so far."

The woman gritted her teeth. "You don't know, though, do you?"

"You're right, I don't know for certain, but—"

"I don't want to talk about this anymore," the woman said as she stood from her chair. "I think I'd like you to leave."

"Ma'am, Reynolds Law is representing the Jones family. We can work with your lawyers on this to make the driver of that eighteen-wheeler pay. We will all be a team."

"There's no *we* in this, Mr. Dawson. I've already told my lawyers that I want to go after everyone."

"It doesn't have to be that way."

"That's the way it's gonna have to be," the woman said as she motioned toward the front door. "Now, like I asked, please leave."

10

Charlotte Acker waited in line at security. She blended in easily with the morning work crowd in her navy-blue jacket and pencil skirt. Men and women in varying combinations of business attire inched along in the line with her. Most stared down at their cell phones or talked with familiar faces nearby. Charlotte listened to pieces of the strangers' conversations while she watched the officers ahead. They worked methodically, ushering the suits and skirts through their row of metal detectors and scanners. Their uniforms bore the insignia of the United States Capitol Police. As Charlotte neared their inspection area, she noticed a portion of their mission statement printed on the wall in bright, bold letters—*Protect the Congress*.

On the other side of security, Charlotte stopped at a welcome desk. A man working the desk handed her a visitor's badge for the day and provided directions to the offices where the interview would be conducted. Charlotte thanked him and set out down the wide hallway with the Monday morning foot traffic.

While the business of voting happened on the floor of the Capitol, much of the work performed by senators, members of the House, and their staff took place in the congressional office buildings that surrounded the Capitol. A system of underground tunnels linked the buildings with one another, allowing those vested with the powers of

Article I to travel safely between their meetings and hearings with one another. The Senate Office Buildings—Dirksen, Hart, and Russell—along with the House Office Buildings—Cannon, Longworth, Rayburn, Ford, and O'Neill—provided cafeterias, gymnasiums, and common areas well suited for the armies of staffers tasked with keeping the legislative machine running.

As Charlotte walked the long hallway, she felt the energy of those bustling by. National policy matters were to be debated, consensuses needed to be reached, and new laws had to be crafted. This was where it all happened, she thought—American history was being written today.

She stopped at a pair of tall doors. Both were propped open. She peered through the doorway into a large room. The two-story space was used mostly for committee meetings and hearings tied to the work of the legislature. She noticed a small group of people standing near the dais at the front of the gallery. They talked quietly, unbothered by her intrusion.

"Can I help you?" a voice asked.

Charlotte turned to her right. A woman sat in a high-back chair with a paperback in her lap. She wore no uniform.

"Oh, sorry," Charlotte replied. "I was just looking to see what was in here. I can be on my way."

The woman smiled. "Well, sweetie, I don't know how much there will be to see in here today. You can stay until the committee convenes at nine, then you'll probably have to go."

It didn't matter, anyway. The interview was at nine. "That's okay."

Charlotte stood in the doorway, scanning the wood-paneled walls of the great room. She noticed there were demonstratives pinned to the back walls of the gallery. They were maps of the grounds around the Capitol. Some had images of rioters on its steps. Charlotte turned back to the woman.

"What is happening in here today?"

"The same thing that happens most days," the woman said. "Not enough."

Charlotte laughed, unsure if the woman was joking. "Well, what happens on the other days?"

The woman smiled as she turned the novel back over in her lap, returning to its pages. "The most amazing things, sweetie. Truly amazing things that make our country what it is."

The office suite's reception area smelled of coffee and freshly baked bread. As Charlotte stepped into the space, she noticed the plate of pastries and croissants at the opposite side of the room. They rested on a table below a large map. A map of where she grew up—South Georgia.

"Good morning," a woman at the reception desk chimed. "How can I help you today?"

Charlotte's eyes searched the map until she found the black dot that represented her hometown of Blakeston. The Chattahoochee River snaked by to the west. The Wiregrass region fanned out to the east. Charlotte turned to the woman at the desk. "I am here for an interview at nine."

"Your name, please?"

"Charlotte Acker."

Charlotte watched the receptionist's face for any hint of a reaction. She saw none.

"Right this way," the woman said as she stood from her desk. "I'll show you to the senator's office."

As they started down the hall, a croissant and coffee were offered. Charlotte declined both. She realized with each step toward the senator's office that she had not anticipated the sudden rush of emotions. She felt a surge of anxiety course through her body, followed by a blitz of adrenaline and uneasiness. Charlotte tried to remember the last time she'd felt this nervous. Maybe the Outdoor Championships her last year at Oregon. She'd prepared her ass off for that, though. Charlotte shook the thought off— she'd been preparing for this morning's meeting for years.

"Take a seat in here," the receptionist said as she turned the knob to a large wooden door. "The senator should be with you in just a few minutes."

Charlotte stepped through the doorway into a handsome office. Her eyes fell on the large wooden desk first. It commanded the room from the far wall. She slowly walked over to it. Stacks of paperwork sat piled on its surface. More books and collapsible folders were stacked on the floor nearby. The clutter surprised her, giving the worked-in office a comfortable feel.

As she waited on her feet, Charlotte inspected the photographs that covered the walls. Captured in the images were snapshots of Bill Collins's life in government service. He was pictured with presidents, generals, actors, and other persons of note. She stared at the senator's face in each of the photos, searching for any similarities to her own. She saw none. Then she saw the picture of his son, Jake. While staring at the smiling picture of a man that died too young—a man that she had quietly accepted as her biological father—she heard the door to the office open.

"I'm sorry that I'm a few minutes late," a voice said. "I was held up on my way into the city this morning. Traffic is a little heavier here than in Blake County."

Charlotte turned to face the familiar voice. It reminded her of painful memories, and it reminded her of home.

"At least you're sorry for something, *Bill*," she shot back. The name sounded much like it tasted in her mouth—disgusting.

A silence settled into the room for a moment as they stared at each other. The senator had the look of a man hell-bent on repentance. Charlotte had that of a boxer ready to exit her corner.

He placed his briefcase on one of the leather chairs at the center of the room. "That's fair."

"Is it, though?"

Bill nodded. "I think that—"

"How do you expect this little interview to go?"

"Well, I'd like to think that—"

"You think I'm going to just come work for you? Is that what you expect to happen, *Bill*?"

The large desk stood at Charlotte's back. She leaned against the edge of its surface, folding her arms across her chest. She felt in control of the room and continued the verbal assault.

"This is downright unbelievable. You come into my school and offer up some sham of an interview in front of basically everyone I know in this town. At first, I was embarrassed, offended really, and I considered not buying into your little game. Then, I thought that—"

"This interview is not a sham," Bill quickly added before being cut off.

"Then, I realized I'd been needing to tell you a few things to your face. Things every coward needs to hear."

"Let's hear it," Bill said with a tone of sincerity. He pointed to an open chair. "Mind if I sit?"

"I do."

"Okay," he replied. "Well, I'd like to—"

"The only man I knew as a father is dead," she hissed. "All because of you."

"I miss Lee every day," he replied. "But I miss Jake, too. I miss my son."

"Well, they are both gone because of your awful family."

"It's your family, too."

"Bullshit."

Bill showed Charlotte the palms of his hands as he sat in the chair, cautiously pointing at the one opposite it. She shook her head and walked over to the picture of Jake Collins. She pulled it from the wall, ripping a nail and hardware from the plaster.

"Look at him!" she yelled. "If this is the way you treat your family, then leave me the hell out of it."

Tears started down Charlotte's cheeks as she tossed the picture frame onto the desk. It bounced from the wooden surface and shattered on the floor.

"I just want to talk," Bill said, his voice calm. "I've wanted to for years. That's all I'm asking for."

Charlotte considered his words, unsure if she'd simply allow him to tap out this early. She felt there were more rounds to go. More blows to be dealt. She wanted him on the ropes, bleeding.

"Talk," she said, finally grabbing the chair across from him. "I'm not sure I'll listen."

"That's fair."

Bill leaned forward in his chair, elbows on his knees. He clasped his hands together in a pleading gesture. "I can't change what my wife did."

"You were part of it."

"If not testifying against her at trial makes me part of it, then yes, I am.

If not divorcing her and leaving her as soon as I knew what she'd done to our son makes me complicit, then—"

"You really want me to believe that you didn't know what she did?"

"I want you to believe me when I tell you that *I didn't know what she was going to do*. Once I knew what happened, it was too late."

"Say it," Charlotte replied. "Say what happened."

"I didn't know she was going to kill Jake."

"Say it."

"She killed my son. Are you happy now?"

"No," she shot back. "What about the night at the cemetery on Parker's Koll? Did you know she planned to kill—"

"I swear it to you, Charlotte. I didn't know Lucy planned to kill Lee that night."

Charlotte sat with her hands in her lap. The adrenaline had somewhat subsided. For some reason, she believed him, and it pained her.

"Is that all?"

Bill paused for another moment, then charged on. "I'm running for reelection, Charlotte."

"I know that," she snorted. "Your campaign stickers were all over town when I was back home for Christmas."

"I'm doing this one without Lucy," he added. "She and I are separated. We have been for the last year or so, and she isn't going to be involved in the campaign."

"You are the incumbent and clear favorite."

"That's true, but this is the first race I've run without her by my side. She's been there for every step, every election for the last twenty-six years."

"You don't want your murderous wife standing next to you at your rallies?" Charlotte said with a laugh. "Pat your campaign manager on the back next time you two sit down to chat."

Bill ignored the comment. "Lucy has been my north star since I was a twenty-year-old kid, Charlotte. We've been together for over forty-five years. If it weren't for her, I wouldn't be sitting in this office."

And two great men wouldn't be in the ground if it weren't for her, Charlotte thought. "So, what does that have to do with me?"

"I'm striking out in a new direction," Bill said. "What I've seen in the world these last years, it makes me want to work to be part of the solution. Not the problem."

"And your wife is part of the problem?"

"Yes, she is part of it. I have been too."

"There you have it," Charlotte quipped. "We've found common ground."

Bill smiled. "Look, I know you may not agree to join my office this summer, but I want you here. You have the best of Lee, and you remind me of my boy. You remind me of what is right in this world."

The senator made his living debating, schmoozing, and manipulating others for personal gain. Charlotte knew she couldn't trust him. Still—she was intrigued.

"What do you mean when you say you are striking out?" she asked. "Are you leaving office at the end of your term or something?"

"No," Bill replied slowly. His words were measured, intentional. "I'm still planning to run in the election this fall. I plan to win, too."

"What then?"

"I'm going to leave the Party after I do."

11

In Blake County, the Sandbar was the only acceptable place to grab a beer on a Monday afternoon. The riverside bar was a favorite among the locals and a mandatory pit stop for Tim and Maggie whenever they passed through the area. The two sat close together on the back deck, a half-empty pitcher of beer between them. They pored over a stack of records and reports tied to the Jones case.

"It's good to be back, right?" Maggie said, looking up from an accident summary she'd received that morning from Crash.

"It sure is," Tim replied, lifting his beer from the table to take a sip. He grinned at Maggie over the edge of his glass. "The Sandbar is the best. I was always able to close the deal here."

"Here we go," Maggie said, shaking her head. "I meant it's good to be back in Blake County."

"I agree," he said. "Hell of a lot of memories here, though."

Maggie nodded. "Lots of *good* memories."

From the back of the restaurant's deck, Maggie could see the waters of the Chattahoochee River. It lazed by under the hot Georgia sky, slowly making its way south toward Apalachicola Bay and the expanse of the Gulf. Near the riverbank, she could make out two sandy volleyball courts. The well-maintained courts played host to a little-known volleyball league called the Chattahoochee Beach Volleyball Club. The members of the Club —affectionately referred to as Hoochies by the bar's patrons—were a competitive bunch of locals that gathered on weeknights to knock around a volleyball and drink cold pitchers of beer. Maggie smiled as she remembered the night she sat on the Sandbar's deck, flirting with Tim Dawson after one of his games.

"What are you smirking about?" Tim asked, pulling Maggie away from the memory.

"Oh, I was just thinking about the first night you asked me out."

"I remember," Tim said with a laugh. "I was nervous as hell."

"You sure didn't show it! Back in those days, I thought you were just a cocky lawman."

Tim raised an eyebrow. "Thought?"

"Uh-huh," Maggie said with a wink. "Back then, when you weren't slapping volleyballs around with your buddies out here, you were out arresting people left and right. I didn't know what to think!"

"What about now?"

She paused. "Now—I just *know* how cocky you are. You just don't get to arrest people as often as you'd like to."

"I'll go arrest somebody right now!"

"Case in point," Maggie replied, laughing. "I'll go out on a limb and say the people of Blake County are safer these days."

"I never heard any complaints."

Still smiling, Maggie returned to the paperwork in her lap. She felt lighter. More relaxed than she had in a while. She couldn't decide whether it was the excitement of a big case to finally latch onto or the change in scenery. Maybe it was a combination of both. As she read, the name of a business caught her attention.

"It looks like Crash was able to pull the inventory on the eighteen-wheeler's trailer. The driver was delivering a load to a company here in Blakeston, then heading over to Jacksonville, Florida."

"What company?"

Maggie paused before stumbling over the name. "Borroka S.A."

"I've never heard of it," Tim said, taking another sip of his beer. "Is there a copy of the bill of lading in there to see what was being delivered?"

Maggie flipped through a few pages in the packet until she found what she was looking for. "Says here that they were set to receive a bunch of metal. Looks like mostly carbon steel and aluminum."

"That driver was just barreling down the highway pulling a trailer chock-full of metal," Tim said, shaking his head. "I wonder how many tons that thing weighed."

"The max, loaded down, is eighty thousand pounds. It's illegal for them to ride heavier than that. Regardless, I can't imagine the people over at Borroka lost much of their product in the wreck."

Tim agreed. "Probably not. I'll spend a little time digging into them, though."

"You mean you'll Google them?"

"That's why you pay me the big bucks," Tim said with a laugh. "Anyway, what's the latest on Maya?"

"Eli says she is still improving. I told him I would go see her again at the hospital before we hit the road."

"Well, it looks like I am certainly going to be putting in some windshield time driving you back and forth from Tampa for this case."

Maggie grinned. "I guess that's another reason why I pay you the big bucks."

"If you will, then, please tell this lowly chauffeur-investigator where you plan to file the lawsuit?"

Maggie thought about what she already knew about the parties to the potential suit. She would represent the plaintiffs—Maya, along with the representative for the estates of Shondra and Jason Jones. They would be bringing the action to the court. They'd sit at the top of the "v" and determine where the lawsuit was filed.

When plaintiffs consider where they can file their claim, three jurisdictional factors must be considered. First, the plaintiffs always must select a court that has personal jurisdiction over the parties involved in the lawsuit. That means the defendant to the lawsuit needs to have done enough of *something* within the jurisdiction of the court so that it can exercise control over the bad actor that is being sued. Second, the plaintiffs must drop their lawsuit in a court that has subject-matter jurisdiction. Meaning, the court needs to be able to hear that type of case being brought by the plaintiffs. Third, the plaintiffs need to file their lawsuit in the right venue—a fancy word for place. In Georgia, a state with 159 counties carved out inside its borders, plaintiffs have plenty of places to choose from.

"The driver of the truck is from Alabama," Maggie finally said. "In Georgia, we are supposed to sue the defendant to a civil case in the county that he or she resides in."

"So, the Joneses can't file in Georgia?"

"No, they can file it here," she replied. "Although the driver is an out-of-state defendant, the Georgia Constitution says we can still sue him here. He caused a wreck here, so the courts will have jurisdiction over him."

"Where does the lawsuit get filed, then?"

"The venue will have to be where the harm occurred—right here in Blake County."

"Damn right."

"Now, they can just remove it to federal court if—"

"Those defense lawyers better look you up," Tim chirped, cutting her off. "Half the scalps in your war chest were taken right in the main court-room of the Blake County Courthouse."

"Yes, but that was a while ago, Tim."

He waved her off. "Is Judge Balk still on the bench?"

"Last time I checked," Maggie said. "This is a civil case, though, and—"

"And this will be a jury trial, right?"

Maggie nodded. "If that's what Maya and Eli want."

"And they will let you actually speak at this trial?"

"Tim, I get what you are saying, it's just—"

"None of those things matter, Mags. Trying cases in Blake County is like going home and playing in your own backyard. You know this terrain—especially in the courtroom."

"Home is in Florida now," she said, deflecting the compliments. "What if things have changed for me here?"

"We are both enjoying being back," Tim said with a shrug. "Let's focus on doing more of that. We can see how much has changed."

"You mean stay here for a while?"

"I don't think we have to make the call just yet, Mags. We can feel it out."

Maggie let the idea sit with her for a moment. It felt right.

"Yeah," she said. "Let's do that."

12

Charlotte looked up at the clock on the classroom wall. In less than fifteen minutes, her first year of law school would officially be over. She'd grinded two long semesters with her fellow 1Ls, and she'd done more than survive —she'd flourished. Now, the next step toward retribution lay ahead: an internship that was set to begin on Monday.

Returning to the screen of her laptop, Charlotte reminded herself that she needed to finish strong. She read over the words of her response to the final exam's last essay question. The question asked for her analysis on the constitutionality of a police officer's warrantless entry into a person's home. She knew the law on the issue, and she knew the exceptions.

When someone does not consent to the government's search of their person, place, or things, representatives of the government, e.g., police officers or sheriff's deputies, are *supposed to be* barred from performing their search. In cases where the government's agents don't have permission—but go ahead with a warrantless search—anything the government officer finds that leads to criminal charges could be thrown out on a proper motion filed by the accused. When a warrantless search is performed by law enforcement, it is the government's responsibility to show that probable cause existed to do so, or that exceptions to the warrant requirement existed at the time of the search.

The hypothetical police officer in Charlotte's final exam question—Officer Tommy Bold—did just that. He entered a home because he was chasing a suspect that fled from a pretextual traffic stop. He mistakenly believed that the suspect ran into a fictitious homeowner's garage. Once inside the garage, Officer Bold did not find his fleeing suspect. Instead, he found a body. The target from the traffic stop got away, but Tommy Bold made the front page of the local newspaper for arresting the homeowner in connection with the murder of his wife. The exam's essay question asked, among other things, "Should evidence of the homicidal husband's crime be excluded from trial due to Officer Bold's warrantless entry into the homeowner's garage?"

Charlotte's analysis of the hypothetical situation was thorough. As instructed, she argued both sides of the problem. She posited that exigent circumstances existed because the police officer was in hot pursuit of a suspect. Then, she reasoned that the Constitution, through the Fourth and Fourteenth Amendments, protected even the guilty from unreasonable searches and seizures by the government.

Satisfied with her response, Charlotte closed her laptop and waited patiently. A few of her classmates' fingers still tapped away frantically on their keyboards. She smiled. They were budding lawyers—they all wanted to win every conceivable point.

"That's time," called the voice of a proctor at the front of the room. His voice spurred a few curse words near the back row of students. "Laptops closed."

The exam takers, most in sweats and T-shirts, slowly rose from their seats to stretch. Charlotte heard a few voices already claiming they'd failed the exam. The rest said little.

"You going out tonight?"

Charlotte turned to a familiar voice behind her. Her friend June Moray inched down the row of desks with a backpack over her shoulder. "Yeah, girl. I'm all for doing something fun tonight. This was my last one."

"Mine, too—thank God."

"I need a serious nap and a shower, though. Should we meet somewhere fancy for dinner before we go out?"

"Yes!" June said, smiling. "I've been eating bagels and ramen all week.

Anything that takes longer than three minutes to cook will be a major upgrade for me."

Charlotte laughed. "How about the Brazz at eight?"

June kept moving down the line of desks, toward the door. "I'll see you there, Charlotte."

Lawton Crane stepped through the front door of Brasserie Liberté at nine o'clock. He wore denim jeans, sneakers, and a dark navy blazer made of Italian wool. A host, standing near the door, greeted him with a warm smile. Crane pointed in the direction of the bar, bypassing any discussion as to a reservation for that evening.

As Crane stepped to the bar, he placed one hand on a brass railing that ran the length of the wide oak drinking surface. Searching for an open seat, he glanced at the legs and ring fingers on a group of women that sat nearby. All were dressed smartly and invested in their conversations with one another. The forty-one-year-old guessed they were in the vicinity of age appropriate. He wasn't there for them, though.

Waiting, Crane continued to survey the French-style restaurant. He knew it not only boasted one of the hottest menus in Georgetown, but it also attracted the professional and unattached from all over the District. The professor had not been back in the game long, but he was catching on. It was a different world than the one he'd met his ex-wife in. It was wider, more digital. Brasserie Liberté met the standard for a restaurant of the modern era, and the packed tables with couples of all shapes, colors, and orientations confirmed it. The restaurant offered delicious fare, excellent drinks, and décor suitable for the social media pages of the trendiest influencers. Crane took it all in, and he liked it.

He spotted an unoccupied seat near the end of the bar and headed in its direction. Moving under the amber-tinted lighting that fell from the ceiling, he felt as if the conversations and music in the room had taken on a sepia hue. Crane smiled as he slid onto the leather-backed barstool. A bartender acknowledged him as he sat, and Crane turned to look through the entryway that led to the main dining area. At its edge, he spotted the profile of a comely young law student having dinner—Charlotte Acker.

"What are you having, my friend?"

Crane turned back to the bartender. "Do you have any McKenna back there?"

The bartender nodded as he placed a small napkin on the bar. "We have the ten-year single barrel."

"Give me that. Neat, with a few drops of water."

"Double?"

Crane nodded. "That'll be fine."

"The only food at the bar on Friday nights is dessert. Do you want a menu?"

Crane shook his head. "I'm fine for now."

"You sure? The crème brûlée is the best around."

"I bet," Crane said, peering back at the entryway. "Maybe later."

The bartender grabbed an order from a couple seated two spaces down the bar, then turned to start pulling bottles from a backlit wall. Crane scanned the labels on the shelves of bottles as he waited. He'd missed drinking liquor. So much so that he'd enjoyed plenty of it the last six nights in a row. The rekindling of his affair with the sauce didn't concern him, though. It was summertime, and affairs were for the married.

The bartender set the glass in front of him. "Here you are, my man."

The professor handed his credit card over. As the bartender went to take it, Crane held the card between his fingers for a moment. "Listen, I'd like to send a couple of drinks across the way to some friends of mine. Can you help me with that?"

"Of course," the bartender said, instinctively looking down the bar at the group of women tiptoeing around forty. Though they were certainly undeserving of the burned-out litigator's baggage, they were at least born in the same decade as Lawton Crane. "What are we sending?"

"We?" Crane asked with a grin on his face. He released the credit card from his fingertips, and the bartender slipped it into his front pocket.

"Yeah, my friend. You appear to be flying solo."

Crane picked his glass up and downed it in a smooth motion. "All right, *my friend*. What would you suggest?"

The barman was at least ten years younger than Crane, but this was his beat. He eyed the now empty glass in front of his customer and turned to collect the bottle of McKenna from behind him. He poured another two fingers in the glass, thinking.

"You can't go wrong with sending another round of what they are already drinking. It's safe, but you may come off as a guy that lacks any creativity."

"I can't have that," Crane said, leaning back in his seat. He considered what his ex-wife would likely want if she were out with friends tonight. "I'll send them champagne, then."

"Get out, son. If that's what you think will—"

The bartender paused as Lawton felt a tap on his shoulder. Without missing a beat, the bartender asked, "What would you do if a guy sent you champagne from across the bar?"

The voice of Charlotte Acker started over Crane's shoulder. "No one has ever done that for me before. I'm guessing it would make me feel a bit like Daisy Buchanan. Nothing wrong with that, right?"

Charlotte's hand stayed on Crane's left shoulder as she spoke. As Crane turned to her, his eyes fell to the flowy neckline on her honey-colored dress, then her long legs and open-toe heels. He quickly willed himself back to eye level. Crane jumped in before the bartender could respond.

"That's exactly how things got off track for poor Daisy. The champagne. The lavish parties. She didn't expect Gatsby to show her the attention he did. Then, before she knew it—*bam!*—there she was, running people over in the street and leaving them for dead."

"Leaving them for dead?" Charlotte said with a grin. "She did no such thing, old sport. The accident was unavoidable, a tragedy by all accounts."

"Spoken like a true defense lawyer."

"Would that be in the defense of criminals or insurance carriers?"

Crane winked. "They are the same to me."

"You would know."

Crane reached for his glass on the bar and took a sip. Charlotte proceeded to order two drinks. Crane insisted on paying for both. As she waited, they talked about the semester. She was a law student on the heels of her first year of school. He had no doubt she was running on fumes. The fatigue from multiple days of limited sleep was a given for a first-year student on the other end of finals week. As she chatted on, Crane could tell she was well into her limit on drinks for the evening. It was evident from her speech, and in her bold approach to her professor seated alone at the bar. As the barman returned with her drinks, Crane pulled the cell phone from his jacket and quickly fiddled with the screen. His good fortune surprised him.

"Don't leave so soon," the bartender said as she started to step away from the bar. "Are you heading back to your table?"

"My friend is waiting," Charlotte replied. "We are here for this round, then heading on to find some music."

The man behind the stick protested. "Don't go back to the stuffy side of the restaurant. Stay here."

"My friend is—"

"Right there," Crane said, pointing to a well-dressed June Moray. She was walking toward the bar.

"What he said," Charlotte added. "Hey, June, look who I found all alone at the bar. I say we—"

"I think my place was just broken into!" June said, holding her cell phone. She typed on the screen as she moved toward the restaurant's front door. "The alarm company just notified me, and the police are supposed to be on their way."

"I'll come with you," Charlotte said as she placed their drinks back on the bar. "I just need to—"

"No, it's okay. My dad is in town, so I'll text him. He will want to meet me there."

"I'm sorry, June. Hopefully it's nothing."

"My Uber is almost here," June said over her shoulder. "I'll text you."

Crane listened to the exchange, waiting. He knew he'd only have a small window of time to make his move.

"Maybe it's nothing," Crane said as Charlotte turned back to the bar. She had her cell phone in her hand. No doubt considering whether to order her own ride home. Crane motioned to the open seat beside him at the bar. "You're welcome to join me for a few more minutes."

Charlotte paused. "Is a few more minutes all that's left of office hours?"

"No, I meant—"

"I'll stay for a while," she said, cutting him off as she climbed onto the barstool next to him. "Did you have dinner?"

"I ate something earlier. I was supposed to meet a friend, but she cancelled on me last minute."

Crane noticed the bartender raise an eyebrow at him as he placed a small dessert menu in front of Charlotte. He stepped away to conspire with other patrons.

"You have to order something," Charlotte urged. "The desserts here are next level."

"Oh yeah? Well, I hear the crème brûlée is the best around."

"Yes!" she replied. "Let's get one."

Crane smiled back at her. "Yes—*let's* do that."

13

Four key areas make up the focus of the United States-Spain Council—trade, investment, education, and culture. Since its establishment in 1996, representatives for the United States have hailed from its highest levels of government. Notable senators, members of the House, and state governors have taken on the work of the Council by partnering with corporate leaders and other top government officials. Their common goal has been to simply promote stronger ties between the two countries, and the Council's annual forum has always been the main stage for those important discussions around trade and investment opportunities set to spark.

Each year—except those that happen to be blanketed by a global pandemic—the forum has alternated between the United States and Spain. The 2022 meeting between the countries—a two-day event scheduled to begin on July 1 in Bilbao, Spain—looked to feature an impressive group of Spanish and American entrepreneurs. Among them, a confident pair of young Basque investors were making noise in the weeks leading up to the event. The young guns wanted a seat at the main table come July, and they believed a meeting with the head of the US contingent, chaired by Senator William H. Collins, was the best way to secure a seat.

"Is there anything specific I need to do during this meeting?" Charlotte asked. She was close to jogging in her heels as she tried to keep up, following the senator's chief of staff through one of the many utilitarian tunnels under the grounds of the Capitol. George Dell, a six-foot-five vassal to Senator Collins, was always moving, but the college track star was determined to keep up. "I would be more prepared, but I wasn't aware this was on his calendar today."

"Don't worry about it," George said over his shoulder. "I just want a second set of eyes and ears in there. These persistent little bastards wiggled onto Bill's calendar somehow."

"They didn't go through the normal channels to set it up?"

"Nope, and no one in the office will admit to adding them without permission. We all know the rules."

"It happens."

"Oh yeah?" George said, turning a moment to look back at her. "Not in our office it doesn't. Bill wants everything controlled by his people now. No one outside his circle is supposed to be meddling."

"I guess the joke's on them," Charlotte replied. "They think they are meeting with Bill. They'll get us instead."

George nodded. "Damn right."

"So, what's their pitch?"

"These guys manufacture firearm components and small armaments. The last couple of years, they've been selling to the big dogs in the firearm industry. Word on the street is, now they plan to start rolling out a new line of long guns to feed the demand in the US."

Charlotte wasn't breathing hard, but one of her calf muscles was starting to cramp. "Like shotguns and hunting rifles?"

"More like assault rifles," George said as they stopped at a bank of elevators. He looked over at Charlotte as she was leaning down to rub her lower leg. "You good?"

"I'm running you down in heels right now, George. Put me in a pair of track shoes and let's make this a fair fight."

George grinned. "No way. It's on you to keep up, squirt."

Both men, standing on the other side of the table, looked to be under thirty. Charlotte considered them as she followed behind George, making her way to the conference table at the center of the room. She knew that the pair of profiteers were just two of the many roaming the complex of bureaucracy that surrounded them. The shorter of the two started with the introductions.

"I am Juan Mari Lazkano," he said, offering a handshake to the senator's chief of staff, then to Charlotte. "This is my brother, Fernando."

As they shook hands, Charlotte eyed the duo's three-piece suits and hair long enough to tuck behind the ears. They didn't look like gun dealers.

"Listen, guys," George began, his tone not aimed at being diplomatic. "I'm not sure how this little meeting found its way onto the books, but the senator won't be joining us today."

Juan appeared surprised. He looked at his brother as if checking in for approval, then turned back to George. "We were told he would be available this morning."

"You were told wrong, and we are very sorry to hear that. Do you guys know how to find your way back out?"

"We still have a proposal that can be discussed. You, or Ms. Acker, should be able to communicate it to the senator for us, no?"

"Sure," George replied. "We certainly would be *able* to do that. That's not how it works, though. If you'd done your homework on how the senator does business, you'd know that. And who are you to treat me like some message carrier?"

Charlotte stepped in. "I think what Mr. Dell here is trying to communicate to you is that the senator's office has a particular strategy that is used when taking in proposals. It isn't written anywhere for the public, but he relies on his team to vet the ideas and proposals that might be of interest to his current agenda. If it doesn't fit, he doesn't really want to hear about it or have us waste valuable time briefing it for him."

"So, the two of you will tell me if our proposal will even make it to the senator's ears?"

"Precisely," George retorted. "So far, it's not going so well for you boys."

"Can we sit?" Juan asked, ignoring the rebuke. The hostility from the senator's career handler seemed to amuse him. "This won't take long."

"I think that—"

"Of course," Charlotte said, cutting George off again. She motioned to the chairs across the table. "We are here. Let's sit and talk about what it is you have in mind."

Juan and Fernando, seemingly in sync with one another, unbuttoned their jackets and took their seats. Fernando spoke for the first time, pivoting slightly on the subject.

"Charlotte, will you be joining us at the annual forum in Bilbao?"

His use of her first name took her by surprise. It sounded natural, though. "I'll be traveling with the senator's team to the event."

He registered his approval with a smile. "Have you visited Spain before?"

"Once," she said. "When I was studying abroad in Paris during college. I flew down with friends for four or five days. I'm very much looking forward to going back."

"Ah, good. Where did you go?"

"Madrid and Seville. They were both wonderful."

The brothers looked at one another, feigning disappointment. "If you have time, my brother and I will show you around our country. Our home is very different from Andalucía."

The Basque Country—*El País Vasco*—has long been a unique region in northern Spain. Its history, climate, language, and culture stand worlds apart from that of Andalucía, a large region in southern Spain. Both are countries within a country, and Charlotte could already tell the two young men were fiercely loyal to their home soil.

Charlotte smiled. "That would be won—"

"I love traveling through Spain as well," George said, interrupting the attention being paid to Charlotte. "After this, you can all make plans to eat tapas, dance Sevillanas, and drink sangria together. Let's just hear what you have to say, though. We have another meeting in fifteen minutes."

The brothers didn't have a notepad in front of them. No laptop or tablet. Their pitch was illustrated only through what was spoken at that table.

Fernando began. "We finished our first manufacturing plant located outside of Spain last year. It is a nice, new facility in Georgia."

"It's state-of-the-art," Juan added. "A very sophisticated plant."

George made a showing of glancing at his watch, but Fernando would not be hurried.

"Our family has been making beautiful, highly sought-after firearms since the early part of the twentieth century. The company has never built a weapon outside of northern Spain. Our Georgia facility will produce the first."

Juan chimed in again. "It'll be the first of many, we hope."

"That's great, guys," George said. "I hope it is the first of many. I am also happy to hear you chose Bill's home state to expand your business into. Let's talk more at the forum because that's sort of what it's for."

Fernando smiled. "As you may know, my government heavily regulates our industry. It is very difficult for my countrymen to purchase our products. Many of the semiautomatic rifles found here in the US are not available back home. They are simply prohibited from being owned unless they are being used for military or security purposes."

Charlotte listened carefully. Gun control continued to be a hot topic in Washington. Many groups from both sides of the debate looked to western European countries as examples of what the results looked like when harsher firearms regulations were implemented. She knew an assault-style weapons ban was being hashed out in the House. She'd not read it yet, but she figured it was a far cry from the regulations that the Spanish government had in place.

"You won't face those kinds of restrictions in this country," George said quickly. "Certainly not in Georgia."

Charlotte nodded in agreement with George. She was curious as to what the brothers wanted. The push to ban assault weapons in the US might have some support in the House, but even if it made it through, she knew it would peter out in the Senate. She didn't know the senator's position on the bill. If she were to put her nonexistent paycheck on it, though, she'd wager that he planned to oppose it.

Fernando continued. "Yes, the United States accounts for much of our sales. That was a big factor in our decision to make the investment in the US. To build the new facility in Georgia."

"Let's get on point," George prompted, still frustrated. "How does this factor in with the forum?"

"My brother and I would like for the firearms industry—specifically our company—to be one of the main topics of discussion in Bilbao. My great-grandfather started with a six-person staff in 1908, making some of the most beautiful *pistolas* in Europe. The company supplied over one hundred fifty thousand units to the Allies in the First World War. We were able to—"

"What about the Second World War?" George fired back across the table.

As the question hung in the air, Fernando and the chief of staff stared across the table at each other.

"The Nationalists seized control of my family's factory during a civil war," Fernando said, after a moment passed. "*La Guerra Civil* was a dark time in my country's history. When the Second World War began, Franco had control of the Spanish government, and my family's factory. Francoists directed the operations of my family's business for a time. My grandfather stayed, along with a few employees, and my father became involved years later. He is who renegotiated full control of our family's company."

"Right, but who did your grandfather make guns for?"

Fernando replied in a cool tone. "*El Caudillo*—Francisco Franco."

"And he sold them to the Reich?"

Fernando nodded. "Yes, our fascist government helped supply the Germans. My family has always been with the Basque people, though."

"I assume you don't want to discuss this part of your company's history at the forum?"

"My brother and I care about the future," Fernando said with a shrug. "We want the senator to show support for our company, for our modern approach to the industry. That is what the forum is supposed to be about. The future."

"How does highlighting your family's company help the senator?" George asked. It was clear the brothers wanted something from Bill. And Bill needed something in return. It was the way it worked.

"The forum's agenda already includes big-picture issues," Charlotte added, trying to clean up the question. "They've slated discussions around major trade initiatives, advancements in renewable energy, partnerships in North Africa, and a lot more. The firearms industry doesn't really connect with the forum's agenda."

"Nor the senator's agenda," George said, reasserting control. "Why would he tap into this idea?"

"Well, we understand the senator has certain barriers in place. That these need to be dealt with, soon. We want to help. If he supports us, we will support him."

"Every politician has barriers. We want to—"

Charlotte interjected with a question that had been percolating in her mind for some time. "You've mentioned your new facility in Georgia. Where is the plant, exactly?"

Fernando looked over at her. Their eyes connected. "It's just outside the city limits of Blakeston. You are familiar with that area?"

Charlotte nodded. "That's right. I was born and raised in Blake County, but you probably knew that already."

The brothers didn't respond. They didn't need to. They'd done their homework.

"Look," George said as he started to lift out of his seat. "This isn't going to be something the senator will be hearing about. I'm sure we'll see you at the—"

"That's not going to be acceptable," Juan said before the rejection was complete. "If the senator isn't even going to be able to consider our proposal, we may have to find another way to get his attention."

George smiled and shook his head. "Good luck with that. You won't get to him while I'm in this office."

The brothers stood. "There are other ways."

"We will be in Blake County next week with the senator," Charlotte said, slowly standing from her chair. There were other ways to reach the senator back home. They had a connection there. She just needed to ask Bill who it might be. "I'll be sure to pass along your proposal."

14

On the morning of June 21st, Maggie Reynolds e-filed a twenty-three-page lawsuit in Blake County Superior Court. The action, brought on behalf of the Jones family, named three defendants: Jimmy Benson, the truck driver; BTF Freight, LLC, the company Benson was driving for on the day of the fatal wreck with the Joneses; and Track Steering, Inc., the manufacturer of the 2010 Toyota Corolla's electric power steering system. A steering system that Maggie's team believed may have failed in Shondra Jones's Corolla on the day of the wreck.

Maggie leaned back in her desk chair, staring at a confirmation page on the screen of her computer. Gone were the days of strutting into the clerk's office of a big courthouse and slapping a lawsuit on the counter for filing. Technology had modernized the paper-laden practice of law, and claims were filed now from anywhere with the click of a button. The exact time, date, and cost of filing the lawsuit stared back at Maggie from the computer screen. Copies of the suit would be shipped out that afternoon, and the defendants would be served within a matter of days. She tried to visualize the steps that lay ahead. Maggie loved the trial work that came with filing a lawsuit, but the truth was, she felt rusty. In her practice, she settled most of the personal injury cases she worked on without ever going to court.

Making the most money possible with the least amount of effort was the way the game worked.

The blueprint for making money in her personal injury practice was simple. A team of paralegals and administrative assistants assembled pre-suit demands on every case brought in the law office's doors. With each case, the team collected as much information as they could from police reports and witnesses, then combined that information with medical records and other supporting paperwork that illustrated their client's injuries. Once they had that information put together, Maggie sent the packages of records out to whatever insurance company was in play, always demanding maximum compensation. The process required little effort from Maggie, and the insurance companies often paid out quick settlements. Maggie kept a third—or even forty percent at times—of the settlement proceeds from each case. It was easy money.

The Jones lawsuit was different, though, and Maggie knew it. Four people had been involved in a gruesome wreck with a tractor-trailer. Only one made it out alive. Maggie represented the estates of two of the deceased, along with the accident's sole survivor. The catastrophic wreck warranted an eye-popping amount of money. One that could never be negotiated with a demand letter and a stack of records. This was her first big one, and, rusty or not, she planned to bring the fight to the courtroom.

The office phone on Maggie's desk buzzed. "Maggie, you have a call on line two."

"Who is it?"

"It's another lawyer," the receptionist said. "Guy says he has a case with you. Said his name is Jack Husto. Do you want me to tell him you'll call him back?"

Maggie looked back at the screen on her computer. The lawsuit against Jimmy Benson and the other defendants had only been filed for a few minutes. Husto couldn't possibly be calling about it.

"No, I'll take it," Maggie said after a moment. "Tell him I'll be right with him."

"Okay."

She took a deep breath, then picked up the receiver. "This is Maggie."

"Jack Husto here," the voice said. It sounded smooth, just like it did on his commercials. "I represent the family of Alvin Hughes, a boy that was killed up in Georgia in an accident with a semi. I hear you represent the rest of the people involved."

"You heard right."

"Sounds like we are on the same side, then. You have a few minutes to talk about the case?"

"Of course, Jack."

Maggie started out by telling Husto that she was glad his firm was involved. They exchanged the normal pleasantries, talking the way lawyers often do about the inherent difficulties that come with representing demanding clients and the stressful business of trial work. That was where the similarities between Maggie and Husto stopped, though.

Jack Husto was more than twenty-five years her senior and had an established presence in the Florida Bar. His well-documented efforts to combat tort reform had put him on a first-name basis with most of the judges and politicians in the state. Although he wasn't considered the most talented in the courtroom, he still ran the largest personal injury practice in Florida. He was connected and respected. A dangerous combination in any rival.

Still, as the two talked, Maggie noticed in Husto's comments that he had done some checking up on her. He knew what part of Tampa her rented office space was in. He knew what committees she'd joined in efforts to network within the Florida Bar. He even knew the names of a few lawyers she'd recently handled cases with. Husto said enough about her little firm to show he'd done his homework. In doing so, he hinted at the fact that he knew more than he was letting on. Maggie knew what he was doing. He was sizing her up. Trying to decide how to play her.

"So, I understand you represent Maya Jones, along with the claims from the estates of Shondra and Jason Jones. Have you sent out your demand yet?"

"I'm not sending a demand letter for their case, Jack."

"No?" Husto said, his tone revealing no position on the strategy. "When will you file suit, then?"

"Just filed this morning."

"That's what I'm talking about," Husto said, a locker-room level of excitement in his voice.

"Let's get after it. Who'd you file against?"

"The suit named three defendants—Jimmy Benson, BTF Freight, and Track Steering."

"Track Steering?"

"That's right. Are you familiar with them?"

Husto laughed. "Uh-huh, I went to the mat with those bastards a few years back. Case was up in Peoria, Illinois. Sleezy bunch of lawyers from Chicago defended the case."

Maggie sensed Husto wanted to tell a war story. She stuck to the facts of the case at hand. "Well, this is a pretty standard negligence action, with a products liability claim mixed in for good measure."

In civil cases involving negligence, a plaintiff, the party bringing the lawsuit, is tasked with proving four elements: duty, breach, causation, and damages.

The first element—duty—is focused on the key question of: *What rule was the defendant to the lawsuit supposed to follow?* When a car wreck is involved, like the one Maya Jones survived, the plaintiff can point first to the rules of the road, i.e., Georgia's traffic laws, to help define what that rule was.

"What do you think about the trooper's report?" Husto asked. "Sounds like this wreck happened out in the middle of nowhere."

Maggie smiled. "There isn't much in Blake County, Jack. Speed limit never drops below sixty-five miles per hour on that stretch of highway."

"I bet lots of people like to just open it up down that road, then."

Maggie nodded, considering his angle. "Benson certainly did."

Once the rule in the first question is defined, the second element of a negligence claim—breach—is directed at the question of: *Was that rule broken by the defendant?*

"How fast does your expert think the tractor-trailer was running?" Husto asked. "I assume you have an expert."

"We do," Maggie replied. "Columbus Davis, and he certainly has Benson speeding. His estimate has him traveling at around seventy-four miles per hour. Maybe a little bit over that."

"That Crash Davis is good," Husto mused. "And that's certainly moving in that kind of weather. I saw in the accident report that the trooper charged the driver of the eighteen-wheeler with a few different traffic citations. Too fast for conditions, failure to maintain lane, failure to exercise due care. It looks like second-degree vehicular homicide is the big one."

"I don't disagree. Those troopers charge anyone involved in a fatal accident with at least VH2 in Georgia."

"I see," Husto said. "Well, I'll defer to you on that. It's been a long time since I've had to get my hands dirty doing any criminal defense work."

Maggie bit her tongue. "That's just the law that's on the books."

The third element of a negligence action—causation—is tasked with a difficult question: *Since the defendant broke the rule, did their actions cause the harm that is claimed by the plaintiff?* The element has long proved troublesome for plaintiffs in civil cases, and it stands as the key line of defense in negligence actions.

Husto started slowly, revealing just a piece of his strategy. "In looking at the accident report, I don't see any mention of your lady failing to maintain her lane on the day of the wreck. No mention of her speeding, either."

"That's because she wasn't."

Husto's tone remained casual. "Our expert seems to think that may be the case, though."

"How so?"

"Well, I haven't read all the reports, but it sounds like your lady—"

Maggie interrupted. "Her name was Shondra."

"No, of course, my mistake," Husto said, unflustered. "From what I hear from our expert, it sounds like Shondra Jones may have been running too fast as well. That she hydroplaned out on that highway, sliding right into another car on the road. We know another driver, other than Benson, was at the scene. He witnessed the wreck and has already stated that Shondra sideswiped him moments before the fatal blow from Mr. Benson's Peterbilt."

"That's one of the reasons the manufacturer of the steering system is involved, Jack."

"I see. Well, you must understand that the family of Alvin Hughes would like a quick resolution of this matter. Helping your client, and her family, understand that Shondra contributed to this wreck would be the most reasonable approach."

The fourth element of a negligence claim—damages—looks at the question of: *How much harm did the rule breaker cause?* When a person is killed because of someone else's negligence, that harm is immeasurable.

"I'm sure you can appreciate the fact that my client, Maya Jones, just lost her mother and brother. Her life will never be the same. Her family will *never* be the same."

"Those are arguments for a jury," Husto said dismissively. "My client's family is just as impacted as the Joneses have been."

"Then, you know we have a responsibility—as advocates for our clients —to get to the truth of who is responsible for this loss of life."

"You are delaying the inevitable," Husto replied, his first mention of a superior position in the litigation. "Shondra Jones's negligence more than contributed to this wreck. My client's family should receive the proceeds from the insurance policies that are in place. It will save us all time and money. It will save your clients a lot of heartache."

"Don't worry about my clients."

"I've asked around about you, Maggie. Most say you are a capable trial lawyer and—"

"I appreciate that."

"I'm just saying, I remember being a young, hungry trial lawyer like you. I pushed cases forward that I shouldn't have. Made promises to clients that I couldn't keep."

"You are overstepping," she said, trying to maintain her composure. The last thing she wanted was a heated scrap in the opening minutes of the lawsuit. Especially with another lawyer she was supposed to be on the same team as. "If you are worried about the money, there will be enough to go around."

Husto paused. "Will there?"

There exists an unofficial fifth element to every negligence claim. A plaintiff certainly must prove the four core elements, but the unofficial fifth element—insurance coverage—can never be overlooked. A defendant to a lawsuit must have the ability to pay the value of the claim.

"Between Benson and BTF Freight, there is two million in coverage,"

Maggie said. "Track Steering will have to kick in the rest if they want to settle the claim."

"You are going to have to drag Track Steering into a courtroom and get a verdict before they will pay a dime. Like I said, I've dealt with them before."

"That's what I plan to do. You can join in the fight, Jack."

A silence filled the phone line as neither had anything else to say. Maggie glanced at the small digital screen on her desk phone. They'd only been speaking for fifteen minutes, but the battle lines were drawn.

Husto spoke first. "You understand that I'll have to file a cross-claim against your clients."

Maggie nodded on the other end of the line, taking in a deep breath before responding. Her clients would face three defendants, no doubt with capable attorneys. Now, they'd also face another challenger from their same side of the aisle.

"Let's get to it, then."

15

Lawton Crane sat up in bed and admired the view. Afternoon light cut through the partially drawn drapes of the hotel room. They bounced from a brass-bordered mirror that held her reflection on the opposite wall. Standing at the end of the bed, her bare back to him, she pulled a pair of jeans up over her long legs. Her tapered waist, sculpted rear, and muscular back were those of an athlete. She turned to him as she slipped her bra on, clasping it in the back with her left hand.

"Is that how you looked at me in class this semester?"

"I've always looked at you as a brilliant law student," he said with a smile. "Now, I am just learning to appreciate other things about you."

Charlotte slipped her blouse on and buttoned it halfway up. The edge of her bra still peeked out from the open neckline. "I'm glad this didn't happen sooner, then."

"Why's that?" Crane asked, readjusting the pillows behind his back. "I'm rather enjoying myself."

"Call me a prude, but I prefer to earn my grades based off of my performance in the classroom."

Crane shrugged. "High marks all around."

"Uh-huh, I bet. I'm guessing it would have been a little hard for you to teach a class full of eighty students while picturing me without my clothes on."

"I'm a professional."

"Right," she replied with a wink. "Should I leave the money on the table over there?"

He laughed again. "The first few are free. Then you start paying."

"I'll bring my money next time."

Crane caught himself before he said something that sounded desperate. The forty-one-year-old was already enamored with the law student. New to teaching, he'd never done anything like this before. Back when he was married—"working late nights"—he'd slept around his old law firm with a few paralegals, but they'd always been younger, and married, too. Nothing close to the beauty that stood before him.

"Where are you headed?" he asked, trying to sound casual. "We have the room until tomorrow."

"I'm catching a flight this evening out of Reagan."

"Where to?"

"Tallahassee, Florida. There is a campaign event back in my hometown. I am going to work a little behind the scenes for the senator and check in with my uncle."

Crane nodded. He already knew she was planning to join the senator's office for the trip to Blake County. John Deese had sent him information about the trip.

"Does your family know you are interning for Collins?"

A cell phone was in Charlotte's hand. No doubt scheduling a ride back to her place through an app. "I really don't want to get into it. It's complicated."

"Aren't they going to know with you being in town at the same time?"

"It's not like I'll be up on stage with him. Honestly, I'm not really all that involved with his campaign activities. I've been focusing more on helping to get things in order for an annual forum set to take place soon in Bilbao, Spain."

He pressed her for clarification. "So, you aren't planning to go to the campaign event in Blakeston?"

Charlotte's phone dinged. "I doubt it. Look, my ride is here, so I'm going to run."

He'd frozen the mood with the conversation about home. She looked up at him and smiled again, buttoning two more of the buttons on her blouse. He made his play to finish on a high note.

"This hotel room is nice, but I liked your place better."

"My place?" she said with a laugh. "We were both pretty tipsy that night after the restaurant. I bet you don't even remember coming back to my place."

"Maybe not completely, but I enjoyed what I can remember about it."

"I know what you enjoyed," she replied as she walked over and kissed him on the cheek.

"Maybe next time."

"Have a great trip."

"I'm just hoping it's not a disaster," she said, smiling as she walked toward the door. "I'll text you when I get back."

Crane watched her go.

16

Early Friday morning, Maggie and Tim woke with plans to return to Blake County for the weekend. As they readied themselves to walk out the door, Maggie typed a quick email on her cell phone. She instructed her team at the office to work until lunch, then to get out of there and enjoy the weekend. She pressed send and shut her phone off. As Tim passed her in the hallway, carrying a suitcase toward the door, she heard the familiar ping of his device.

"Check your cell phone," she said, slapping him on the rear as he passed. "Little surprise for the staff at Reynolds Law."

Tim put the suitcase down and pulled his phone from a pocket. "Payday *and* an early weekend. Look who is finishing the week out as everybody's favorite boss."

"That directive includes you, big guy."

He laughed. "I already planned on taking the whole day off."

"Oh yeah?"

"Don't worry, it's cool. I'm sleeping with the boss."

"I guess I'm without a driver for the morning, then."

Tim walked over to her and put his arms around her waist. "I can certainly go to work in other ways."

"Yeah, yeah," Maggie said, rolling her eyes. "Toss me those keys."

As they drove, the two talked about things other than work. They laughed, listened to music, and took the journey at a leisurely pace. Maggie couldn't deny the fact that the closer she was to Blake County, the more relaxed she felt. She realized that a force had been pulling her back for some time now, and there was no use resisting. She turned to look over at the passenger seat.

"Tim, I think we should move back to Blakeston."

"I've been talking to a Realtor for the last couple of weeks," he said, without looking up from his phone. His tone was beyond casual. "I already planned to take you to see a house tomorrow."

"Are you serious?"

Tim turned to her. "It was supposed to be a surprise."

"What about Tampa?"

"What about it?"

"That's not an answer."

"Okay, Mags. Blake County just feels like home. How's that for an answer?"

It wasn't a well-tooled argument. It was more the simple explanation of a gut decision. She loved that about him. "Well, what about the practice?"

"Look, I can't tell you what to do there," he said with his palms up. "I can tell you that we have been chasing whales down there for the last five years, though. Not a one has been anything close to the Jones case. People want you to represent them here. People with real cases. I don't know how much more of a sign we need."

She nodded. It was simple, really. They didn't own the office space in Tampa. They didn't have a close group of friends to leave behind. The house would sell in no time, and there weren't any kids to worry about uprooting—yet.

Blake County was where they belonged.

The traffic surprised them as they pulled into downtown Blakeston. Cars and trucks lined the city streets. Maggie drove around, looking for an open space. She found one four blocks from the downtown's main drag and eased the car in between two lifted pickup trucks.

"What in the world is going on downtown tonight?"

"Who knows," Tim said, stepping out of the car's passenger side. "Maybe there's some kind of concert tonight?"

They locked the car and made their way toward the quaint brick buildings of downtown Blakeston. They had reservations for 7:30 at Juno, a favorite restaurant on the main square. They held hands as they walked along the sidewalk. Merchants still had the doors open to their shops, and a few artists had exhibits set up on the barricaded streets. Maggie nodded to a few of the familiar faces that passed. She knew she had not been forgotten in the small Georgia town. She was the lady lawyer that represented Lee Acker. The person they believed kept the truth about the murder of Jake Collins. A truth that the rest of the town still yearned for.

"Look," Maggie said as they approached the downtown's square. Both eyed the rows of political signs that lined an elevated stage in front of the Blake County Courthouse. "Looks like there is a campaign event for Bill Collins tonight."

"Great," Tim groaned. "Let's just dip into Juno. They'll tuck us somewhere in the back. That way we don't have to listen to that rascal's speech."

"Rascal?" Maggie said, turning to Tim with a grin. "Really?"

He winked. "I'm a Black guy that's house hunting in Blakeston. I'm trying to blend in, Mags."

They checked in at the restaurant, but their table wouldn't be ready for another fifteen minutes. The bar was full, so they stepped back outside to watch the rally begin. A crowd had gathered around the stage, and music played from tall speakers. An Allman Brothers favorite had many of those in attendance singing and talking excitedly among themselves. Tim joined in with the crowd, belting out the lyrics in a high-pitched voice and playing air guitar against his waist.

Maggie bobbed her head, swaying along until the music lowered. The crowd turned its attention to the stage and the historic courthouse that stood behind it. Maggie spotted the head of what looked like Bill Collins. She and Tim were near the back of the crowd, but the front steps leading to the door of the restaurant were elevated just enough. She could see him clearly from her vantage point. He was waiting at the edge of the stage, getting ready to step into his element. Even from where she stood, she recognized the moment. The few seconds before climbing into the ring. That excitement, mixed with an uneasy energy. She often felt the same way before she stepped in front of a jury.

The crowd started to clap and holler as they sensed the candidate was ready to address the group. He took the stage, and the applause rose another octave. He egged his supporters on with large hand motions, allowing the adulation to continue for a time, then signaling for the group to quiet. As he did, sirens could be heard wailing in the distance.

"I have a table for Dawson," said a voice from the doorway. "Table for Dawson."

"Perfect timing," Maggie said as she turned to the voice. "We'll be right in."

The speech began as Tim and Maggie started toward the front door of Juno. The sirens in the distance continued. They served as an eerie instrumental soundtrack tucked in the background of the senator's words. Tim held the door open to the restaurant.

"Apparently half the force is out running somewhere."

"It sure sounds like it," Maggie said as she stepped through the door. "Hopefully everyone's okay."

Charlotte cut down the path that ran along the river. She slowed her pace, carefully choosing where to place her feet as the trail descended along the steep bank. She knew the route well. She'd fallen hard on a spot of slick clay the summer before her senior year of high school. The spot had been well hidden below a heap of pine straw on the downslope. It rolled her four times at full speed. She'd also been kidnapped on the trail later that same year. She hadn't been back to run it since.

Charlotte opened things back up as the trail flattened out. Her running shoes pounded against the ground, and her legs burned from the dead-out sprint. She flipped her wrist over and checked her watch—sixty-three minutes in.

Time to kick, she told herself. *Only one more mile to go.*

When Charlotte needed to push herself on a run, she took her mind elsewhere. She dissociated herself from the pain in a manner that allowed her body to cross the threshold to elite performance. A level that only a select group of runners could ever dream to compete at. For her, it often felt like an out-of-body experience when she went to that space. There, she reinserted herself into old memories, reliving the fear, excitement, and anger from a different time in her life. All to tamp down the intense exhaustion that waited at the end of a run. All to fill that void that waited in her life when she wasn't running.

She breathed in deep, counting the foot strikes to the ground. *Home-stretch.*

She thought back to the day she fell on the trail. She remembered how it scared her in the moment. Her body smacked the ground, dazing her as she flipped down the bank. She should have broken several bones that day, but she stood up after the fall and walked the rest of the way home. There, she found her dad waiting for her on the front porch as she came up the drive. He never told her he timed her runs, but she knew he did. He always had a mental stopwatch running. Just in case something went wrong.

She eyed the watch again—sixty-five minutes in. *Almost there.*

Two weeks later, he brought her back out to the same trail with him. Her first run in the woods since the fall. She'd been reluctant to go, but she didn't want to disappoint him. She could still hear his voice as they walked toward the trail together. His cadence slow, encouraging.

There's nothing to it, Charlotte. Your mind wants you to be scared. It wants to protect you. Your body won't quit on you, though. Remember that. It will go as far as you will it. Trust it. Push it.

They ran the trail together. She remembered how satisfied he looked as she pushed ahead of him in the woods that day. She left him behind in that training session, and each one after that. He never was able to keep up with her again. He told her that day to always remember the strength inside of her.

You are fierce. You are strong. You are an Acker.

She eyed the end of the trail. A steep incline awaited, so she dug her shoes into the dirt and charged the bank. As she did, she thought back to the night they kidnapped her. She remembered the truck as it raced along beside her. Its headlights bouncing as it skidded to a stop at the head of the trail. They'd waited until she was near the end of her route, tired and running on fumes. She remembered how they jumped from the truck and started yelling for her to get down on the ground. Both had guns drawn. Both—John Deese and the other man—grabbed her body as they forced her toward the truck. She'd tried to break loose. She'd tried to run from them. She couldn't fight the two of them, though. They'd been too strong.

Never again, she told herself. *I'll never let it happen again.*

Both legs screamed as Charlotte crested the edge of the bank. They immediately thanked her once her shoes met the gravel road. There, she began walking toward the lights of home. Her heavy breathing was all that she could hear as she walked along the edge of the quiet woods. She sucked in air through her nose, then blew it out through her mouth. In through her nose. Out through her mouth.

What would he think? she thought as she turned up the drive. The tall house was lit up, but the front porch sat empty. No one waited for her. *What would he think about my decisions?*

She considered this as she climbed up the steps on the front porch. Off in the distance, she heard a sound that didn't belong in the woods. She turned to look out into the darkness and quiet that surrounded her home.

He would be proud, she thought. *I know it.*

Before she turned to go into the house, she heard the sound again. Drifting through the night sky—she heard the blare of sirens.

17

Lawton Crane stood in his boxers in front of the bathroom mirror. He ran water over the blade of his razor, half listening to a CBS news segment that played from the television in the other room. He placed the razor on the bathroom counter and bent down to splash the warm water on his face. He let the warmth from the sink wash over him as he massaged his tired, puffy eyes. When he stood back up, he assessed his appearance in the mirror. He stared at the reflection, shaking his head at what he saw. He looked like a fraud.

The newscast changed in tone as the on-screen reporter declared that she had breaking news out of Georgia. Crane cut the faucet off and stepped to the doorway of the bathroom. A large "Breaking News" banner was plastered in bold letters on the TV screen. Information was still coming in, but the reporter notified its viewers that CBS had been able to confirm the details of a shocking tragedy. The banner on the screen changed to: *Wife of US Senator Found Dead Outside Georgia Home*.

A photo of an ornate iron gate appeared on the screen. It pictured what looked like the entranceway to a large, wooded estate. The reporter described the photo as the main entrance to Kelley Hill Plantation, the family estate of Senator Bill Collins and that of his late wife, Lucy Kelley Collins. The correspondent's voice described the property as a large hunting preserve in Blake County, Georgia. A secluded piece of private land that was only accessible by the Collins family and their guests.

Crane walked over to his bed and sat at the end. He stared at the screen, listening as the only available details from the homicide investigation were stretched out for dramatic effect. A photo of Bill and Lucy Collins appeared on screen. The image of the classic-looking couple was most likely plucked from the countless images CBS already had on file. The two were pictured smiling at a ritzy gala hosted at the White House. The senator dressed in black tie. Lucy Collins wearing a dark evening gown that shimmered in the light.

"Last night, authorities with the Blake County Sheriff's Office responded to a 911 call placed from Kelley Hill Plantation. There, deputies found Lucy Kelley Collins unresponsive. Cause of death has not been formally announced, but reliable sources have indicated that Collins suffered multiple gunshot wounds. She was rushed to the hospital by ambulance, and it is believed she was pronounced dead on arrival."

Crane heard his cell phone vibrating on the nightstand beside his bed. He continued listening to the recap of the events in Georgia.

"Authorities say that the 911 call was placed by a housekeeper. Her initial statement seems to indicate that she returned to the Collinses' vacation home to drop off an order of groceries that was requested by Mrs. Collins. The housekeeper told deputies at the scene that she left the house for the supermarket around 6:15 p.m. that evening and returned to the property around 7:50 p.m."

The cell phone buzzed again on the surface of the nightstand.

"The office of Senator Bill Collins has yet to release an official statement on the death of his wife. However, it is widely known that the Collinses were in town for a campaign rally. The rally took place in the downtown area of Blakeston, Georgia. Authorities believe that the attack on Mrs. Collins took place while Senator Collins was speaking at the rally. The investigation is ongoing, and the local authorities are exploring all possible suspects. They are asking for anyone with information about this incident to please step forward to assist investigators in apprehending the perpetrators."

Crane pressed a button on the remote and muted the television. He didn't move from his seat as he tried to process the events that had been set in motion. His Washington apartment felt worlds away from the woods of South Georgia. He'd met Senator Bill Collins on two occasions. Once while working at his former law firm, and once in his classroom at Georgetown. He'd never met Mrs. Collins, though, and he never would.

The cell phone started vibrating again. Crane stood and walked over to collect it from the bedside table. He hesitated, then pressed the green button on the screen to answer the call.

"You've called three times already," Crane said, paying close attention to the tone in his voice. He wasn't sure who was listening. "Can't you leave a voicemail?"

"I wanted to talk to you, Professor."

"What the hell about?"

"I'm sure you can guess."

Crane could feel a knot growing in his stomach. "I don't know what you are talking about."

"You say that, but you do."

Delta Flight 5149 touched down a few minutes after eleven at Reagan National. The plane landed uneventfully on the airport's main runway, then began taxiing toward its gate. Charlotte sat at a window seat in the main cabin. As she waited, she took in the activity around the busy airport. Catering trucks, pushback tugs, and other ground vehicles loaded down with luggage and supplies zipped by on the tarmac. Personnel wearing reflective gear and ear protection signaled to the commercial jetliners that navigated the area like ships on the water.

As the plane pulled to a stop near its gate, the captain's voice came over the intercom. He notified the passengers aboard that they were being asked to wait a few minutes for the ground crew to fix an issue on the jet bridge. The calm Midwestern voice assured all those on board that if the repairs took longer than fifteen minutes, he would find them another gate. Several passengers nearby groaned in frustration.

Charlotte reached down to the bag between her feet and fished her cell phone out of an inside pocket. She powered on the device and waited as it booted up.

"Holy shit," she murmured as the screen came to life. Her reaction was just loud enough to catch the attention of those seated by her. "This can't be real."

The woman seated next to her turned and asked if everything was okay. Charlotte assured her everything was fine, then began scrolling through a news app with the latest on the situation. An article from the *Washington Post* confirmed it. Lucy Kelley Collins, dead at sixty-four. Found facedown on the ground outside her family's estate in Blake County, Georgia. No witnesses to the crime. No leads to speak of. Only an inarguable manner of killing—two fatal gunshot wounds.

Charlotte read through the details of the murder again, then scanned the remainder of the article. It provided a succinct summary of the victim's most notable accomplishments. Born in Blakeston, Georgia, October 9, 1957. Attended the University of Georgia for undergraduate studies. Second runner-up in the Miss America 1978 Pageant of Beauty and Talent in Atlantic City, New Jersey, as representative for her home state of Georgia. Married in 1979 to William H. Collins, a recent member of the United States House of Representatives and current member of the United States Senate. Mother to one child, Jacob K. Collins. Her suspected role in his murder, along with that of Lee Acker, didn't make the cut, though.

Charlotte closed the article out and flipped over to her messages. She had seven texts from her mother. Another four from her uncle. One message from Bill, and an email from his chief of staff, George Dell. They all encouraged her, in one way or another, to speak with them before making any comments to reporters on the matter. None of them mentioned law enforcement.

The captain's voice chimed in again over the intercom. "Looks like they are going to finally lower the drawbridge for us, folks. The crew here is going to pop the hatch in just a moment, and we will get you on to where you need to be. On behalf of Delta, our partners, and wonderful crew, thank you for flying with us. We hope you have a wonderful rest of your day."

Charlotte suddenly felt uneasy in the tight surroundings of the aircraft.

People were already standing in the aisle, adding to the cramped feel of the cabin. Charlotte leaned over to look around the seat in front of her and checked for movement from the flight attendants at the front of the plane. They whispered to one another, eyes directed toward the passengers at the rear of the aircraft. Charlotte pushed back in her seat and took a deep breath in. *Lucy Collins was a killer that got what was coming to her. It was a good thing, right?*

Passengers near the front of the plane started to file out of the aircraft. Storage bins above the rows of seats popped and creaked as suitcases were retrieved. Charlotte allowed a few eager passengers to push by her in the aisle, then started toward the exit. She eyed the flight attendant and captain as she neared the cockpit. The senior attendant pulled a radio to her mouth and spoke quietly into the instrument. Still, they both smiled and nodded to Charlotte as she passed.

She made her way down the jet bridge and through the door that led to the terminal. As she entered the airport, she noticed three police officers in uniform standing near the gate counter on her right. She considered their faces.

"Charlotte Acker?" a voice over her left shoulder asked.

Charlotte turned to it and found a man in a suit leaning against the wall.

"That's me," she said. "Who are you?"

The man pulled a badge from his jacket and showed it to her. "I'm a detective. Can I speak with you for a moment?"

Charlotte studied him. Thin, maybe early fifties. Blue suit of a polyester blend. No socks and brown loafers.

"I don't think you told me your name, Detective."

"Pete Baggett," he replied. "Arlington County Police Department."

A few people waiting at the nearby gates had taken notice of the small group of police officers serving as a welcome party. The curious onlookers kept their distance, but Charlotte noticed a gangly teenager had his phone up and was filming the interaction. She considered her options.

"And what exactly do you need to talk to me about?"

The detective looked to his left and noticed the interested bystanders. He straightened his tie before responding. "The Metropolitan Washington

Airports Authority has an office here that we can sit down in. It could be a little more private. How about we go there for this talk?"

"Do I have a choice?"

"Of course," Baggett replied. "You aren't under arrest."

Charlotte paused. "But?"

He shrugged his shoulders as if he wasn't the one calling the shots. "Look, Charlotte, come talk to me a few minutes. Answer some questions, and you will be on your way."

"That's the first option," Charlotte said with a smile. "Tell me about the second."

He nodded. "If you aren't open to talking about where you have been for the last twenty-four hours, I'll be forced to make this a more formal inquiry. You understand?"

"Sure," she replied, nodding her head as well. "I understand."

"Good," the detective said. He turned slightly to his left and motioned to the group of officers standing at the desk. "Let's get an interview room lined up, guys. Can one of you show her the way to—"

"Lawyer," Charlotte said, interrupting the detective's directions. "I'd like to speak with my—"

"I heard what you said. You aren't under arrest, Charlotte. Do you understand that?"

She offered her own shrug. "I still want to speak with my lawyer."

Baggett looked down at his loafers. He shook his head from side to side, smiling. "Let's go for a ride, then."

18

Charlotte sat in the back seat of the unmarked Chevrolet Malibu. The detective drove, while a female police officer rode in the front passenger seat. A marked Ford Explorer followed closely behind. Charlotte stared out the passenger-side window as the vehicles exited the concrete perimeter of the airport and made their way out onto the George Washington Parkway. The Potomac soon appeared out her window, glistening under the afternoon sun.

"I'd like to call my lawyer on the way. Is that all right with you?"

The detective lifted his eyes to the rearview mirror. "Fine by me."

The officer in the front seat handed over a cell phone. Charlotte looked at it, realizing it wasn't her own.

"I'll need mine. I don't know the number by heart."

The detective nodded to the officer. All part of their game. "Go ahead and hand back her cell phone."

Charlotte wasn't handcuffed. She took the phone and unlocked it. Still, the female police officer eyed her as if she might somehow call in a hit on their vehicle at that very moment.

"Who are you calling?" the detective asked. "Just out of curiosity."

Charlotte ignored the question as she pressed the phone to her ear. She waited for it to begin ringing, but it didn't. The call went straight to voicemail. *This is Maggie Reynolds. I'm not available right now. Please leave a message after the tone.*

"Come on," Charlotte murmured. She knew Maggie's law office would be closed on a Saturday, so she mashed the number for her cell phone again. She achieved the same result. *This is Maggie Reynolds. I'm not available right now. Please leave a message after the tone.* Charlotte obliged. "Hey, this is Charlotte—um, Charlotte Acker, that is. I need you to call me back as soon as you can. It's kind of urgent."

She left her number and ended the call. The vehicle slowed to a stop in traffic, and Charlotte noticed the detective was watching her in the rearview mirror again.

"Know any other lawyers?"

He opened the door to the interview room and found her alone. She sat at a small table, a plastic bottle of water and a single slip of paper placed nearby. She offered him a cautious smile. He returned one of his own.

"Thanks for coming," she said in a quiet voice. "I really didn't know who else to call."

Lawton Crane took a seat on the other side of the table. "I came as quickly as I could. It was a mess getting an Uber over from the stadium. Place was packed."

"Who's in town?"

"Orioles," he replied as he added a stick of gum to his mouth. "The Nats looked good today, though."

"I'm glad."

The door to the interview room opened, and the detective poked his head inside.

"How long do you two need?" he said, some irritation in his voice. "My grandkid has a birthday party this afternoon that I'd like to get to. I already told my daughter I'd be there."

"You want us to come back tomorrow?" Crane asked as he turned in his seat. "Monday might even be better."

Baggett shook his head. "I got called in on a Saturday to do this. We are doing it today."

"And I left a good ball game on a Saturday afternoon to be here for your questioning."

The two men stared at one another a moment, sizing the other up.

"Take another ten minutes. Shouldn't take me long if you'll let me ask my questions."

"What is this all about?" Crane asked, catching the detective before he closed the door.

"We will get into that, counselor. I'll be back in ten."

The door closed with a slam, and Crane turned back to Charlotte.

"Do you know what this is about?"

"I think so," she replied as she folded her arms across her chest.

He chewed his gum some more, waiting. Crane hoped she was considering whether she could trust him.

"This room isn't supposed to be recorded at the moment, right?" she asked. "I mean, Baggett knows this is an attorney-client consultation."

"Look," Crane began with a sigh. "You know I have never handled any criminal defense work. In my old firm, we had a white-collar defense section, but I steered clear of the stuff. This is the first time I've ever even been in an interrogation room."

"So, do you think we should talk in here?"

"My understanding is these rooms aren't *supposed* to be recorded when a lawyer is meeting with a client. There are plenty of stories about police stations surreptitiously recording attorney-client conversations, though. I recommend you only tell me what I need to know today. Nothing more."

Charlotte nodded. "I know the detective wants to ask me where I've been for the last twenty-four hours. He told me that much."

"You flew back from home today, right?"

"That's right. I was back home in Blake County a few days visiting family, helping the senator with a few things behind the scenes. Nothing too exciting."

Crane nodded. "I'm sure the detective will ask you if you saw Lucy Collins while you were there."

"That we can assume."

"I'm sure he will also ask you if you know anything about her murder."

"Aside from what I've heard in the news?"

"Of course."

"What do I tell him?"

Crane paused a moment. He wasn't sure what a true criminal defense lawyer would advise a client to do in this situation. "I don't know, Charlotte. You can tell them the truth. You can tell them that you had nothing to do with this whole mess. You can also keep your mouth shut and tell them that same exact thing later. It's going to be up to you."

"If I don't answer Baggett's questions, he is going to consider me a suspect."

"Again, I'm not very familiar with this process. I know what you have told me about Blake County, though. I'm pretty sure you will continue to be a suspect regardless of what you do or don't say."

"I'm not going to answer his questions, then," Charlotte replied. "At least not today. I want to know more about what happened back home. I want to know why they picked me up."

Crane knew it was the right decision. "I'll let him know."

"Before you do, see if you can get any other insight on what the hell is going on."

Crane stood to step toward the door. Before he could get to it, it opened, and the detective reappeared.

"Can I come in?" Baggett asked.

"Sure," Crane replied. He walked around to the other side of the table and sat next to Charlotte. "Let's hear it."

"I don't think I know you," Baggett said as he took the last open seat at the table. "I've been doing this job for a little while. I know most of the criminal guys that do this kind of work. I've not heard your name before."

"It's a big city."

"That it is, Mr. Lawton Crane."

Crane quickly asked, "Are you even investigating a crime here in your jurisdiction?"

Baggett smiled. "Nope."

"So, why are we here, Detective?"

"Is your client going to talk to me?"

"She might," Crane snapped. "Once we know what this is all about."

"Oh, she knows what this is all about, counselor."

"Enlighten me, then."

Baggett stared at Crane. "The wife of a sitting senator was murdered last night in South Georgia. The authorities down there are looking at all angles. My department was simply asked to assist in looking at one of those angles for them."

"Which is?"

"Your client, and the fact that she literally flew the jurisdiction of the law enforcement agencies running this homicide investigation down in Georgia."

"I still haven't heard how this murder has anything to do with my client?"

"Look, they know she was in Blake County last night. They just want to know where."

"I've never been down there, Detective, but we can assume a lot of people were in that community last night."

Baggett turned in his chair to speak directly to Charlotte. "Your lawyer here is obstructing this *very* simple process. Tell me about your whereabouts for the last twenty-four hours. That's all I need to know. Then you can go."

Crane put a hand up. "Hold on, Charlotte."

"Are you instructing your client not to answer?"

"I am right now."

"Okay, I'll need to place a hold on her," the detective said as he began to stand. "And we can resume this little discussion on Monday. By then, I'll have heard back from the crime lab and investigators down there."

"You're going to keep me here at the jail?" Charlotte exclaimed. "Why?"

"Your fingerprints were found at the scene of a murder, along with hair that looks a lot like yours," Baggett said as he made his way toward the door. "The DNA results will take time, but the prints are apparently a solid match."

"Fingerprints?" Charlotte said, her voice rising. "Don't just walk out the door. Explain to me what the hell is going on!"

"Your prints were on two shell casings found at the scene," Baggett said coolly. "Someone from the jail will be over to escort you to a holding cell. We should know soon if—"

The door opened to the interview room, and the same uniformed officer that rode over from the airport stepped inside. She held Charlotte's cell phone.

"I've been sitting up at the desk in intake, and Ms. Acker's cell phone keeps ringing. Her mother has called eight or nine times in the last thirty minutes. I thought you may want to let her—"

The phone began ringing in the officer's hand.

"Is that her calling again?" Baggett asked.

The officer checked the screen. "It says the call is from a Maggie Reynolds."

"That's my lawyer," Charlotte said. "Let me talk to her."

Baggett took the phone from the officer and pressed the button on the screen to answer the call. He placed the phone to his ear.

"Good afternoon, this is Pete Baggett. I'm a detective with the Arlington County Police Department in the Commonwealth of Virginia."

He paused, listening to the voice on the other end of the line.

Charlotte motioned with her hand. "Give me the phone, Detective."

He put a finger up. "Yes, ma'am. I'm sitting here with Charlotte Acker now. She has a lawyer with her, though. They have already refused to answer some questions about Ms. Acker's whereabouts over the last twenty-four hours."

Crane interjected. "Detective, if you will give us the room, we will—"

Baggett shook his head at Crane. He spoke back into the phone. "Ms. Acker will probably be transported back to Georgia in the next few days if that—"

He stopped, listening again.

"Yes, ma'am, that is correct. She will be charged down there."

"Charged?" Charlotte yelled at the detective. "With what?"

Baggett stared at Charlotte as he spoke into the phone. His voice remained calm. "From what I hear—an arrest warrant for malice murder will be signed today. They should have her back in Blake County by the end of next week."

19

Maggie pressed the button on the intercom to the right of the metal door. A faint beeping tone sounded from deep inside the labyrinth of concrete walls and steel. It was just after midnight, and all appeared to be quiet around the county jail. Only the sound of crickets chirping in the thick woods filled the air. She pressed the button again, this time holding it down a second longer. Still nothing. She glanced up at a camera positioned above the jail's fortified entryway. As she did, a voice crackled from a small speaker beside the door.

"I about don't believe my eyes," the man said. "I'm staring hard at my video monitor in here. I want to make sure I'm not seeing a ghost. Is that *the* Maggie Reynolds standing outside my jail?"

"You'll have to let me in to find out," Maggie said, speaking directly into the metal facing of the intercom.

"Who do you need to see?"

"Don't you know I'm here to see you?"

"Don't be giving me that sweet talk, Maggie Reynolds. You'd have gotten around to visiting me years ago if that was the case."

"I'm getting around to it now," she said with a laugh. "Let me in there. I need to see the Acker girl, too. I heard they dropped her off here a couple of hours ago."

"I figured that's what you were here for. I'll buzz you through."

An electric buzzing sound vibrated from the large door. Maggie pushed against it, and the metal latch gave way. From there, she entered a small room surrounded by reinforced windows. In one corner of the anteroom stood an old wooden pulpit. A faded cross was etched in the wooden stem, and a thick logbook lay open on its tilted surface. The book kept records of all outsiders that entered the jail, regardless of the reason. Maggie stepped to it and wrote her name and the time under the day's date—July 2, 2022.

Through one of the windows, she saw the wave of Elroy Monroe, the lead on the jail's night shift. The second steel door at the other side of the small room buzzed, and Maggie pressed against it. She stepped through the doorway into the jail's booking and intake area. In one breath, she took in the familiar smell of her past. The antiseptic tang of a county jail was an all too familiar odor to those that worked at one time or another as public defenders. It was a smell they had to endure often in client consultations and busy court days. It wasn't unbearable for Maggie—it simply stank of regression.

The steel door slammed behind her, and she turned to the man at the desk. "Elroy, I really do love what you have done with the place."

"I'm glad you like it," he said. "We had a few of the inmates paint the booking area about a month ago."

"Looks like you went with the beautiful eggshell beige again. Excellent choice."

"That's what the county wanted. It's the best at keeping the stains off the walls."

"Gross," Maggie said with a shake of the head. "That's an image I didn't need to add to my evening."

Elroy smiled. "You asked."

Maggie took in the area around her. Stacks of paperwork from the day's bookings of criminal defendants cluttered the long desk that ran the length of the intake area. Elroy Monroe stood on the other side. For as long as Maggie worked in Blake County, Elroy had served as the lead on the jail's third shift. She would often visit her clients in the evening to avoid the commotion of the daytime's arrests and other activities. Elroy was always there for a good chat. Plus, he treated her, along with her clients, with a level of courtesy befitting of a small hotel. For that reason, she always referred to him as the night manager at the county jail.

"How is my girl doing?"

Elroy shrugged. "They brought her in through the sally port about an hour ago. Hasn't gone back into the women's dorm yet. She'll have to go through medical first."

Maggie knew the process well. "Did they bring her in by bus?"

"Yes, ma'am. Last night, they flew her into Atlanta. Drove her down today with some other inmates. I believe they had stops in Columbus and Americus on the way down."

Inmate transport—especially across state lines—can be a dangerous process for everyone involved. Some inmates consider the time in transit as an opportunity to escape, and a few have been successful over the years. For that reason, law enforcement and correctional officers assisting in the transport are constantly on high alert. Buses carrying inmates often shackle the accused at the wrists, waist, and ankles to prevent them from staging an attack on those handling the transport and the other inmates along for the ride. Maggie was glad that Charlotte had arrived in Blake County. At least here, they would try to keep her safe.

"Does Sheriff Clay want her put in general population?" Maggie asked.

"I don't know," Elroy replied. "The sheriff has been real buttoned up about the whole thing. I suspect he'll have to eventually move her to gen pop. That's a decision above my pay grade, though."

She nodded. "I hear he's going to consider keeping the investigation with his office. Is that true?"

Elroy rubbed the back of his neck, clearly mulling over the question.

In Georgia, the sheriff is a constitutional officer elected at the county level. Serving in terms of four years, the sheriff acts as a county's chief law enforcement officer. The position is not subject to oversight by the county government because the sheriff is bound only by those responsibilities laid out by statute and those set forth in the Georgia Constitution. The modern-day sheriff's office is tasked with maintenance of safety in the court system and service of legal papers; administration of the county jail; and most general law enforcement matters in unincorporated areas of the county.

As the work of homicide investigation has grown more complicated over the years, the sheriffs of Georgia have routinely requested the assistance of the Georgia Bureau of Investigation—the GBI—to assist in the more complicated murder investigations. Still, it is the sheriff's decision whether to request the assistance of the GBI for an offense that occurs in the county—jurisdiction over the investigation rests only in the sheriff.

"You know, Sheriff Clay goes way back with those Ackers," Elroy said after a long pause. "He and Charlotte's daddy played ball together. They finished school up the same year."

"The same goes for Jake Collins, too. Weren't they all in school together?"

"All I know," Elroy said, lifting a hand with the index and middle fingers wrapped together, "is that Clay and Acker were like this at one point."

Maggie understood. "I didn't get a chance to meet Sheriff Clay when I was working up here. He hadn't been elected yet. I think he was still stationed elsewhere, serving on active duty."

"That's right. He came home the year after Lee was killed. He ran in a special election for the Blake County Sheriff in 2019."

"I hear good things."

Elroy nodded. "I wish he would have been the sheriff back when Lee was in here. Clay would have looked out for him."

Maggie didn't say anything. She knew what Elroy was thinking. If Maggie hadn't gotten Lee out on bond, he might still be alive.

Maggie decided to air out the question. "You think Lee would still be alive if Sheriff Clay had been in town?"

"Probably not," Elroy replied. "The Collinses seem to always have a way of getting what they want."

Maggie considered the obvious flaw in the night manager's theory—Lucy Collins was now dead. Her streak of influence had run out.

Maggie made a showing of looking at her watch. "Let's wake Charlotte up. I'd like to talk to her for a few minutes."

Elroy's hand went to the keys on his belt. "Yes, ma'am."

Charlotte closed the door to the visitation room. She straightened her oversized jumpsuit, then pulled a collapsible chair out from under the table to sit on. Her hair was up, tied into a neat ponytail with a rubber band. She looked remarkably rested for someone that had just made an eight-hundred-mile trip in shackles. The Acker cool clearly on display.

"You are a hard person to get in touch with."

Maggie smiled. "I'm here now."

"This is true."

"How are you holding up?"

"I'm fine," Charlotte said, waving her hand in a dismissive manner. "Let's skip all that, though."

"Sure," Maggie replied, leaning forward to rest her elbows on the edge of the small table. "What do you want to talk about?"

"Are you going to represent me in this?"

"That's what I'm here to talk about."

Charlotte sighed as she looked down at her fingernails on her left hand. "My mother told me you weren't doing criminal defense work anymore. Is that true?"

Maggie readjusted herself in her seat. "That's mostly true."

"Why?" Charlotte asked, eyes still down as she picked at a thumbnail. The light pink polish had begun to chip. "You were one of the best, right?"

"It's complicated."

"Is the money not good enough?"

"In what?"

"In criminal defense work," Charlotte said, lifting her eyes to Maggie's. "It's not as lucrative as all the personal injury stuff, from what I hear."

"No, not as a whole."

Charlotte kept her eyes on Maggie. "You know my family can pay your fee, right?"

"I know."

"Is that why you're here, then? To get the terms straight?"

"No," Maggie said, careful with the edge in her voice. "I'm here in this rural jail, well after midnight, because I want to make sure you are okay. I told your mother that—"

"My mother," Charlotte laughed. "I'm sure she is very worried."

"Look, Charlotte, I am here because I want to help you through this. You are in some deep—"

"Are you going to represent me?"

"I don't do criminal defense work anymore, and I—"

"Unbelievable," Charlotte said with a sigh. "You are beyond ungrateful. My dad's trial—my dad's death, really—put you on the map, and now you—"

"Let me finish," Maggie hissed.

Charlotte motioned with a hand and looked away.

"I was going to tell you that I am willing to consider taking the case. It must be because that is unequivocally what you want, though. I was never able to see your father's case through. I told him I would take him to a verdict. I intend to make good on that promise."

"I want you to represent me."

Maggie replied slowly. "Okay, then that's what we'll do."

"With one condition."

"What's that?"

"I want you to handle my defense with co-counsel."

Maggie stared across the table at her new client. Her small law firm was more than well equipped to handle a single criminal case.

"I don't want to put together some large defense team, Charlotte. If you want me to handle your defense, I want to do it my way. I've tried a lot of cases right here in Blake County. I know the terrain."

"I know," Charlotte said. "I just want to bring one other lawyer on board."

"I'll consider it."

Charlotte smiled. "Good."

Maggie started to stand. "I'll reach out to them and feel it out."

Charlotte nodded. "Give me a piece of paper. I'll write his name down for you. He shouldn't be hard to find."

Tim Dawson walked into the Blake County Sheriff's Office a few minutes after 8:00 a.m. As expected, the reception area sat empty. He made no attempt to ring the bell at the warrant clerk's desk. Instead, he pushed through the door that divided the lobby area from the suite of offices and started the familiar trek down the hallway to the employee break room. He knew the layout of the building well. During his time with the GBI, he often interviewed suspects being held in the county jail and assisted deputies of the BCSO in their investigations. The office space had changed little in the years he'd been gone.

As Tim walked the hallway, he scanned the framed portraits that lined the walls. Each one was the face of a sheriff that had once held office in Blake County. True snapshots of South Georgia law enforcement. All men. All white. All except the last photo on the wall.

Tim stopped in front of the portrait of Sheriff Charles Clay. It looked much like his own. A small amount of pride swelled in Tim's chest for the first Black sheriff of Blake County. He eyed the emblem at the bottom of the frame: *January 2019–present.*

A woman spoke from behind him. "This year is an election year for him."

"That's what I hear," Tim said as he turned around. Tracey Howell, all five feet of her, stood leaning against the door to the break room. She'd been handling all the important administrative duties in the building for the last twenty years. "Who is running against him?"

"Kevin Bond," she said, a terseness to her voice. "That prick ran against Charlie back in the special election in 2019. Lost by a little less than three hundred votes."

Tim whistled. "That's pretty damn close."

"Too close," Tracey said. "He has been complaining about some stupid voter fraud scheme since he lost."

In Georgia, the standards to qualify in an election for sheriff are minimal. The person must be a US citizen that is at least twenty-five years old; they must have resided in the county for at least two years immediately preceding the date of qualifying; they must be a registered voter that possesses a high school diploma or an equivalent; and, of course, they cannot possess a felony record.

"Is he accusing Charlie of going out and buying votes?"

"No, he knows no one would ever believe that. He challenged Charlie's residency in Blake County during the years leading up to the last election. He claimed Charlie lied about being a resident of the county. Said he had a home in Virginia Beach. A rental house he received mail at while he was deployed overseas."

Tim nodded. "That's politics for you. When you lose, just accuse the other side of cheating."

Tracey nodded along in agreement. "You are sure a sight for sore eyes, Tim. It's been a little while. What brings you in here?"

"I'd like to see Sheriff Clay if he is in."

"Your wife working the defense for the Acker girl?"

"It looks like it."

"What do you need to talk to Charlie about?"

Tim knew that Tracey was the gatekeeper when it came to appointments with her sheriff. If he froze her out, she'd refuse to facilitate the meeting.

"I need to talk to Clay about the investigation into the death of Lucy Collins. I've heard a lot of rumors, and they can't all be true."

"We call it a murder around here, Tim. Sounds to me like you've been working for defense lawyers too long." She said this with a wink. "And what rumors are you talking about?"

She was probably right. "Like the one saying the sheriff isn't going to bring the boys from the GBI in on this one."

"I don't know anything about that."

"You sure?"

"I don't know anything about anything when it comes to the murder of Lucy Kelley Collins. Everyone in this building knows that's the rule. No reporters, no lawyers, no handsome private investigators."

"I get it," Tim said with a smile. "That's why I need to talk to him. Can't you help me out?"

A burst of morning laughter exploded from the break room behind her. The interruption allowed her time to consider the request.

"He'll be in after lunch," she said. "I'll pencil you in for one o'clock with him. No promises, though."

Just after 10:00 a.m., Maggie placed a call to one Lawton Crane—the name of the attorney Charlotte scribbled on the piece of paper. On the fourth ring, a man answered.

"Hello? This is Lawton." The voice sounded groggy.

"This is Maggie Reynolds. I'm an attorney out of—"

"Yes," Lawton said. He cleared his throat with a cough. "Hello, Maggie —good morning."

"Morning," she replied, diving right into business. "I got your name from Charlotte Acker. She is in jail here in Georgia. As you may know, she is charged in a rather serious criminal matter down here. She has asked me to represent her in connection with it."

"I'm familiar with her problems down there, and I know of you, Maggie. The other day, when Charlotte was picked up at the airport in Arlington, she called me to come sit in on the interview with the detective. I was in the room when you called her phone."

"Right," she said curtly. "Charlotte asked me to call you and get up to speed on things."

Maggie didn't have a problem misrepresenting the purpose of the call. She needed to feel this guy out. Yes, Charlotte was a grown woman now, and she certainly was entitled to her choice of legal counsel. Maggie wasn't about to just bring anyone into their camp, though. Maggie would consider the ask to bring him on board—but that's all she agreed to.

"How is she?" he asked. "I mean how is she holding up?"

The sound of the question struck her as being oddly personal. "She is in jail," Maggie replied slowly. "Otherwise, she seems to be doing fine. I've encouraged her not to dwell too much on what she cannot control. She understands that she'll be in there until we have a bond hearing. Probably longer."

"I was worried about her when they carried her off at the station in Arlington. It has to be a terrible experience. Especially for someone with her kind of upbringing."

"Jail is an awful experience for anyone, Lawton."

"Of course. I just meant that—"

"By the way, how do you two know each other?"

"She took one of my courses this semester."

The short answer left much to be desired. "So, you are a law professor?"

"That's right."

Maggie smiled to herself. Law professors worked in the abstract, far away from the real work in the courtroom. No top-tier professor would come down from their ivory tower to handle a criminal trial in South Georgia. They wouldn't know where to start. "Do you have any trial experience, Professor Crane?"

"Plenty," he quickly replied. "Probably somewhere in the neighborhood of sixty jury trials over the last fifteen years. Mostly in federal court, though."

Surprised by his answer, she fumbled over her words. "And—how long have you been out of practice?"

"Eight or nine months. My last trial was in October of last year. Over in the Eastern District of Pennsylvania. Essentially right there in Philly. A nasty products liability case in front of Judge Neely."

He had her full attention.

"Good outcome, though. It was one of those crazy defective tire cases.

Plaintiff filed against Firestone and some other defendants. The guy drove a set of tires down to the nubs and had a blowout on I-95. Rolled the vehicle and died, of course. Family tried to claim Firestone sold him a bad tire."

"Those can certainly be some tough cases," Maggie said, as if she'd handled a dozen tire cases herself. She knew she had on the phone a true insurance defense man. Someone that knew the game of defending big-time lawsuits. Someone she could learn something from. "Have you done a lot of products liability work?"

"It's pretty much the only thing I did for the last fifteen years. A senior partner at my old firm plucked me out of the bullpen and trained me up during my first year as an associate. I never had a chance to do anything else."

Maggie looked over at the stack of binders she'd started lugging around with her. All information being collected for the Jones case. The more she looked into how to attack the defendants, the more she started to feel she was out of her depth. She needed guidance from someone with experience in high-stakes civil litigation.

"Did you do a lot of work for Firestone?"

"Most of my clients were from the automotive sector, but my firm regularly handled a portion of Firestone's business."

Maggie couldn't believe her good fortune. "That might be useful in—"

"I know what you are going to say," Crane said, stopping her midsentence. "I understand I had no business stepping into that interrogation room the other day with Charlotte. Other than a clinic I worked in during law school, I have no experience in the practice of criminal law."

"That's okay," she said. It wasn't, but she certainly didn't plan to tell him otherwise. "Charlotte was your student, and she was lucky to have a lawyer with your extensive trial experience available to step in on short notice."

"That's very kind of you to say."

Maggie was done considering Charlotte's request. The girl had excellent instincts as far as her choice of counsel. He probably wouldn't help much in the defense of Charlotte, but he'd be a key resource for Maggie in her work on the Jones case.

"Now, before we get into exactly what happened in the interrogation room with Detective Baggett, let's talk about something Charlotte wants you and me to discuss."

Maggie hoped she wasn't moving too fast.

"What's that?" Crane asked. "Is something wrong?"

"She would like us to explore the prospect of working together as co-counsel."

"I don't know if—"

"I think it could be an excellent idea," Maggie quickly added. "And I know Charlotte wants you there at the table."

"She does?"

"Absolutely, Lawton. She'd be crazy not to. You have a distinguished career as a litigator."

"I don't know, Maggie. Do you think it's a good idea? I have no experience working as a criminal defense lawyer."

"I have enough for the both of us."

"Okay," Crane said slowly. "I'm on board if that is what Charlotte wants. I want it to be clear to her that I'll be sitting second chair, though."

"I wouldn't have it any other way."

"Should we just plan to meet a day or two before the bond hearing?"

"That'll be perfect," Maggie said, unable to pull the smile off her face. "We can just catch up then on what was said in Arlington. I'm sure we have a lot to talk about."

"Sounds like a plan."

Maggie hung up and placed her cell phone on the desk. Alone, with no one watching, she stood from her chair and started a little dance.

Tim sat at the end of a leather couch in Sheriff Clay's office. As he waited, he took in the spartan quarters around him. In one corner, a mini fridge with a gym bag stacked on top hummed noisily. Beside it sat two pairs of running shoes and a canister of protein powder. The only photo Tim could find in the large room was an old picture of Clay and his wife on their wedding day. No certificates or awards hung on the walls to commemorate Clay's accomplishments, nor were there any signs up to pledge his loyalties in the world of college football. The only piece of arguable décor was a large American flag pinned to the wall behind the sheriff's desk. It hung proudly, watching over the simple workspace.

Tim turned as the door to the office opened. A few inches below the head of the doorframe entered the image of law and order. He strode toward the couch and extended a hand. The sheriff's short-sleeve polo did little to hide the two pythons he had for arms. Tim stood and braced himself for a handshake befitting of a man that deadlifted somewhere north of five hundred pounds.

"I'm Charlie Clay," he said, his accent slightly out of place for someone that hailed from Blake County. "Has anyone offered you something to drink?"

"Tracey offered me water and coffee earlier, Sheriff."

"Good," Clay said, taking a seat in one of the two chairs opposite the couch. "Did she complain to you about me outlawing soft drinks in the office?"

Tim smiled. "In fact, she did mention the policy to me. I think she may be getting up a petition."

"I don't allow any vending machines in this entire facility. Everything you find in the break room is free to my deputies and staff, but there is no junk allowed. No sodas, energy drinks, or anything like that will be found in the fridge. If my people want that stuff, they can buy it somewhere else."

Tim noticed that the sheriff smiled easily, but there was no doubt that his words were those of a military man.

"I imagine a policy like that was met with some resistance."

He grinned. "I'm not saying we have to eat like rabbits around here. I just can't have half my deputies carrying around thirty or forty bills of extra weight. It's embarrassing."

"I agree. When I was with the GBI, I always pushed for higher standards around physical fitness."

"It's the only way to keep everyone safe," Clay said with enthusiasm. "I have my team on the mats training jiu-jitsu twice a week now. They need to be ready to roll when breaking up a honky-tonk brawl."

"Being able to hit a heavy bag didn't do me much good in the few scraps

I found myself in," Tim added. "Knowing how to properly execute a rear chokehold did."

The smile widened on Clay's face. "See, you get it. Those are the kind of practical skills my team needs to stay safe out there on the roads."

"Nobody is messing around here at the BCSO anymore."

"No time to," Clay replied. "The toughest hurdle we have in law enforcement these days is the limited opportunities to get training hours in."

Tim nodded. "People want better policing, but our police are over-worked and undertrained. The standard line officer is just picking up bad habits on the job, making the issues worse."

"You hit the nail on the head," the sheriff said, pumping a fist. The swift motion seemed to displace the air in the room, then he settled back in his chair. "Anyhow, what can I do for you?"

Tim had spent much of the morning thinking about how to approach the sheriff on the investigation. Normally, Tim gathered his information from lower-level personnel. The officer on desk duty, or a secretary in the records department, always had the inside line on the hot gossip. Tim suspected that wouldn't work with this case, though. It was a given that the BCSO was already being hammered with requests for information on the murder of Lucy Collins. A private investigator snooping around on behalf of the defendant would be stonewalled with pleasure by the people on the front lines. The only way to get reliable information was to come straight to the brass.

"I need to talk to you about this murder case."

The sheriff's forearms flexed as he leaned back in his seat. He paused a moment, appearing to consider his words before he spoke. "I asked around about you, Dawson."

Tim felt no need to respond.

"A couple of the guys around here told me you used to be a rising star with the boys out of Atlanta."

"I don't know about all that, but I put some time in with the GBI. I gave them everything I had. It just didn't fit with where life was headed."

The sheriff nodded, serious now. "Still, you understand the rules around disclosing information that forms part of an active investigation."

"Of course."

"This case worries me, Dawson, and it puts me in a bit of a predicament. See, I knew Charlotte's daddy well."

Clay stood from his seat and walked over to the mini fridge. He pulled two bottles of water from it, tossing one to Tim.

"Lee and I lost touch after high school. I wasn't half the athlete he was, and my family didn't have any money to send me to college. Like a lot of guys around here, I left and joined the Army."

Tim twisted the top on his bottle, listening. He hoped the narrative might lead to something Maggie could use.

"I was stationed at Camp Darby when the whole deal went down around the murder of Jake Collins. I hadn't seen Lee in fifteen years, but I didn't believe it for a second."

"You ended up being right, too."

"I know I was. I read your reports from the investigation, too. There was barely anything tying Lee to the murder, and it was clear you weren't sold on the theory of Lee being the killer."

Tim shrugged. "I couldn't see it then, but the Collinses framed him. Plain and simple."

The sheriff took a deep breath in. "This case is different, though. *Way different.*"

"How so?"

"For one, there is plenty of physical evidence," Clay said cautiously. "Charlotte's prints are on both casings found at the scene. Not partials, either. They are clean as hell."

"Okay," Tim said. "What else?"

"A few strands of brown hair were found on the victim at the scene— they match Charlotte's DNA. Footprints were found all over the ground around where the body fell. They are a match for a pair of running shoes owned by the girl."

"How many pairs of that shoe would have been made?"

"We got a search warrant for her mom's house here in Blake County and found the exact shoes. Hell, they still had dried clay stuck to them. The same kind you will find if you drive over to the murder scene today."

"That's not good."

Clay nodded. "Not good at all."

"Anything else?"

"There is motive, too. You know the history."

Tim nodded. "Sheriff, it's still possible that it's just another Acker accused of killing a Collins. There is always more with these people."

Clay folded one arm over the other, unmoved.

Tim continued. "You were never convinced Lee was a murderer, right?"

"That's right," Clay said, his tone somber. "This one is different, though. This Acker is a cold-blooded killer."

21

As Maggie approached the back door to the Blake County Courthouse, a deputy waited for her with the door open. He waved her inside the building, hoping to avoid detection from any reporters nearby. Around front, parked on the main square, several news vans waited by the courthouse's public entrance. They were ready for the events of the day to unfold.

"The judge is waiting for you, ma'am," the deputy said as he led her up the back stairwell. "He and Mr. Hart."

"Judge Balk's calendar doesn't start until 9:30 a.m. What's the rush?"

"No, ma'am, not anymore. All his court calendars start at 9:00 a.m."

"Since when?"

"Been that way for at least a few years now."

Maggie picked up her pace as she reached the top of the stairs, cursing herself for not double-checking the start time for the hearing. As she started down the hallway, she glanced at her watch—8:48 a.m.

The deputy called after her. "The judge's chambers are in the last door on the right."

Maggie thought about telling the young deputy that she knew more about the courthouse than he did, but she thought better of it. It had been five years since she'd stepped foot inside the building. Apparently, things had changed.

She knocked on the door to the judge's chambers. Laughter could be heard from inside. She knocked again.

"Come in!" a deep voice called. "The door should be open."

Maggie stepped inside the room. She found the Honorable Judge John Balk seated at the head of his conference table. His robe was off, hanging on a nearby coatrack. He wore a light blue dress shirt and a red polka dot tie.

"Good morning," Judge Balk offered from his chair. "I was hoping you might sneak in here before we got started."

Maggie strode in the judge's direction to offer a handshake. "Of course, Judge, and good morning."

He took her hand and pointed to his left. "You remember Michael, right?"

At the judge's left sat the prosecutor, Michael Hart. The familiar face—and capable adversary—stood and offered a handshake of his own. The two hadn't seen each other since the trial of Lee Acker. Though the trial never reached a verdict, most in the local legal community viewed the event as a loss for Hart. A blemish on his impressive trial record. Maggie could only imagine how hard he'd lobbied to take over the prosecution of Charlotte Acker.

"How could I forget?" she said as she shook the prosecutor's hand with a smile. "I see you are still with the DA's office."

"I see you can't seem to quit defending murderers."

"Children," the judge interjected in a light-hearted tone. "You can catch up on your own time if you need to. Now, have a seat, both of you. We need to talk about Ms. Acker's bond hearing this morning."

Hart winked across the table at Maggie as he returned to his seat. "It's good to see you, Reynolds."

"You as well, Mike."

As Maggie took her seat at the table, she tried to put her finger on what was different about her opposing counsel. She remembered him as being rather reserved during their last trial, somewhat methodical to a fault. He constantly had a stack of documents in front of him, and he would furiously review them during any available breaks. Today, he didn't even have a notepad in front of him. All he had was a cheap-looking coffee mug in hand that read: *Lock Her Up! Lock Her Up!*

Maggie dove right in. "We are asking for the State to stipulate to a bond in this case, Judge. Ms. Acker is from here, she has no criminal record, and she is—"

"We know who she is," Judge Balk grunted. "No need to get into all that in here. You can argue it out in the courtroom if you need to."

Maggie couldn't help but notice the judge's frequent use of the word "we" when he referred to himself and the prosecution. If the court was already leaning toward the State's position, it would not bode well for Charlotte's request that she be released from jail pending trial.

"Judge, you know the State is in opposition to the defendant's petition for bond. The details of this crime are just too serious and too clear for all to—"

"Again, we don't benefit from either of you grandstanding in private," the judge snapped. "There is no jury here. There are no reporters to write down what you say."

"Yes, Judge," Hart replied. "To reiterate, the State will not stipulate to a bond of any kind in this matter."

The judge turned to Maggie. Her old ally hadn't so much as smiled at her since she walked in the room. She sensed that in her absence from Blake County, there might have been more changes than she realized. Maybe even some hurt feelings.

"Do you still want to move forward with the bond hearing?"

"Of course," Maggie replied, somewhat surprised by the question. It wasn't unheard of for a judge to blatantly signal their opinion on a matter before reviewing the evidence and hearing argument—but this was a murder case. Maggie had a responsibility to her client. A hearing had to be held. "The defense is ready to proceed with a hearing."

"Very well," the judge said as he checked his wristwatch. "Please arrive earlier next time if you want to thoroughly discuss anything in chambers."

"Yes, Judge."

He started to stand. "Is there anything else we need to discuss?"

"There is one other matter," Maggie replied slowly. "A rather unusual one."

"And what would that be?"

"The matter of co-counsel, Your Honor."

As a rule, attorneys are confined to practicing law in the states they are licensed in. However, with permission, an out-of-state lawyer may appear as counsel in a jurisdiction they don't practice in by filing a request to appear *pro hac vice*—for this occasion only. As courtroom procedure, and the law for that matter, can vary greatly from state to state, an application to appear *pro hac vice* is a unique request. When lawyers seek to join an action in another state, they are required to do so with sponsorship by an attorney licensed in that unfamiliar jurisdiction. In Georgia, this sponsor is often referred to as local counsel.

Judge Balk reviewed the application from his seat at the bench. In his twenty-one years as a superior court judge, he'd granted only three such applications. Most had been filed by out-of-state personal injury firms that relied on one of the local lawyers to sponsor their application. The same small-town lawyers that failed to adhere to the letter of the law on a regular basis in their own practices. He'd never considered an application to appear *pro hac vice* in a murder case, though. He certainly hadn't considered one with local counsel as qualified as Maggie Reynolds.

"Good morning, ladies and gentlemen," the judge said after a few moments. He smiled at the circus before him. "Before I begin with the day's calendar, there's a rather unique matter that needs to be addressed."

The judge had read the carefully worded document, and he agreed with the spirit of the applicant's argument. Though state and federal constitutions offer guaranties as to a criminal defendant's right to choose their counsel, they don't necessarily provide a criminal defendant with the absolute right to have an out-of-state attorney admitted to represent them. However, for a court to deny a criminal defendant's request to be represented by an attorney from out of state, the judge would need to first determine that the admission of the defendant's counsel—on a *pro hac vice* basis—would prejudice the defendant or disrupt the orderly processes of justice. As the loss of life and liberty are at stake in criminal matters, a higher level of deference could be awarded to the accused.

"I see we have a full house this morning," the judge said, continuing his introduction to the crowd on hand. "I am glad that the public has an interest in the proceedings in this court. I simply ask that you all be respectful of this process by maintaining proper decorum."

The judge scanned the faces before him. He knew several of the individuals packed into the pews in the gallery. Most were there because they wanted a glimpse of the spectacle. They wanted to see Charlotte Acker, the local darling, dressed in all orange. They wouldn't be the only ones that would catch a glimpse of the murder suspect, though. The judge eyed the row of cameras positioned along the back wall—cameras that would broadcast the scene for all to see.

"I also see that we have members of the media with us. I received your properly filed request to appear this morning and tape these proceedings. As you already know, your privilege to record and report on the events in this building can be revoked should your work interfere in any way with my courtroom."

After the trial of Lee Acker, the county commissioners had hastily diverted money from other areas in the budget to renovate the historic courthouse. Most of the dollars went to modernizing the main courtroom. A move to better accommodate the technology used to try cases of this century. A move that also carved out more space along the back row of the courtroom for members of the media. Judge Balk showed little support for the changes in his courtroom, but he understood that progress was inevitable—even in South Georgia.

The judge turned his attention to the parties. Maggie Reynolds stood ready at the lectern. An out-of-state lawyer by the name of Lawton Crane sat at the defense table. Across the aisle, Michael Hart waited at the prosecution's table.

Maggie spoke first. "Your Honor, would you like the defense to now address Mr. Crane's application?"

"Certainly, counsel. Please proceed."

"I believe the court has reviewed the application filed by Mr. Lawton

Crane to appear as co-counsel in *State of Georgia v. Charlotte E. Acker*, a criminal case now pending in the Superior Court for Blake County."

"I've reviewed Mr. Crane's verified application for *pro hac vice* admission, and my clerk has confirmed that the application fee was tendered this morning."

Maggie nodded. "And Mr. Crane is present this morning, Your Honor. He is seated here at the table for the defense."

Judge Balk's eyes shifted to the unfamiliar lawyer. "Mr. Crane, have you appeared in any judicial proceedings in this state?"

Lawton stood to address the court. "No, Your Honor. I've made applications to appear in other jurisdictions throughout my career, but I've not had the privilege of appearing as counsel in the state of Georgia."

The judge immediately recognized the calm demeanor of a courtroom lawyer. He also noticed the accent, a sub-variety of some mid-Atlantic metropolitan area. Somewhere far north of Blake County.

"So, you would agree that this would be a privilege to appear as counsel in these proceedings?"

"Without question, Your Honor."

"Your application says that you are in good standing with both the Virginia Bar Association and that of the District of Columbia."

"That's correct. I've been a member of both for some fifteen years."

Those in the packed courtroom had come for a first glimpse of the murder suspect, Charlotte Acker. They weren't there to listen to a stuffy discussion about a big-city lawyer's qualifications, certifications, and degrees. The judge had a responsibility to vet the applicant, though.

"Throughout your practice, Mr. Crane, have you handled any trial work?"

"I've been a litigator since the first day I stepped into a law office. I was the youngest member of my firm in Washington to try a case to a verdict as lead counsel. Since then, I've handled a number of collective actions and cases involving large-scale litigation."

"How many jury trials have you been involved in?"

"I'm not certain of the exact number, but more than sixty."

"And how many of those were criminal trials?"

Lawton shifted in his stance and glanced over at Maggie. "I've not been involved in a criminal trial. However, I'll be serving as—"

"You said none?"

"That's correct, Your Honor."

Maggie inserted herself into the discussion. "Mr. Crane will be serving as my second chair in the defense of Charlotte—"

"I understand, counsel. You are listed on Mr. Crane's application as both lead and local counsel."

Maggie folded her arms across her chest. "And that is how Ms. Acker has asked that her defense be organized."

"I see," the judge said, still considering the request. He turned back to the out-of-town lawyer. "Mr. Crane, I expect you still have a rather busy schedule with your practice in Washington. Won't your involvement in these proceedings interfere with your case load?"

Dealing with scheduling conflicts is one of the many issues that a trial lawyer is forced to grapple with. If the lawyer has a large number of cases in litigation, he or she is bound to face weeks where several cases are set for a hearing or trial during the same week. As the attorney cannot be in multiple places at once, attempts must be made to resolve the scheduling conflicts by notifying the courts involved. In Georgia, pending criminal matters almost always take priority over civil cases. An issue the silk-stocking firms rarely worry about, as most elect to keep their hands out of matters involving criminal law.

Lawton glanced at Maggie again, then back to the judge. "At this moment, Your Honor, I don't have any cases in litigation. I recently made a change to focus on a career path in academia. I'm no longer in private practice."

"He is currently a professor at Georgetown," Maggie added. "A member of the law school's faculty."

"I see," the judge said again. He understood the connection now. In a small town, by the time a hometown kid was accepted into law school, every member of the local bar association knew about it. Charlotte Acker was no exception.

"Did Ms. Acker take any of your courses at Georgetown?"

"She took my course in Constitutional Law this past semester, Your Honor."

"And you don't feel there is any conflict given your relationship this past year?"

Crane paused a moment, considering his response. All lawyers are trained to look for conflicts when taking on new clients. Attorneys aren't supposed to represent a client when there is a significant risk that their own interests—or their responsibilities to another client—will adversely affect the representation. The rules around conflicts of interest varied from state to state, but most ethics committees agreed on one thing: *No sex with clients*. "My position as her law professor during this past year isn't a conflict. It won't prevent me from being able to participate in her defense."

"Very well, counselor."

The judge turned to the prosecutor. "Does the State wish to be heard?"

Hart stood from his seat and glanced back at the media along the wall. He smirked as he buttoned his jacket. "The evidence in this case could not be more compelling, Your Honor. Ms. Acker can hire an army of lawyers if she so chooses. It won't matter—"

The judge lifted a hand. "Mr. Hart, is there an objection to Mr. Crane serving as second chair for the defense?"

Hart glanced over at Lawton, sizing him up. "The State has no objection."

With a deputy on each side, Charlotte stepped into the courtroom. She'd been inside the wood-paneled room more than most. She'd watched hearings and trials from the seating in the gallery, even testified as a victim from the witness stand. She'd once considered those difficult days to be part of her repertoire. Valuable experiences that set her aside from other young lawyers entering the profession. Law school classmates often asked about her experiences in the Blake County Courthouse. They asked because they'd read the news stories or had seen the docuseries on her father's trial. They all wanted to hear about it. To find out what she'd seen. What she'd learned. Charlotte always lied, though, acting as if those tough days were no big deal.

She took a deep breath in. *You can do this.*

Charlotte once believed that those days watching her father stand trial had made her battle tested. That they better prepared her for what was ahead in the challenges that awaited her in the practice of law. She'd been wrong, though. She now knew what those days were meant to prepare her for. They were meant to prepare her for the challenge of her life—the experience of being the accused.

The deputy placed a hand on her back to move her along. "Let's go, Charlotte. Take a seat over there with your lawyers."

Charlotte felt the eyes on her as she took short, intentional steps in her shackles. Throughout her years training for track and cross country, she'd undertaken countless long-distance runs without flinching. Now, it pained her to walk the short distance to the defendant's table. *Her table.*

As she walked, Charlotte noticed the familiar faces in the courtroom. The black-robed judge sat atop the bench, the witness stand and an elevated desk composing his tiered fortress. Below him sat the clerk of court, a court reporter, and several other court personnel. Charlotte kept her chin up, shoulders back, as she absorbed their stares. At the defense table sat Maggie Reynolds and Lawton Crane. Behind them waited her mother, uncle, and the rest of the world.

Another deep breath in as she scanned the room. *This is it—the room where everything will be decided.*

Maggie pulled a chair out at the table. "Have a seat next to me."

Charlotte nodded to her. "Okay."

Lawton slid a piece of paper in front of her as she sat. "The judge granted the request for me to join the case."

Charlotte looked down at the copy of the court's order. A bright spot in what would no doubt be a tough day. "That's great news," she whispered. "Thank you for being here."

Maggie leaned in close. "Are you ready?"

22

Maggie started to make her way out of the courtroom. As she walked toward the exit, she was careful to avoid eye contact with the reporters that waited along the back wall. She'd overheard their short interaction with Michael Hart as he exited through a side door to the DA's office. He'd offered no comment on the proceedings. A move that surprised her given his decisive win in the opening skirmish of *State v. Acker*.

A journalist in a blue blazer called out to her first. "Hey, Maggie, do you have time for a quick comment on the hearing today?" Maggie mustered a smile as she turned to the correspondent. A late twentysomething reporter that probably handled the court beat and local crime reports for one of the regional news stations. He needed a sound bite from the defense—the side fighting a losing battle.

Maggie slowed her pace, allowing her time to calculate her response. The media could be a powerful weapon for the trial lawyer. It helped shape the opinions and biases surrounding high-profile cases. Voices from the six o'clock news had the opportunity to speak to potential jurors well before the lawyers did. Still, Maggie knew that traditional media sources weren't the only way to speak to a jury pool in the modern era. Other weapons in the war of information had emerged, and a targeted social media strategy was quickly becoming the weapon of choice for trial lawyers that wanted to shape the narrative before a trial. The right message, depending on which side of the aisle you sat on, could plant the seed for defeat.

She started to beg off. "I need to get going—"

"I just have a few questions," the reporter said, cutting her off. "I'm with WXFL, and we'll be covering the lead-up to the trial."

"I'm with Fox 5," another voice said. "Can I get your thoughts on the ruling today?"

The other reporters nearby sensed there was blood in the water, and they converged on the aisle that ran down the middle of the courtroom. Maggie stood there, trapped.

"I have five minutes," she finally said, placing her briefcase at her feet. "I'm not in a position to comment on much more outside of today's bond hearing."

Cell phones and other handheld recorders were produced from the five or six reporters left in the room. Two cameras stood positioned nearby, ready to capture any sliver of disappointment in her face. The tall bench at the front of the courtroom—the major hurdle from the morning's proceedings—loomed behind her.

Determined to hit the high points first, she took the lead. "We respect the court's decision to remand Ms. Acker to the custody of the Blake County Sheriff's Office, but we will be filing a motion for reconsideration of bond this afternoon. Ms. Acker is an innocent woman that is being accused of a heinous crime. She should be granted a bond of some sort."

The young reporter in the blue blazer jumped in with his next question. "The prosecution stated this morning that the State believes this was a killing carried out in revenge. Your client's family has been very public in their opinion that Lucy Kelley Collins should have been held responsible for the murder of Lee Acker. How will your client deal with these very public statements about the need for the victim to be punished?"

"Collins was tried years ago in this very courtroom for the murder of Lee Acker," Maggie replied, motioning to the bench and jury box behind her. "A jury decided not to hold her responsible. Ms. Acker's family doesn't speak for her on all matters. My client respects the juries of Blake County— and their decisions."

"Why do you have an out-of-town lawyer serving as co-counsel,

Maggie?" another reporter asked. She shoved her recording device closer to capture the response. "Who made the decision to bring Mr. Crane on board? Was it you or your client?"

Maggie smiled. She wasn't about to offer any insight into that discussion. "I try all my cases with a team, and Lawton Crane will be an excellent addition. He brings a lot of knowledge and experience to the table. Next question."

The same reporter pressed on in her line of questioning. "Who will be making the final decisions as far as trial strategy?"

"I will," Maggie said, ending the discussion on the topic. "Next question."

Blue blazer shot another question her way. "Sheriff Charles Clay testified today that he didn't want Charlotte Acker released on bond because there would be no way to ensure her safety. Given the fact that Lee Acker was killed during the last case you tried in Blake County, do you agree with the sheriff's concerns?"

Maggie had pressed the sheriff during his testimony at the hearing. He served as the lead witness for the State, and he performed beautifully. He focused on the potential flight risk faced when any murder suspect is allowed on bond. He touched on community safety and intimidation of potential witnesses in the ongoing investigation. His main point, however, was the safety of the defendant. Maggie couldn't remember ever questioning a member of law enforcement so focused on the protection of the accused.

"Sheriff Clay's concern for Ms. Acker's safety appears to be genuine. He is well respected in the community, and that's because he looks out for the citizens of Blake County. No jail can ever be completely secure, though, and we know Ms. Acker would be safer at home."

Blue blazer finally tossed her a softball. "It is widely accepted that Charlotte's father was framed in the murder of Jake Collins. Is it your theory that Charlotte Acker has been framed as well?"

"Yes," Maggie replied, reaching down for the briefcase at her feet. "Time is up. Last question."

A new voice fired a question her way. "Do you recognize the name Alvin Hughes?"

"Of course," Maggie said as she turned toward the questioner, a woman with large glasses on and a silk scarf around her neck. "Earlier this summer, Alvin Hughes was killed in a terrible car wreck along with two other people —Shondra and Jason Jones. That's all I have time for—"

The reporter persisted. "Have you seen any of the social media posts put out by his mother?"

The reporter shoved a tablet in front of Maggie with an image of Mrs. Hughes's latest post. The smiling picture of young Alvin Hughes had over ten thousand interactions with it. A caption at the bottom of the image read: *This is my sweet boy. He was killed this summer because of the negligence of Shondra Jones. The Jones family has hired Maggie Reynolds to represent them. Maggie Reynolds represents murderers in the courtroom. That's what she does. She represents Charlotte Acker, and she represents the family of the woman that killed my son. Don't believe a word she says. She is a liar. My lawyer—Jack Husto —is going to expose her. Her Acker client is going to get exposed, too! Better believe that!*

Maggie tried to conceal the shock on her face as she read the social media post. After a moment, she slowly handed the tablet back to the reporter. Her mind raced as she tried to develop a response. She took another second to think—a mistake.

"Do you represent the family of Shondra Jones?" the reporter pressed, ready to take a prized scalp to display on her next segment. She wasn't about to let Maggie respond. "An accident report was included with that social media post I just showed you. It sounds like Shondra Jones veered off US 84 and caused a wreck with another vehicle, then an eighteen-wheeler."

"That isn't true," Maggie replied defensively. "The Joneses have already filed their lawsuit in Blake County Superior Court against the driver of the eighteen-wheeler and—"

"I have a copy of the answers filed by the defendants to your clients' lawsuit," the reporter quickly added. "The Hughes family also entered their cross-claim. Everything was filed this morning during the bond hearing, and *all* the other parties say your client caused the wreck."

Maggie hadn't reviewed the answers and cross-claim in the Jones case. She'd been busy with the bond hearing. The reporter knew this, of course.

Maggie shook her head. "Is there a question?"

"Do you expect Charlotte Acker—or the Jones family—to take responsibility for what has happened?"

Maggie pushed through the line of reporters. "We're done here."

23

So long as an inmate behaved, Sheriff Clay allowed for his temporary residents at the county jail to exercise visitation on the weekends. Those inmates with last names beginning with A through M were allowed to see family and friends on Saturday. Inmates with last names beginning with N through Z were allowed the same on Sunday. No other in-person visitation was allowed for inmates during the week, aside from visits with legal counsel or select medical personnel. The jail kept track of all visitors, recorded all phone calls, and monitored all non-legal mail received by inmates. For an inmate at the county jail, there was no expectation of privacy.

Outside of visitation, the only way an inmate interacted with the outside world was through the limited number of group services offered through the jail. Those struggling with substance abuse were allowed daily meetings with facilitators of the Alcoholics Anonymous and Narcotics Anonymous programs, and twice a week, inmates interested in obtaining their GED could sit in on courses with instructors from the local community college. On Wednesday nights and Sunday mornings, a twice-convicted, born-again preacher led worship in the library.

Fighting was prohibited, gambling was discouraged, and, unless the Bulldogs were playing football, the televisions in the jail stuck to movies and sitcoms. Breakfast was at six in the morning and lights-out was at nine o'clock sharp. The jail's rules were simple, and no inmate received special treatment. No matter who they were.

"How much longer?" Charlotte asked, her finger pressed down on the intercom's metal button. The call system connected her to some control room deep inside the jail. A room the jailers called "central command." She'd never seen the room, but she envisioned it as a dark little space full of television monitors, empty take-out containers, and stale donuts. "The lieutenant sat me in here almost twenty minutes ago."

The guard on duty smarted back from her side of the intercom. "Just sit in there and wait, Acker. Lots of folks have people visiting them today. It isn't just you in here."

It was Saturday, Charlotte's first in the county jail. Turning away from the intercom on the wall, she stared through a thick plastic divider that cut the closet-size room down the middle. A door opened on the opposite wall, and two familiar faces finally entered the room.

Cliff Acker walked straight to her and put a hand on the divider. "Hey, Charlie girl."

Charlotte placed her own hand on the other side of the plastic and smiled at him. She was happy he was there. "Thank you for coming."

"We wouldn't miss seeing you!" he said, his voice muffled by the protective plastic.

Charlotte's eyes moved to the other face in the room. Her mother had barely entered the space. Her feet were still planted by the door as she appeared to take in the cramped room, the image of her only daughter dressed in prison garb.

"Come on, Grace," Cliff said as he sat in an open chair. He pointed Grace to a black telephone receiver that hung close to the divider. "We only have fifteen minutes here with her. You two should talk."

Grace walked to the receiver and picked it up. She held the lower portion of the phone as far away from her mouth as possible. "How are you doing, Charlotte?"

"I'm doing just great, Mom. I sure appreciate you coming all the way over here. I hope it didn't get in the way of whatever else you have going on."

Cliff knocked on the divider. There was only one receiver to speak through, but he got the gist of what was said.

Charlotte shot him a glance, but he just leaned back in his flimsy chair. He looked right at home.

"Charlotte, I'm here because I want to support you," her mother said. "What else are you asking me to do?"

Charlotte knew her mother wasn't the type to mince words. They'd not spoken directly about the murder accusation, but Charlotte suspected her mother would tell her how she felt about the situation if asked. She might even tell Charlotte she'd been stupid for getting caught.

"I need you to support me like you supported Dad."

Grace switched the phone to her other ear. "Is the two hundred grand I just shelled out to fund your defense not enough? Is me testifying at your bond hearing that you will be a good little girl not enough?"

"I need you to believe me," Charlotte hissed into the phone. "Like you believed Dad."

Cliff knocked on the divider again. He looked more serious this time.

Grace waved him off. "I'm not talking about the case, Charlotte. You know the deal."

Charlotte nodded. She knew the phones were all recorded. The only privacy she would have while in jail would be in the meetings with her attorneys. Nowhere else.

"Have you heard from Maggie since the bond hearing?"

Her mother shook her head. "Not a word. I've called her office in Tampa, but she is in the process of relocating it to Blakeston. I've called her cell phone a few times. It has been going straight to voicemail."

"Have you called Lawton?"

Grace paused a moment. "I've spoken with him."

"Okay," Charlotte said slowly. "Has he spoken with Maggie since the bond hearing?"

"He told me they were meeting next week to discuss some personal injury case she has filed here in town. Apparently, she has been consumed with it as of late. He told me he may help her out with it. I'm sure they will be working on your defense, too."

Charlotte had not seen a news article since being escorted from Reagan

National Airport for questioning. She knew nothing about the coverage surrounding her case. She hadn't heard any of the commentary from Bill Collins's camp, nor had she seen any of the interviews with the lawyers involved.

"That's strange," Charlotte said after a moment. "They haven't told me anything about working together on another case. I mean, as far as I know, Maggie only met Lawton a week ago."

"You know she has other cases, right?"

"I know, Mom," Charlotte said after another moment. "I guess she handles a lot of car wrecks and stuff now. I just figured this would take priority and all."

A correctional officer opened the door and poked her head inside the room opposite the divider. Charlotte couldn't hear what the woman said. Cliff appeared to say something in protest, but the woman shook her head.

Her mother turned back to her. "It's time for us to go," she said softly. "I'll come back next weekend. I want us to keep talking. I hope things can get better between us."

Charlotte was in no mood to argue. She really just wanted a hug. "Me too, Mom."

Cliff took the receiver from Grace. "Be good in there, Charlie girl."

Charlotte nodded to him. If he could do time in a federal prison, she could do a few months in the county jail. "Make sure you take care of her."

"I can barely take care of myself," Cliff said with a wink. "I'll do my best, though."

The correctional officer was speaking to Cliff's back, but he paid her no mind. The con knew at what octave he needed to take a jailer seriously.

"Keep fighting for me out there."

He nodded. "Take care of yourself."

The door to the outside world closed, and Charlotte sat for a moment. She took in the silence of the room, a rarity in her caged environment. She'd once been able to maintain a serious meditation practice while competing for the Ducks of Oregon. Her coaches encouraged each of the athletes to practice some form of mindfulness training to cope with the anxiety and stress that came with preparing for major competition. Now, she could barely find a moment in the day when the inmates around her weren't talking or arguing with one another.

A voice poured from the metal speaker on the wall. "You still in there, Acker?"

Charlotte stood and walked over to the intercom. She hit the call button. "I'm still in here. My visitors are gone." She wasn't about to request that anyone take her back to the dorm. She'd sit alone in the visitation room all day if they'd allow it.

"What were you waiting on?" the jailer asked. "You know the rule. Once visitation is over, you buzz us here at central command."

What am I waiting on? Charlotte spent all her time waiting. Waiting for lunch. Waiting for dinner. Waiting for lights-out. Waiting to go home.

"Sorry," Charlotte quickly added. "This is my first Saturday with—"

"I'll get someone to you. They'll take you back to the female dorm."

Charlotte had experienced some of the best years of her life while in college at the University of Oregon. Her first year as a student, she lived in the dorms. She met wonderful people from all over the country. She'd walk out the doors of Carson Hall and go for a run along the banks of the Willamette River, or a day hike with friends in the nearby Cascades. After freshman year, she moved to a house near campus with a few of her teammates from the track team. She never planned to return to living in the cramped quarters of a dorm room, nor did she plan to return to live in Blake County—certainly not the women's dorm at the county jail.

The voice chirped again from the speaker. "Actually, you just sit tight, Miss Popular. You have another visitor coming in there to see you."

"Who is it?" Charlotte asked. "I don't think I—"

The door opened in the room opposite the plastic divider, and a man in a twill blazer entered. It took a moment for his face to register. The man turned and said something to the guard, then made his way over to the two empty chairs. He chose the one that had been occupied by Cliff some ten minutes earlier. He picked up the receiver hanging nearby. She returned to her seat and did the same.

"I hope you don't mind me visiting you," he said in an easy tone. "I was in town on business. Checking in on our manufacturing facility."

"I don't mean to be rude," Charlotte began. "But, it's Fernando, right?"

He nodded. "That's correct."

She noticed his eyes glanced a moment at her orange jumpsuit. She instinctively ran a hand over her waist area to straighten out the wrinkles in the material. As if doing so would change her appearance in the slightest. She'd not taken a shower in two days, wore no makeup, and had not been out in the sun for what felt like a month. The last time they'd seen each other, sitting across from one another in a conference room on Capitol Hill, she'd been dressed as a professional. Charlotte felt the surge of embarrassment as she tried to think of something to say.

"I guess we—"

"We missed you at the conference in Bilbao," he said, interrupting the awkward moment. "I was hoping to show you around in between the events."

She'd been hit on in some strange places. Jail would be a new one for the list, though.

"I was unexpectedly detained," Charlotte said with a smile. "It's unfortunate, too. I was looking forward to going. I'm pretty sure it would have this place beat."

Fernando forced a small laugh as he glanced around the depressing room. "I would say so."

"How did the conference go?"

He shrugged. "Much of the US delegation was unable to attend given the senator's circumstances. The loss of his wife was terrible, unfortunate really."

Charlotte considered the comment. "I'm not sure what you want me to say other than—"

"Right, of course. She seemed like a wonderful person, an intensely motivated woman."

"Did you know the senator's wife?"

"My brother and I worked with her on the location for our facility here in the US."

"The manufacturing plant here in Blake County?"

"Yes," he said with a nod. "Borroka S.A. has only one manufacturing facility outside of *Euskadi*. It's the one here in Blake County. We make everything else back home."

Charlotte thought for a moment. After the sit-down with the brothers, Charlotte and George Dell recapped the meeting with the senator. She explained to the senator that the brothers intimated that there was some kind of quid pro quo involved. Bill told Charlotte that he was aware of the new firearms manufacturing facility in Blake County but told her that he had not been involved in the courting of the company. He told her he'd never met the owners.

"Did you ever meet with Bill Collins about the construction of the plant?"

Fernando shook his head. "We were supposed to on several occasions but were never able to connect. He is a very busy man. We met only with Mrs. Collins, John, and their team."

"John Deese?"

"Yes, the same."

Charlotte nodded, absorbing the information.

"When did you see him last?"

"The conference in Bilbao," Fernando said. "He came and helped us meet some of the remaining members of the US delegation."

In the time Charlotte worked with the senator, she never once saw John Deese in his office. Bill never confirmed whether John was still involved with his work. She'd mentioned to the senator that if she ever saw him in the office, she'd quit her internship that day.

"Did Bill Collins send him over?"

"I believe so," Fernando replied. "That's what he told us. I think there was—"

A door opened in the room opposite the divider, and the guard entered. She told Fernando something.

He turned back to Charlotte. "The guard tells me it's time to go."

"Wait," Charlotte said. She'd been beating around the question too long. Now there was little time to get a response. "Why are you here?"

He stared at her a moment. "I'm in town for business."

"But *why* are you here in this jail to see me?"

"I had a few meals with John while we were at the conference. We talked of the murder of Lucy often. As I mentioned earlier, it is terrible."

"It is," Charlotte said. "I didn't do it."

Fernando continued. "John seemed quite convinced you did do it. He told us you'd hated the Collins family for years. That you blamed them for—"

The door opened again, and the same guard waved for Fernando to get going.

Charlotte raised a hand to stop him. "So, you just wanted to stop in and tell me this?"

"I just wanted to see you again," Fernando said as he stood, holding the receiver against his ear. "And see something for myself."

"See what for yourself?"

"John assured my brother and me that you had the look of a killer. He promised us that it was true."

Charlotte tried to keep her cool. "Well, what's the verdict?"

"I'm not sure yet."

"What the hell is that supposed to mean?"

Fernando ignored the question as he placed the receiver on the desk in front of him. He looked over his shoulder at the closed door, then pressed a hand against the plastic divider. The gesture reminded her of her Uncle Cliff's greeting earlier that morning. She stared at the hand for a moment, unsure what to do. In his palm was a small piece of paper with four words written on it.

"I'll come back and see you again," he said, his words muffled. "Bye for now."

Charlotte nodded.

He pulled his hand from the divider and turned for the door. Charlotte mulled the four words over in her head as she watched him leave.

Collins set you up.

24

Tim stepped around stacks of boxes as he made his way down the hallway. The new house in Blakeston had been lived in for nearly a week. The first night in the house, he and Maggie unpacked the kitchen and the bedroom. The rest of the house was still boxed away, but Tim knew it wouldn't stay that way for long. It was Sunday, and Tim sensed he was in for a full schedule of unpacking, moving furniture, and carefully avoiding a back injury.

"Let's get this stuff unpacked later this week," Tim said as he entered the kitchen. He wanted his intentions for the day put on the record. "We already have everything we need out."

Maggie looked up from a checklist she was hard at work on. "No way, big guy. It's Sunday, and we have the whole day to get the house in order."

He walked around behind her and glanced down at the list of moving-related honey-dos. He needed to mentally prepare for the day ahead. He also wanted to get his arms around her before she put pants on for the day.

"If purgatory exists, I'll be spending it moving heavy furniture and boxes ad infinitum."

"At least there isn't any football on," Maggie said as she looked up at him. "Not that there will be any on in purgatory."

Tim smiled. "I think they let you watch Canadian football, though."

"I'm pretty sure they just call it hockey."

A cell phone rang on the counter next to Tim. The number for the Blake County Sheriff's Office flashed on the screen. He handed the device to Maggie.

"It's probably Charlotte calling from the jail. You want to answer it?"

"I can't talk to her today," Maggie said, returning her attention to her checklist. "I'll go see her later this week. It's better to talk to her in person."

"She's been calling since her bond hearing on Tuesday, Mags."

"I know she has," Maggie said. "I've been busy wrapping up other cases. She can wait until later in the week."

Since they worked together—in fact, he worked for her—Tim tried his best to avoid arguing about work-related matters with Maggie, especially on the weekend. She was the attorney. He was the investigator. Charlotte was her client, and he respected that relationship. Tim didn't need to be told his place in their professional hierarchy. He pushed back at times on her decisions, but he tried his best to offer sensible alternatives only when it appeared his input was needed. Most of the time, though, he stayed away from trying to direct Maggie on how to handle her clients. She knew what she was doing. At least—he hoped she did.

"She just paid a heck of a lot of money for you to represent her, Mags. I'll pick up and tell her you'll see her next week. I don't mind doing a little hand-holding for you."

"Her family paid a lot of money," Maggie said, not looking up from her list. "There's a difference."

Tim held the phone until it stopped ringing, then placed it back on the counter. He recognized the tone in her sharp response. A signal that he usually took as an indication to proceed with caution. He decided to speed by the caution flag. "What's that supposed to mean?"

"It means her family paid me to represent her on the charge of murder. It doesn't mean I have to hold her hand every time she gets worked up about her case. I'm her lawyer. Not her therapist."

Tim shook his head as he turned toward the coffeepot. "You don't even know what she's calling about."

"I know what she is calling about, Tim. They all call about the same thing while they are in jail. I've represented countless criminals."

"You're right, and—"

She interrupted him in a condescending tone. "And I certainly know a lot more than you do about how to deal with these criminal defendants."

Tim knew a version of this argument had been brewing for a while. He'd watched Maggie's approach to the practice of law change over the last years. With each case she settled in her personal injury practice, she only wanted more. More money. More respect. More of things she would never get enough of.

"*These* criminal defendants? Do you hear yourself, Mags?"

Maggie snapped back at him. "Are you saying she isn't a criminal defendant? Are you saying she isn't calling me four times a day asking for an update on getting a bond?"

"Look, that's not what—"

"I love you, Tim, but you're not going to speak to me about how I counsel my clients in *my* law practice. That's crossing a line that—"

"How many calls have you taken from Eli Jones this week?"

Maggie started down the hallway. Tim followed her. Their bare feet pounded on the hardwood floors. Their voices sounded amplified in the half-empty house.

"I don't have to answer to you!"

"I've seen you talking to both Eli and Maya multiple times this week. I know you also met with Crash Davis on Friday about the depositions coming up next week. You're telling me Charlotte Acker doesn't deserve ten minutes on the phone?"

"The Jones case could net *me* millions, Tim. It's the largest case of my career. If you don't recognize that, then get off my team."

"This is Charlotte's life!" Tim shot back. "It's the biggest case of *her* life, and she has trusted you to handle it. You shouldn't have taken the case if you weren't going to be able to take it seriously."

The door to the bedroom slammed. Tim stood in the hallway for a moment, considering whether he wanted to argue anymore. He couldn't hear anything from his side of the door. If she was crying, she wouldn't let him see it. If she was angry enough, she'd soon be out for another round.

He turned and walked back down the hall. He grabbed a set of car keys from the counter and walked out the door.

Tim sat at a table in the back of the downtown diner. He sipped his coffee and watched as groups of churchgoers eased in from the early services. Most were white. Not because the diner didn't cater to Black folks, though. No, it mostly had to do with the fact that the Black churches in town still hadn't warmed up yet. They'd be rocking well into the early afternoon.

A familiar face walked in the front door with a woman and two teenagers. A waitress at the breakfast counter quickly recognized them and pointed to a booth near the front window of the diner. The VIP offered her a smile as he scanned the restaurant, no doubt an old habit he'd picked up in his years as a soldier. He noticed Tim in the back, the only other similar face in the place. The man directed his family over to the booth, then made his way toward Tim.

"Good morning, Sheriff."

"Call me Charlie," the sheriff said as he offered a hand. "You already get your breakfast?"

Tim nodded. "I got here early and had something. I plan to get on out of here in a bit."

After the argument with Maggie, Tim walked out the door in a T-shirt, basketball shorts, and a pair of slides. The sheriff eyed his appearance with some interest.

"You and your wife found a church yet in town?" The question was mandatory interrogation material for Sunday morning in a small South Georgia town. "Lots of great options around here."

"Not yet," Tim replied as he took another sip of his coffee. The liquid was cool now. "We just closed on our house last week, so we still aren't completely moved in. We'll start looking, though."

"My family attends Crossbridge most Sundays. The two of you should join us next weekend. It's a nondenominational outfit. A good mix of folks."

The sheriff's coded language was not lost on Tim. They both understood that small-town worship remained the most segregated day of the week in the South. It made things difficult for a married couple that looked like Tim and Maggie.

"That might be nice. She and I'll talk about it."

The sheriff looked back over his shoulder at his family. His wife was laughing with their two kids, obviously waiting on him before getting their order in. No other tables were within earshot.

"Look, I know your wife filed a motion asking that Judge Balk reconsider a bond for Charlotte Acker. I want you two to both know that while she is in my jail, we will be making sure she is safe. My predecessor could have done the same for Lee."

Tim sensed there was more. "Sure, we understand. You know how the pre-trial process is. These clients want to be home on bond, regardless of the charges."

"My jailer that works the night shift has considerable leeway during his time at the desk. The place is usually quiet, other than my deputies bringing the drunks in from the road. He asked me about making some accommodations for young Acker."

"You're talking about old Elroy?"

The sheriff nodded. "He is still my night manager."

"What kinds of accommodations are you thinking?"

"I don't make exceptions for any of my inmates. You need to know that."

"That's what I've heard."

"Charlotte was Lee's little girl, though, and she—"

"Or Jake's little girl," Tim added with a smile. "Not that it matters now."

"In my mind, she was raised an Acker. That makes her an Acker, through and through."

"Fair enough," Tim said as he thought for a moment about what the layout of the county jail looked like. The women had one dorm that housed around fifty inmates. The men had four separate dorms that could hold close to two hundred at maximum capacity. The place could get crowded.

"I'd like your camp to withdraw the motion to reconsider bond if we can make Charlotte more comfortable."

The sheriff didn't have the authority to make any calls in the courtroom, and neither did Tim. That was for the lawyers. The sheriff controlled what happened in his jail, though. Outside of the basic human needs, any privileges offered to inmates were within the discretion of the sheriff. Tim understood who held the power while Charlotte waited for her trial.

"What are you thinking?"

"It's Elroy, really," the sheriff replied. "He is concerned about some of the other inmates threatening Charlotte while she's in gen pop. Rich kid. High-profile case. You know the deal."

"We don't want that."

"Right, and we have a few individual holding cells near the front of the jail. Elroy usually puts the crazies in there when they come in doped up."

Tim nodded. He knew the area.

"My man told me he could set up an individual bed in there and make sure Charlotte has everything she needs. She made a request to my office to allow her to do some online legal research. I guess young lawyers don't really use books anymore to do all that."

"They don't."

"Anyway, my idea is for your wife to bring her a laptop. Elroy will make sure it's tucked away safe. She can work and sleep in peace in a more private area."

"I'm sure she would be grateful, Charlie."

"She has also asked about something that I'm not sure about. I may need your assistance if I'm going to be able to accommodate her."

Tim tried to conceal his surprise as he listened to the sheriff. The man in charge of keeping Charlotte locked away was doing everything he could to make her more comfortable.

"What do you need?"

"She sent me a letter a couple of days ago. She laid out how long she'd been a serious runner. How she has leaned on running over the years to get through tough times in her life. I'll be honest, Tim, it was a beautiful tribute to exercise, and it really resonated with me."

Tim smiled. "The girl was certainly an assassin while on the track team at Oregon. Plenty of awards and all—"

"I'm trying to help your wife's client out here," the sheriff replied with a laugh. "And, look, I can't go a day without getting into the weight room. It has helped me deal with what I've seen in my past life. It's my therapy, and—"

"And running is hers."

The sheriff nodded. "I don't have any deputies that can keep up with the girl. Most of my guys barely get a mile in under ten minutes. I was thinking that—"

Tim knew what the ask would be. "I'll run with her, Charlie."

"Good," the sheriff said, pleased. "I want all the running at night. I'll have a deputy follow you on the roads in a marked vehicle. No running through the woods. You'll need to get the routes pre-approved by my office, and we'll put an ankle monitor on her while she is out running with you."

"No problem."

The sheriff glanced back at his family again. He'd kept them waiting long enough. He turned back to Tim. "I knew what they said about you was true."

"Don't believe everything you hear, Charlie."

"I don't," the sheriff said as he extended a hand. His stout forearms bulged from under his dress shirt. "You are still one of the good guys, though. If you ever want to come back to law enforcement, come talk to me about a job first."

25

The parties sat around a large table in a dated conference room. The large alcove on the ground floor of the Blake County Courthouse was referred to as the law library, though little research took place within its walls. The books lining the dusty shelves were out of date and rarely touched by the lawyers of Blake County. Occasionally, a hapless soul that didn't have access to the internet, or enough money to hire a lawyer, would wander into the law library searching for answers to their legal questions. When Maggie served as a public defender in Blake County, she used the library on occasion as a hideaway of sorts. A private office just down the hall from the busy courtroom. So, since she didn't have an office established in Blakeston, she felt the law library fit perfectly for the depositions of Maya Jones and Columbus Davis.

At one end of the table sat Jack Husto. Husto wore a seersucker suit, an outfit he claimed to wear only when he handled cases in the small towns of South Georgia. Two lawyers from large law firms in Atlanta sat at the other end. They spoke casually with Husto. They'd worked on cases together in the past and chatted like old fraternity brothers, recounting war stories from glamorous courtrooms in grander cities. A court reporter sat at the table with her laptop and cup of coffee at the ready. She tried to offer some small talk to Maggie, an effort meant to ease the tension caused by the men intentionally ignoring them at the table.

"Are we ready to proceed, gentlemen?"

"Of course, Maggie," Husto said with a phony smile. He looked over at her as if she had interrupted serious discussion between adults at the dinner table. "I am just here to support my client. It is these fine lawyers that are doing the questioning today."

They were only fifteen minutes into the morning and Maggie wanted to hurl her first insult. "Let's get started, then. Who do you intend to depose first?" She directed the question at the other end of the table to not confuse things for Husto. "Both Ms. Jones and Mr. Davis are seated in the hallway."

The younger of the two Atlanta boys spoke first. He couldn't be much older than she was. "As you may remember, in exchange for our clients' agreement not to remove this action to federal court, we've agreed to press through the discovery process quickly."

"Right," Maggie replied. "That's why we are here."

The Atlanta boys exchanged a glance. "We believe Jack's client here has a rather strong claim. Our clients feel a responsibility to make the Hughes family whole. Your action is interfering with our ability to get this entire dispute resolved quickly. We may be able to convince our clients to offer *something* to avoid the nuisance and expense of going through discovery."

In civil litigation, the discovery process is oftentimes the most burdensome aspect of working up a claim. Discovery usually takes place before the plaintiff and defendant reach the courtroom. The parties to a lawsuit are entitled to engage in the exchange of information through several discovery tools. Litigants can send written questions to one another in the form of interrogatories. They can request documents and physical evidence from one another in the form of requests for production of documents. They can inspect property, places, and things by providing notice and an opportunity to object to those involved. They can also take the oral depositions of witnesses to the action. Depositions can be crucial in the success of a civil case, and they provide the parties a preview as to what they can expect at trial.

"The Jones family is grieving alongside Mrs. Hughes," Maggie said calmly. "Their actions are on the same footing."

Husto huffed down at his end of the table, then whispered something in his client's ear.

"Let's take Maya Jones's deposition first," the older of the two Atlanta lawyers said. He straightened his red tie as he spoke. "I don't expect this one to take very long."

Maya Jones sat near the middle of the conference table. Her brother, Eli, sat in a chair to her left. Maggie sat to her right. A small microphone had been clipped to Maya's yellow blouse to capture the audio. Maya raised her right hand. They were on the record.

"Do you swear, or affirm, that the evidence you shall give today in this deposition shall be the truth, the whole truth, and nothing but the truth?"

Maya nodded.

"Please answer out loud."

"Yes," Maya replied. Her voice sounded strong, clear. "I do."

"You may lower your hand."

Red tie started in on the questioning first. "Good morning, Ms. Jones. My name is Gilbert Wesley, and I'm an attorney with the law firm of Spear & Donovan. I represent Jimmy Benson and BTF Freight, LLC, the company that owned the truck your mother was in a wreck with earlier this year."

"The same eighteen-wheeler that killed my mother and brother?"

Atta girl, Maggie thought. *Let this guy know he can't push you around.*

Wesley paused, then scribbled something on the legal pad in front of him. "I'm going to be asking you a series of questions today about the lawsuit your attorney filed for you in Blake County Superior Court. A lawsuit that named Jimmy Benson, BTF Freight, LLC, and Track Steering, Inc., as defendants."

"Okay," Maya said slowly. "You didn't answer my question, though."

"That's not how this process works, young lady. I ask the questions. You provide me the answers."

Maya kept her eyes on her interrogator. "I guess that means that you do represent the people that are responsible for killing my mom and brother."

Maggie had not expected this kind of boldness from Maya. She'd seen the fire in her brother on occasion, but it had not presented itself in Maggie's conversations with Maya. There were worse traits family members could share.

Wesley made a production out of turning a few inches in his chair. "Maggie, have you not taken the time to speak with your client about how this deposition process works?"

Maggie ignored the question and turned to her client. "Mr. Wesley represents the company that owned the semi that ran into your mother's car. He also represents the driver of that truck. You're right to ask for clarification."

"Objection," Husto spouted from his end of the table.

"I'll add my own objection to the record as well," Wesley said. "I represent Jimmy Benson and BTF Freight, young lady. That's all. Now, do you intend to answer my questions today?"

Maya turned to Maggie. Maggie nodded.

"Yes, sir."

"Good," Wesley said. "Now, when I'm done with *my* questions, these other gentlemen at the table, Mr. Husto and Mr. Lock, they may want to ask you some questions as well."

"My lawyer can ask me questions, too."

"I guess you're a smart little cookie, then. Sounds like your lawyer has talked to you about how this deposition is supposed to go?"

"Don't answer that," Maggie said with a palm raised. "Don't answer any questions that Mr. Wesley has about what you and I have discussed. That is privileged communication, and Mr. Wesley should know better than to ask questions like that."

"I'm not going to argue with you or a sixteen-year-old girl," Wesley shot back. "Now I—"

"I'm fourteen, Mr. Wesley," Maya said in a strong tone. Her eyes were fixed on the highly paid defense lawyer. "My brother that died in this wreck would be sixteen if he were still alive. You'd better get your facts straight."

Wesley shouted back across the table, "Listen here, you little—"

"Whoa!" Eli said, standing from his chair at the table. He started to walk around to the other side. "You aren't going to speak to my little sister in that tone."

Wesley stood from his chair and pointed at Eli. "Stop right there!"

"Control your clients," the other Atlanta lawyer added, no small amount of panic in his voice.

"Or what?" Eli said as he rounded the table. "Or one of you two will?"

"I'm calling the police," Husto exclaimed from his end of the table. "This is out of—"

"I want you to apologize to my sister," Eli shouted as he came within feet of Wesley. He grabbed the lawyer's red tie with one hand and yanked on it. "And I want you to apologize right now."

"Get the police on the phone," Wesley said as he tried to back away from his aggressor. The knot from his tie pinched at the skin on his neck. He cried out in a whimper. "This deposition is over!"

Eli released the tie and grabbed the lapels of Wesley's blazer. He pushed the older lawyer up against one of the bookshelves in the library. Their noses were within inches of one another. The whites of the Atlanta lawyer's eyes were visible for all in the room to see.

"Cut it out, Eli," Maggie shouted from across the room. "This isn't the way for you to get your point across."

The door to the law library burst open, and one of the courthouse deputies was through it. Another followed him with surprising speed. A pistol was drawn.

"Get off him!" the first deputy shouted. "Now!"

Eli put his hands up and backed away from the lawyer. Maggie couldn't see her client's face, but she knew he had to still be glaring at Gilbert Wesley.

"Hands behind your back, Eli," the second deputy shouted. He said the name with a tone of familiarity. "You're coming with us."

Eli moved his hands to his lower back. "No one is resisting. I'm complying with your commands."

"I'm going to the judge," Wesley shouted, now emboldened by the presence of the deputies. "I'm also going to have you prosecuted, bud."

"You do that, *bud*," Eli replied. "We'll see where that gets you."

"Shut up, Eli," Maggie added. "Don't say another word."

"Listen to your lawyer," Husto said from his end of the table. "Criminal defense work is all she knows."

26

When Judge Balk heard that there had been a dust-up in the law library of his own courthouse, he summoned the lawyers involved to his office on the building's second floor. The judge instructed his judicial assistant to have the lawyers wait in his conference room until he arrived from the local country club's golf course. The attorneys—Maggie Reynolds, Jack Husto, Gilbert Wesley, and Hinson Lock—did as they were told. Like school-children anxious for the principal to arrive, they waited around a conference table in the judge's chambers. As expected, Judge Balk looked less than pleased when he came through the door. Jack Husto spoke up first.

"Judge, I want to be the first to apologize for you having to come in here like this on a Friday. Frankly, I'm embarrassed by the—"

"I'm going to be doing most of the talking," the judge said as he took a seat at the head of the table. "I'm also going to have this meeting added to the record."

The same court reporter from the morning's depositions came through the door. She found an open seat at the conference table and started to set up her station. As she worked, the judge scanned the faces at his table.

Gilbert Wesley tried to break the awkward silence with an introduction. "Judge, I don't believe we've had the pleasure to meet. I'm—"

"I want every word on the record," the judge said with a finger lifted. He turned to the court reporter. "Are we ready?"

"Yes, sir," she replied, lifting a stenomask to her face to begin taking down the meeting verbatim.

Judge Balk looked at Maggie first. He nodded in her direction as he spoke. "I'd like all counsel to go ahead and state their name for the record."

"Maggie Reynolds here on behalf of the plaintiffs."

The judge then nodded to the men on the other side of the table; all three sat opposite Maggie.

"Gilbert Wesley, on behalf of Jimmy Benson and BTF Freight."

"Hinson Lock, on behalf of Track Steering, Your Honor."

"Jack Husto, Your Honor, and if I may—"

"No, you may not," the judge replied. He frowned at Husto's seersucker suit jacket as he spoke. "Who do you represent, Mr. Husto?"

Husto and the judge looked to be around the same age. Husto clearly didn't like being spoken to harshly by a man that would be considered one of his contemporaries, especially not one that was a lowly trial judge.

"I represent one of the plaintiffs involved, Mrs. Hughes. She is also a cross-claimant in this matter."

"Very well," the judge said. He folded his arms across his chest. His thick arms struggled against the sleeves of his knit polo. He looked over at the attorney with the red tie first. "Mr. Wesley, you called my office this morning after an altercation occurred during a deposition. Tell me what happened."

Wesley lifted a legal pad from the table. Like a good insurance defense man, he'd scribbled notes on the pad to memorialize the event. A small portion of the billable time that would be added to his client's invoice. "This morning, during a deposition of one of the plaintiffs, I was assaulted by—"

"Assaulted?" Maggie chuckled from across the table. "Really, Gil?"

The judge lifted a finger and held it up as a warning. "No one should be speaking unless I ask them to. Is this clear?"

Husto raised a hand. The judge nodded in his direction.

"Your Honor, maybe we could ask Maggie over here to give us the defin-

ition of simple assault here in Georgia. She seems to understand the criminal process rather well and has been defending the—"

"Mr. Husto, I'll give you the elements of simple assault if you need to
write them down. If not, I suggest you keep quiet."

Husto's phony smile remained on his face. It refused to crack under the
pressure from the judge. "No, of course not, Your Honor."

"Proceed, Mr. Wesley."

"Like I was saying, Judge, I was assaulted by a young man in this morning's deposition of one of the plaintiffs. He threatened me, choked me, and
threw me up against the wall. It was—"

"Just another Friday night?" Maggie mused from her side of the table.

Judge Balk couldn't help but smile a second at the comment as he
turned to growl at Maggie. "Final warning, counselor."

Wesley continued, sheepishly. "Not only did it disrupt the discovery
process, Your Honor, but it has put me in a rather unique position as
counsel for my client."

"What position would that be?"

"Well," Wesley said, readjusting his tie. "I asked that the deputies have
this young man prosecuted for his attack on me this morning. I instructed
them that I didn't want any contact with him while his criminal case
remained pending."

Maggie sat on the edge of her chair, trying to maintain her composure.
"Judge, if I may—"

"You will have your chance to speak," the judge said, not even looking
over at Maggie as he spoke. "Now, Mr. Wesley, please proceed."

"Thank you, Your Honor." Gilbert Wesley had practiced law long
enough to know that you needed to cook when the pan was hot. "I have two
requests to the Court. First, I am asking for sanctions tied to the plaintiff's
conduct. This young Black man is a party to this case. He is the adminis-
trator of his mother's and brother's estates. His attack on me caused us to
cancel the depositions today and waste my client's money on travel, along
with my time and efforts."

Judge Balk made the obligatory note on a legal pad of his own. "What is
the second request, Mr. Wesley?"

"As this young man will be charged with assault—a matter I hope this county will take seriously, as I'm an officer of the Court—I think these proceedings should be dismissed for the time being. I won't be in the same room with this young man, and my client shouldn't have to change lawyers because of this attack."

Maggie couldn't resist. She was burning now. "You can't be serious, Gil. This is complete and utter bull—"

"Counsel!" Judge Balk shouted. "Say another word and I'll hold you in contempt. I'll put you in the same place your client is being held until you can respect this court."

As a public defender, Maggie had practiced in front of Judge Balk for five years. During that time, she put together a well-respected reputation built upon her fierce and creative defense work. Not once had a judge ever threatened to throw her in jail, though. The rebuke surprised her, and the words hung over the silence of the room.

"Now," the judge said after taking a deep breath. "This is what I'm going to do."

All the lawyers at the table—expect Maggie—had a legal pad at the ready. She was focused only on keeping her cool. Judge Balk continued.

"I'm going to order a fine in the amount of five thousand dollars be paid by the plaintiffs. Half of that sum will be paid to Mr. Wesley's office. The other half will be paid to Mr. Lock's office. The cost of the court reporter's services will be covered by the plaintiffs."

Husto spoke up, this time in a more deferential tone. "Your Honor, will my client be required to contribute to this fine?"

"No," the judge replied. "Only the plaintiffs represented by Reynolds Law will be responsible for this sum."

"Thank you," Husto said. "I assumed that would be—"

"As for your request to dismiss this case, I am going to deny your verbal motion."

Maggie exhaled slightly as she processed the news. She was still in the game.

Wesley quickly spoke up. "Your Honor, would you consider granting a stay in these proceedings, then?"

When a judge issues a "stay" in court proceedings, the judge's order halts any further litigation until the stay is lifted. In certain situations, especially in matters involving civil litigation, a stay is a device that is used to allow other matters that impact the case to play out first. An indefinite postponement of civil proceedings is as good as a win for defense lawyers. Their client is protected from a verdict, and the defense lawyers are still able to periodically bill their client's file while the stay is in effect.

Judge Balk looked over at Maggie. She knew what was coming.

"I'm going to order a stay in these proceedings," he said, a hint of disappointment in his tone. "When the criminal matter is resolved for your client, you can notify the court. I'll then consider anew whether to allow this lawsuit to continue."

27

Charlotte stepped out under the August evening sky. The heat from the day had somewhat subsided, leaving only the familiar weight of the South Georgia humidity hanging in the air. She knelt and tightened the laces on her running shoes. The routine felt familiar, like catching up with an old friend she hadn't seen in a while. When she finished with the laces, her hands moved to the new monitor that sat just above her right ankle. The ankle bracelet was mandatory running equipment—a demand that she offered zero resistance to. It had been explained to her that the monitor would allow the BCSO to track her location in real-time. Fine by her. She had no plans to attempt an escape. She just needed to run.

"There you are," Charlotte said as a familiar face approached from the dark parking lot. "I was over here praying you wouldn't stand me up."

"See, I was just over there praying you'd take it easy on me tonight," Tim replied, a smile on his face. He wore a tank top, workout shorts, and a reflective running vest. He tossed Charlotte a vest that was identical to his. "Put this on. That way I'll at least be able to see you while I'm chasing you during this five-mile run."

Charlotte cocked her head to the side. "You only put in a request for five miles? I've been in jail for over a month, Tim. My legs are ready to go."

Nearby, a young deputy leaned against the hood of his patrol car. He'd been tasked with following the running duo's every movement while on the roads that night. Any small deviation from the pre-approved route would warrant an immediate call into dispatch. He reminded them of this.

"We're sticking to the route that was approved, y'all. Those are the sheriff's orders. I can't have us changing anything now."

"Yes, sir," Charlotte said as she turned to wink at the deputy, an old classmate that'd been a year ahead of her in high school. "I'll go wherever you tell me to go, Thomas."

The deputy turned to walk to the driver-side door of his patrol vehicle. No doubt trying to conceal the reddening in his face. "Let's get going," he said over his shoulder. "We only have an hour set aside for this little outing."

"You heard the man," Charlotte said as she turned back to Tim. "Lead the way!"

Tim pointed in the direction of the main road that fronted the county jail. The patrol vehicle behind them groaned as it shifted into drive. With its headlights shining on the path ahead, the group took off for their first sanctioned run along the roads of Blake County.

Shortly after ten o'clock, Tim pulled into the driveway of the new house. Lights had been left on by the front steps. A glow from the television danced on the drapes that guarded the living room windows. Tim cut the vehicle off. He didn't reach for the handle, though. She was waiting up for him, and he needed to weigh his options. They'd not spoken for five days. A brutal stretch of silence brought on by their fight the Sunday before. The argument needed to happen, but that didn't mean he should continue to punish her. He knew what he needed to do.

Tim stepped out of the car and headed for the front porch of the house. As he made his way up the brick steps, the front door opened. Maggie appeared in the doorway, wearing shorts and an old T-shirt from his glory days. He spoke first.

"Look, Mags, I'm sorry about what I said last weekend. I have no place telling you how to handle your business. I'm not getting—"

"No," she said slowly. She took a step toward him. "It's my fault."

One of the little surprises that Tim came across after he married Maggie was the fact that she was horrible with apologies. She had a competitive spirit buried deep within her that drove her to excel at most things she put her mind to. While she could recognize those moments when she was wrong, she often fell short in explaining how. She was a wordsmith by trade, and he'd watched her present compelling, heartfelt arguments to twelve-packs of strangers. She couldn't do the same for the people she loved, though. A small thing. One Tim decided years ago he could live with.

"I think we can agree there was a better way to discuss how to handle Charlotte's case. I'll do better next time."

"Maybe so," Maggie replied with a laugh. "I still need you to call me out on my shit, though. If you don't, who will?"

"I'll keep at it, then," Tim said, wrapping his arms around her. "At least until you fire me."

She leaned into the embrace. "There's an idea."

They stood there on the front porch, arms around one another. They listened to the unfamiliar sounds of their new neighborhood. A streetlamp buzzed at the edge of the road. Dogs barked in the distance. Bass boomed from a car full of teenagers riding aimlessly nearby. Their neighborhood sounded like a thousand others peppered across the state. It sounded like home.

"You're smelling ripe," she said, face still buried in his chest. "You been at the gym?"

Tim held her in his arms. He hadn't told her about the conversation with the sheriff. He hadn't told her about the deal. "Not exactly," he said. "I've been over at the jail."

"What was going on over there?" she asked, taking a step back to see his face.

"You're not going to believe me when I tell you."

Maggie considered him. "Try me."

"I went for a run with Charlotte. One approved by the sheriff."

"I'll admit, I didn't expect you to say that. Your idea?"

Tim shook his head. "Not mine. She has Charlie Clay to thank for this little accommodation."

"Our sheriff is letting murder suspects go for runs around the county?"

"Only the ones that he likes," Tim replied with a grin. "And he has a soft spot for our girl."

"He and her dad were apparently close."

Tim nodded. "The sheriff told me that much when I met with him the other day. I think this is his way of trying to take care of her."

Maggie started walking along the edge of the front porch, thinking. "Any strings attached to this little accommodation?"

"Well, we made a little deal this week."

"We?"

He nodded. "Charlie and I did."

"And that would be—"

"So long as Charlotte remains in custody at the county jail, she gets to run."

"That's it?" Maggie asked, an eyebrow raised. "I need to get you enrolled in a class on negotiation."

"She also gets a private space in the jail, along with some other perks."

"Okay," she said. "Not bad. Is she happy with the deal?"

"Mostly," he replied. "She wants to see you, though."

Maggie nodded. "I'll go this weekend."

"Otherwise, she's fine. I explained to her that you were tied up this week with the Jones case. Told her all about the wreck while we ran tonight. She understood."

Maggie looked out on the quiet street. Concern filled her voice. "I may have already messed that case up, Tim."

"What are you talking about? Maya's case is just getting started."

Maggie turned back to him and started in on her narrative. She confessed to him that her aggressive approach to keeping the case in Blake County had backfired on her. That she'd allowed Eli and Maya to go into the depositions unprepared for the other side's tactics. She described in colorful detail how Eli proceeded to not only threaten one of the lawyers for the defense, but somehow managed to get himself arrested in the process. The ordeal had produced a conundrum, one that would probably mean the end for the family's case.

Maggie capped off her narrative with the worst of it. "So, Judge Balk just decided to put the whole case on hold until Eli's criminal charges get sorted out. The case is dead in the water."

Tim ran a hand through his hair, thinking. "Can Husto's client go ahead and settle her claim while everything is on hold?"

"He's certainly going to try," Maggie said after another long moment. "I haven't had the heart to discuss that possibility with Maya yet."

Tim stepped over to her side and put an arm around her shoulders. "So, what's the plan?"

"There is only one thing to do," Maggie said, still looking out on the stillness of the night. "We have to show the people of Blake County that I still know how to win big."

28

Maggie stood in the jail's anteroom, waiting to be let inside. She signed her name in the visitor's log, then flipped through its pages, scanning the names of all that had come and gone over the last few weeks. The log required the name of the visitor, reason for the visit, and name of the inmate receiving said visit. She was familiar with most of the attorneys listed in the visitor column and also recognized several of the family names printed in the column set aside for the inmates. Old family names with roots that stretched far into the less desirable parts of the county, areas where the business of methamphetamine had long since taken the place of small-town farming. The large metal door buzzed, and Maggie pushed against it to enter the jail. As she stepped inside, Maggie took in the familiar smell and the opportunity that awaited her.

"Welcome back," Elroy said from his seat at his desk. He hopped to his feet and started moving toward one of the doors tucked in the corner of the intake area. "Ms. Acker is in here."

"Thank you, Elroy. How are things here tonight?"

"Quiet," he said with a pleasant nod. "You and the other lawyer have been my only visitors."

"The other lawyer?"

"That's right," he said. "The one from up north, Mr. Crane."

Maggie hadn't noticed Lawton's name scribbled in the visitor's log. She considered this as she waited for the night manager to open the door to Charlotte's cell. She'd spoken with Lawton the day before, but he'd not mentioned his plans to return to Blake County so soon. To be fair, though, she hadn't asked.

"I'm not sure how long I'll be," Maggie said, switching her bundle of paperwork from one arm to the other. "I imagine we'll have quite a lot to discuss tonight."

"Should I leave the door cracked?"

"Is that what you did for the other lawyer?"

Elroy shook his head slowly. "No, ma'am. They asked me to close it."

Maggie absorbed this as she watched Elroy pull open the heavy door to the cell. Though he was up in age, he still maintained the strength and sturdiness of a working man. A necessity for his charge that included keeping watch over the county's more dangerous men as they slept. Maggie knew he had other unofficial responsibilities in his job, though, like keeping tabs on what was really happening in the sheriff's jail.

"Just holler if you need something."

Maggie thanked him and stepped into the small cell. In a matter of moments, she was able to take in the entirety of the seven-by-twelve space. As expected, it had only the bare necessities. A bed and metal toilet took up most of the room. In one corner sat a stack of textbooks waiting to be read. In the other, a pair of running shoes peeked out from under a small bundle of clothes and towels. One light had been placed at the center of the concrete ceiling, and it illuminated every inch of the depressing little space.

Charlotte was stretched out on her bed, staring up at the ceiling. "It doesn't look like it, but this place is a nice upgrade for me."

"I bet," Maggie said, giving the cell another look around. She tried to think of something that might lighten the mood. "At least you get to potty in privacy."

Charlotte swung her legs out of the way and made room for Maggie at the end of the twin bed. "Surprisingly enough, that part didn't bother me too much in the dorm. It was the having to sleep near all those strangers at night, the incessant talking during the day."

Maggie sat. "Aren't you lonely in here?"

"It can get a little boring," Charlotte said with a shrug. "I do have my running dates to look forward to at night, though."

Maggie smiled. "You trying to move in on my guy?"

Charlotte laughed. "He's the only one I get to see while I'm in here. Everyone else I meet with from one side of a plexiglass divider."

Maggie nodded, making a mental note of her client's lie.

"I see you have some light reading in here," Maggie said, pointing toward the stack of books. "Are they for your classes this fall?"

"That's every book on criminal law that I could get my hands on. Most are right out of the bookstore back at school."

"There is high-level, academic discussion of the law. Then there is how it is practiced in the real world, Charlotte."

"I understand," she replied. "I still want to be able to discuss it from both angles."

If Charlotte wanted to meet separately with Lawton to discuss due process, individual rights, and the limits on government power, that was her choice. It didn't change anything with Maggie. It just didn't make sense to hide it.

"Have you heard from Lawton recently?"

"I have," Charlotte said after a pause. "Talked to him today. Classes are starting up next week, but he's doing well. He has some interesting ideas for the defense."

"Don't talk trial strategy over the phones," Maggie said, prodding around the details of how her client spoke with co-counsel. "I've told you that no one is supposed to record attorney-client phone calls, but it's still best to be careful."

"I know."

"What does he have in mind?"

"He hasn't given me the specifics yet. We've just been talking about my decision to testify."

"A big decision. One you and I will need to discuss, too."

Before a client takes the stand to testify—in any kind of case—they must be thoroughly prepared by their counsel. Maggie had always coached her clients to only answer the question that was asked of them. Never anything more. This simple rule forced the lawyer handling the questioning to work harder in their cross-examination of the witness. A well-prepared witness can result in a labor-intensive exercise for the attorney asking the questions. A talented witness, that is also well prepared, can turn a cross-examination into a difficult task. Maggie knew that Charlotte would prove to be a witness adept at slipping, sliding, and avoiding answers to the important questions.

Maggie pressed on. "When was the last time you saw him?"

"Not that long ago," Charlotte replied. "He brought me all the books, actually."

"Is there a—"

"I see you brought me something, too," Charlotte said, pointing to the bundle of documents at Maggie's side. "What's all this?"

Maggie glanced down at the paperwork. Below it was a large, glossy box. Her client obviously didn't want to talk about Lawton.

"The State handed over some of the discovery this morning. I went ahead and printed out copies of the reports for you."

"Looks like there was plenty to report on."

"They have quite a bit of evidence against you," Maggie said slowly. "We can walk through it tonight if you'd like to. I reviewed it all this morning and have some questions for you."

Maggie handed the stack of documents to Charlotte. A thick rubber band bound the stack of reports, lab results, and photographs into one rectangular brick of paper.

"I'll page through it first," Charlotte said, placing the brick below her bed. "Anything else we need to talk about?"

Maggie glanced at her watch. She'd only been at the jail for about fifteen minutes. She'd planned for a long meeting, poring over the information provided by the prosecution. She'd prepared herself to deal with a client frayed by emotion as they discussed the mountain of incriminating evidence. The kind of tough discussion that Maggie always had to have with her more guilty clients.

"I also brought you a laptop to do research on," Maggie said, flipping the box over. "It's another accommodation from our favorite sheriff. It's not much, but it—"

Charlotte leaned across the bed and hugged her with both arms. The sudden gesture took Maggie by surprise. The two had been all business with one another since their first meeting at the jail. While a cold approach to the attorney-client relationship proved effective in some cases, it had not produced a healthy dynamic for the two of them.

"Thank you," Charlotte said, almost in a whisper. "This—along with the running—will keep me sane in here."

Maggie let her client hold the hug for as long as she wanted. As Maggie waited, she tried to remember the last time she'd done something for a client that provoked this kind of a reaction. She'd settled a few car-wreck cases that resulted in large paydays for her clients. The checks exchanged in those meetings prompted smiles all around. No one flashed this level of gratitude, though. No one hugged her and thanked her for making their lives bearable again.

"It's just a laptop," Maggie said after Charlotte released her. "It's not like it's an acquittal or—"

"It's the first step toward one," Charlotte quickly said, wiping moisture from her eyes. "I can do the research now. I can start to figure out how the hell I ended up in this mess."

Maggie nodded, listening. She reminded herself that Charlotte was from a younger generation, one that had always experienced life supported by the most modern technology. Laptops, smartphones, and tablets had been essential tools in her education and exploration of the world around her. To fight back, she had to have access to that technology.

"I have some ideas where we can start, but I'll need to go through the discovery and see what lines up. Do you have a digital copy of the file?"

"I'll bring you a thumb drive next time I see you," Maggie said, amazed at the sudden transformation of her young client. "We have a couple more weeks before things ramp up, and I can—"

"I'll need Tim to investigate a few things for me. Do you mind if I discuss those tasks with him on our run tomorrow night?"

"Of course not. We work for you."

"I know this isn't your only case, but I—"

Maggie lifted a hand to stop her mid-sentence. "This is my most important case, Charlotte. I have some other cases, but my focus is on you."

"Do you mean that?"

Maggie did. "I'm all in."

Charlotte nodded, satisfied. "How fast can you get me back into a courtroom?"

29

Michael Hart pulled up to the main gate at the edge of Kelley Hill Plantation. A security guard holding a clipboard walked over to Hart's vehicle. He glanced in the back seat as he asked for identification. Hart reached inside his jacket and produced his driver's license.

"Thank you, Mr. Hart," the large man said as he scrutinized the license. He lifted his eyes to Hart's face, comparing it with the photo on the ID. Before he returned the plastic, he referred to his clipboard. Everything by the book. "I see your name here on the guest list."

Hart got the impression that the man was accustomed to kicking in doors, not working them. The many hats one must wear when they enter private security.

"How big a crowd are we talking tonight?" Hart asked. "I was told it would be a fairly small gathering."

The man ignored the question. "Do you know where you're going on the property?"

Hart shook his head. He hoped this grunt wasn't about to hand him GPS coordinates. "The senator's aide told me to ask for a map at the gate."

The man pulled a glossy slip of paper from his clipboard. He clicked on a small flashlight, then leaned down close to the window of the vehicle, close enough for Hart to make out several small scars on the man's jawline. He proceeded to explain the route to the building where the party would be hosted. The map showed a simple diagram of the clay roads that snaked throughout the massive property, but the man explained the route in impressive detail.

"How long is the drive from here to the house?"

"Approximately twelve minutes."

Hart thanked the guard, applauding him for his attention to detail, then started to roll up his window.

"Mr. Hart, you know this is a black-tie affair," the man said with a hand up. He was looking at the navy-blue suit jacket, the yellow tie around the prosecutor's neck. "I thought I should give you a heads-up."

Hart grinned. "My tux is at the cleaners."

"Right," the man said with a nod. "Well, be safe out there tonight."

Hart kept the window open as he pulled his vehicle forward through the opening of the plantation's elaborate wrought iron gate. Two newer-model Land Rovers sat parked in a staggered manner on the entrance road. They created a sort of barricade that Hart had to weave through in his mid-size sedan. When he cleared Rover number two, Hart spotted a second individual near the edge of the drive. This member of the senator's security personnel held an assault rifle in one hand and offered a short wave with the other. Hart kept his eyes on the dark road ahead. He felt as if he was heading out into deep water, out to play with the sharks.

Hart walked through the front door of the main house and found the home bustling with activity. The event was in fact black-tie all the way, and Crane scanned the Waspy room full of impeccably dressed guests. A tray passed nearby, and he lifted a champagne coupe from it in an attempt to blend in. Another tray passed with a delicious-looking assortment of small bites, but Hart waved the server off. He'd snag a plate and find a quiet corner to hide out in later.

As a career prosecutor, now with some twenty-one years on the job, Hart rarely had the opportunity to visit grand homes for private events.

He'd cleared forty-eight thousand after taxes and child support last year, and that number would improve little over the remainder of his career. He was regarded by his peers as a solid prosecutor. One that understood the system better than most. And some years ago, when Hart took the lead on the prosecution of Lee Acker, he'd been considered a man with modest political ambitions that extended beyond the office of the district attorney. Those dreams crumbled, though, with the storm that followed the elder Acker's death. The press painted the outcome as a blunder of sorts, and Hart somehow became the face of the investigation's mishandling. It wasn't until recently that redemption even seemed possible, but there he was, back in a room full of powerful people. Back in the game.

"Mike Hart!" a deep voice called from nearby. "How in the hell did you find your way out here?"

Hart turned at the sound of his name. Leaning against the wood banister of the foyer's grand stairwell was the Honorable John Balk. He held a lowball in one hand and an unlit cigar in the other. In his audience was a pair of young women, neither of them Mrs. Balk. The judge waved Hart over for an introduction.

"This is the man that I mentioned to you earlier," the judge said after releasing Hart's hand from a strong grip. "He will be prosecuting the Acker girl later this year."

While Hart liked the idea of his name being spoken in the presence of such fabulous-looking people, it surprised him that the judge was choosing to speak so openly about a case he would soon preside over. Hart offered a modest smile to both women. They appeared interested in him for a few minutes as he spoke about the case, but they soon started looking around the room for more exciting prospects. Being relevant in your chosen profession wasn't enough in this room. One needed money as well.

"Excuse us a moment," the judge said, pulling Hart aside. He placed the cigar between his teeth and pulled a handkerchief from his jacket. He spoke with the cigar in his mouth, a low rumble to his voice. "Mike, I'm not so sure you should be here. These little events are far away from the public eye, but these folks aren't exactly known for their restraint when it comes to spreading gossip."

Hart considered telling the judge something similar. "I'm only stopping by, Judge. I missed the funeral for Lucy Collins earlier this summer. I figured I'd pass along my condolences in person."

"That funeral was closed off to only family and close friends," the judge replied, glancing over his shoulder to see if anyone hovered nearby. "Besides, I've not seen the senator here tonight."

"Look at all these donors around here, you know he's—"

"I'm sure he's here," the judge scoffed. "He's just rather private, even at events like these."

Hart drained his glass, ignoring the comment. "Where can I find something stronger?"

"There's a bar in the next room, but listen to me," the judge said, placing a hand on Hart's shoulder. "I know how these people can be. They are going to ask you about the case and what they can do to help."

"I know how the rich can be with law enforcement, Judge. I'm not going to report anyone for offering me some vague amount of money as a bribe."

"You won't take it, either," the judge added curtly. "Wouldn't even think about it."

Hart laughed. "I'd think about it, Judge, but of course I wouldn't take it."

The judge nodded, pleased.

Hart left the magnificent entryway of the home and made his way toward the next room full of guests. He eased through groups of important people, all in deep conversation. As he passed through their respective orbits, eyes lingered on his misplaced attire. He ignored their silent judgment and found a space at the nearest bar, one of three assembled throughout the large room.

"Any pricey bourbon back there?"

"Yes, sir," the bartender replied. "Plenty."

"Pick one and give me a double."

"On the rocks?"

Hart nodded. "This room is something else, by the way."

"You're telling me," the bartender replied as he handed over the drink. "They call it the game room. These people aren't playing around, though."

"No kidding," Hart replied. "I'm not sure there is much the senator hasn't killed."

"From the chatter I've heard at the bar tonight, sounds like most of them belonged to his late wife."

Hart considered this as he slid to the end of the bar. There, he found a comfortable spot to take in his surroundings. Peppered along the walls, stretched out on the floor, and hanging from the high ceilings were the colorful, life-like trophies. Hart had never seen so many animals on display. He spotted a warthog, two different kinds of buffalo, a wildebeest, he believed, an impala, hyenas, and a full-size giraffe. He counted at least seven different kinds of deer but gave up when he overheard someone mention that the room's counterpart sat on the other end of the house. As Hart sipped his drink, he tried to decide whether the huntress responsible for all these kills could have appreciated the sport involved in tracking her game. He hoped she enjoyed the sport. If she didn't—it meant she only enjoyed the kill.

A hand tapped him on the shoulder. "Are you Michael Hart?"

A blonde in a strapless dress led Hart down a long hallway, away from the commotion of the party. He listened as the steady hum from the mixture of conversation and laughter faded. The woman made polite small talk as she guided him through the house. They passed a security guard, one that looked slightly larger than the man at the front gate, then arrived at a door. The woman knocked twice and entered.

"The senator will join you in a few minutes," she said with a nod that stated her intention to leave him there, alone. "Can I get you anything?"

Hart eyed a wet bar in the corner. "I'll manage to find something while I wait."

"Very well," she said. "If you will, please hand me your cell phone."

Hart considered her for a moment. The request didn't come off as one that was optional. "May I ask why?"

"It doesn't really matter why."

She was right. "Okay," Hart said, pulling his phone from his jacket. "How do I get it back?"

"You saw Ted out in the hallway?"

Hart nodded as he handed the phone over. "Is his real name Ted?"

She winked as she turned for the door. "He'll return it to you when you are on your way out."

30

Bill Collins appeared from a door on the opposite wall of the study. He offered his patented smile as he started across the room. He looked at ease in his tux, a classic black tie loose on his collar. A haberdasher's dream customer.

"Don't get up," he said with a hand extended. "I'm coming to you."

Hart was already halfway out of his seat. "Good evening, Senator Collins. I'm humbled you—"

"Drop all the formalities, Mike," the senator said as he shook Hart's hand, a solid grip perfected through his work in Washington. "I convinced Jimmy and Rosalynn to do the same when I had dinner with them last month in Plains. I hope you can do me the same courtesy."

"Of course," Hart replied, unsure why the senator had a need to justify his request. "Thank you for having me, by the way. Your home here is incredible, and the party is just that."

"Are my guests having a good time?"

"Absolutely," Hart replied, a grin on his face. "Some more than others. Your bartenders are making sure no one goes thirsty."

"How about our friend John?"

"The Honorable John?" Hart replied, sensing the senator wanted to rib the old judge in his absence. A game that good old boys played from time to time, not so different than the gossip exchanged between girls. "Last time I saw him, he was taking in some conversation with some of your more, let's say, attractive guests. I left him in their seemingly capable hands."

"I see," Bill mused, an eyebrow raised. He probably had a few professionals working the party that evening. Guests with a skill set that his big donors appreciated. "Did the old boy seem to be taken by these ladies?"

"I'd say so."

"I've known Big John Balk for years," the senator added in a conspiratorial tone. "He may prefer to play the role of the sober judge while in the courtroom, but he rather enjoys himself when he is allowed out of the house."

Hart nodded along, listening. He'd noticed the judge's red, swollen eyes on occasion. A detail that was hard to conceal under the fluorescent lighting of their small-town courtroom.

Bill continued. "I've met a few of his outside interests over the years. I thought he'd slowed down, though."

"I don't want to assume anything based on the little bit I saw," Hart said, the lawyer in him eager to preserve the record. "I'm sure he was just networking."

Bill winked. "Assume away, ADA Hart."

The senator clapped his hands together as he rose from his seat. He offered a drink to Hart as he made his way over to the wet bar in the corner. Bill selected two glasses from a shelf and began pouring from a large decanter. Hart noticed the window by the bar that sat half-open. It allowed the occasional burst of laughter to float in from groups of guests that congregated outside. The senator returned with the glasses, handing one to Hart.

"I know you are busy," Hart began. "And I certainly don't intend to take up a lot of your time. I've just been trying to get in touch with you. To discuss the case."

Bill took a sip of his whiskey before responding. "I've received the requests from your office to interview me about the murder."

Hart nodded. "It's not so much about interviewing you. I like to interview the families of my victims. At least those closest to the deceased. It helps with building my cases out."

"I remember we did the same when you handled my son's murder."

Hart sipped, unsure whether he wanted to go there. "I've made some changes with the way I approach my cases."

"Good," Bill said with a sharpness that closed further discussion on the past. "Let's talk about my wife's murder."

"Yes, sir," Hart said as he readjusted his position in his seat. He knew the details of the murder scene by memory. He'd reviewed the file at least ten times, always combing through it for a flaw in the case. He still hadn't found one. "Where do you want to start?"

"Let's start with your suspect—my granddaughter."

"Well, of all the murder cases that have landed on my desk over the years, your wife's murder is the most straightforward of them all. Charlotte Acker is our shooter. I have no doubt."

Hart knew the statement wouldn't come as a surprise to the senator. It had been well publicized that Acker faced a mountain of incriminating evidence. They'd tried to protect the details of their investigation, but the media had been relentless. As Acker was the prime suspect in a revenge killing, she was receiving all kinds of attention. A kind of circus-level intrigue swirled around the case. The kind that had long followed the notable murders in American history.

"No other possible suspects?" Bill asked. "I'd rather you tell me now if there are any other possible leads."

"None."

"Okay," Bill said slowly. He sipped some more from his glass as he appeared to consider his next inquiry. "Tell me about the evidence."

"It's difficult to know where to start."

"You're a prosecutor, Mike. Where are you going to start in your opening statement?"

Hart smiled. "I always start with motive. That's what drives every premeditated killing."

"And you believe my wife's murder was premeditated?"

"Of course."

"All right. So, Charlotte was getting payback for Lee. For her family."

"Clearly," Hart said, gaining confidence. "She lawyered up from the beginning, so she never agreed to an interview. She didn't need to, though. We knew motive from the get. Everyone did."

Bill nodded. "Where to next, ADA Hart?"

"Opportunity."

Bill stood from his seat and walked toward the open window. He pointed out toward the dark woods that surrounded the large home. "She ran the trail up from the river, right?"

"That's right," Hart said, still in his seat. "We have the exact route that she ran the night of the murder. My tech guy believes Acker was within a few hundred yards of your house, maybe closer."

Bill turned from the window. "And this was near the time you believe Lucy was murdered?"

Hart nodded. "There is also plenty of physical evidence. DNA, fingerprints, footwear impressions, and—"

"I understand," Bill said with a hand raised. "There is little doubt."

Hart shook his head. "Based on the evidence, there is no doubt."

"I assume that statement will find its way into your closing argument?"

"I may marshal the evidence first, but it'll be at the core of my message to the jury."

Bill didn't say anything else. He finished the liquid in his glass, then placed it on a nearby side table with a sigh. Hart sensed it was time for their meeting to end. Still, he felt compelled to ask the obvious question.

"I ask this of all my victims," Hart said as he stood from his chair. "It seems foolish in a case like this, but I've not had a chance to speak with you."

"What do you need to know?"

"I assume you want us to prosecute this matter to the fullest extent of the law, right?"

Bill paused, then extended a hand. "I'm not sure I can answer that question, Mike."

He made his way down the front steps of the house. The valet recognized Hart as he approached, the workingman's suit a dead giveaway. The young man grabbed a set of keys from his cabinet and hustled away into the darkness, in search of the least expensive vehicle in his lot. While Hart waited, he replayed his conversation with the senator in his head. He'd met with the family of victims for years in his work as a prosecutor. The meetings were an awful part of the job, but they were necessary. Plus, they always taught him something new about the human condition.

Some victims were angry, shocked by the sudden loss of their loved one. Others simply cried as they confronted the news, receding into their shells as they were asked to speak about their traumatic loss. Oftentimes, though, the families were numb to the impact of a senseless killing. To lose someone you love in a violent manner—at the hands of another human being—is an experience that no one is prepared to endure.

Hart tried to help them, though. He grieved with them, fought for them, and won with them. It felt good, and he could still remember the faces of countless families he'd helped, faces that clipped through his mind on occasion. As Hart waited, he flipped through the catalog of those people he'd worked for, trying to remember just one person that reminded him of the senator. He was still searching as he watched his car pull up to the curb.

"Here you are, sir," the young valet said, stepping out of the car. "I like this Malibu. I actually learned to drive on one. My mom still has it."

"It's state issued," Hart said, then nodded to the rear of the vehicle. "Does hers have the spoiler?" He smiled as he said this. "The spoiler makes all the difference."

"I bet," the valet said with a laugh. "Honestly, I've never noticed."

Later that night, the kid would be behind the wheel of vehicles that were sportier, more European. He'd take in every inch of the shiny toys as he drove the short distance. An experience he'd tell his friends about, bragging about being behind the wheel of six-figure machines. That was how people were with fancy things. The eye candy was enticing. It shifted your attention. It forced you to overlook the simpler details in life.

"Don't forget what you learned to drive on," Hart said as he handed the valet a couple of small bills. "It's a small thing, but now you know to look."

The prosecutor climbed into the vehicle and started down the drive. He looked back at the lights from the large house as they faded in his rearview mirror. He knew that the senator was going through a difficult experience.

One that was not being shared with his loyal supporters. The great man was alone, in a lavish house that rocked with revelry. In a way, Bill Collins's predicament probably seemed fitting to his harshest critics. The man had championed controversial causes throughout his career in politics, some-times fanning the flames on the fringes of his party. He'd lost a son, a wife, and would soon lose a granddaughter to prison. Yet, he would probably still be reelected come November because that was the way murder cases were. They touched the lucky, just like the cursed. The grief that followed the senseless violence cared little for how much power one had. It cared little for how much money had been amassed. It was indiscriminate and always struck hard.

Hart pulled back up to the front gate of Kelley Hill Plantation. It was closed, and another vehicle sat on the outside of the entranceway. Its head-lights cut through the bars of the gate, casting shadows that stretched across the hood of Hart's vehicle. The same large security guard from earlier stepped over to the window of the Malibu.

"Hold on a moment, sir," he said in a gruff tone. "We are dealing with a little situation here."

"What kind of situation?"

"An unwelcome guest is all. My partner is going to move him out of the way."

"Is that Ted?"

"No," the security guard replied, confused. He looked back in the direc-tion of the gate. "The man out there in the car is a guy by the name of John Deese."

"I meant your partner," Hart said with a grin. "The guy with the assault rifle. I think I met him up at the house earlier. I heard his name was Ted."

The large man shook his head. "Just sit tight, sir."

"What's the deal with the Deese guy?"

The man ignored the question and turned to walk toward the gate. With his back to Hart, he pulled a sidearm from somewhere inside his jacket and held it pointed down at the ground. Hart watched as the silhou-ette from the large man's partner neared the uninvited vehicle on the oppo-site side of the gate. Deese stepped from the driver's side and began shouting at the two men. With the Malibu's window down, Hart could make out some of the words being said. Threats were dispensed easily, and soon the partner on the other side of the gate had Deese by the throat. Hart assumed that the security guards didn't know they were in the presence of a local prosecutor. Hart stepped out of his vehicle.

"Take it easy!" Hart shouted, safely behind his open car door. "I can get law enforcement out here if this guy is a real problem."

The sound of Deese's head striking the hood of his car sounded loud from where Hart stood, so he reached back into his car to find his cell phone. A deputy could be out to the gate in ten minutes. They'd sort it out.

"Leave the phone in the car, counselor," a voice said from nearby. "No need for the police to get involved."

"It's kind of too late," Hart said as he stepped back away from the car. The large man's handgun was up and trained on Hart's chest. Hart thought about his words. "I'm with the district attorney's office. You don't want to do what you're doing."

"DAs have been shot around here before."

Hart watched as the gate began to open. The partner on the opposite side had shoved Deese back into the vehicle. The driver's face was visible for a moment in the headlights of the Malibu. He had blond hair, a grimace on his face, and blood covering the area around his nose. He backed up quickly, then spun the tires as he sped away. The pistol stayed on Hart until the sound of the fleeing car faded away.

"Listen," Hart began in a calm tone. "Maybe we need to all just settle down and—"

"You didn't see anything, right, ADA Hart?"

Hart paused a moment. He knew there was only one appropriate response. "Of course not, gentlemen. I've had a couple tonight, so I'm just a little out of sorts."

"Lots of good bourbon at that party," the large man said, tucking his sidearm back inside his jacket. "That probably explains the mix-up here."

"Absolutely."

"It's just a small thing, anyway."

Hart nodded. "You're right—nothing to see."

31

Maggie eased into the main courtroom of the Blake County Courthouse. Lawton followed a step behind, a briefcase in hand. In the front row, directly behind the defense table, sat Tim and the two remaining Ackers. They, along with everyone else in the courtroom, would serve only as spectators to the day's hearing. Maggie had no plans to call a witness, and neither did her friends at the district attorney's office. They all knew the hearing would be short because the request was simple, aggressive. The defendant wanted her trial. She didn't want to negotiate. She didn't want to argue about the evidence. She didn't want to engage in any pre-trial maneuvers. She just wanted a twelve-pack of jurors in the box, and she wanted it as soon as possible.

As expected, the courtroom had visitors from the media positioned in the back row. Maggie nodded in their direction as she walked down the courtroom's center aisle. They continued their conversations with one another, discussions centered around the mundane news of rural South Georgia. Maggie knew her frenemies from the press were watching, though, and trying not to appear too eager.

A pleasant voice called from the line of reporters. "Maggie, do you have time for a quick comment before the hearing?"

"Sure," Maggie said as she slowed her pace. She turned to her questioner, a bald reporter in a red jacket. "I'll tell you exactly what I'm going to tell Judge Balk. Charlotte Acker wants her trial. She's even willing to foot the bill if that's what it takes."

"How soon will—"

"The prosecution has maintained that the evidence against my client is overwhelming. Let's all quit talking about how good their case is against my client and have a jury decide her fate. Charlotte trusts that the people of Blake County will find the truth."

"And that truth would be—"

Maggie lifted a hand. "That's all I have for now. I need to prepare with my team."

"I have just one more—"

Maggie waved the reporter off, continuing down the aisle. She smiled at the three suits huddled close to one another at the table for the prosecution. All three men turned to glare at her. She'd violated an unwritten rule among trial lawyers: *No pre-hearing grandstanding for the media from within the courtroom.* Maggie knew the custom well, but she held firm on Michael Hart's glare as he watched her. His sidekicks whispered instructions to him, but his gaze stayed with Maggie. In it, she saw something she recognized. The serious expression had returned to his face. The one that reminded her of the prosecutor she faced five years ago. The change in his demeanor comforted her. It was better than the nonchalance with which he had approached the case for the last few months. It meant the day's hearing had the prosecutor's full attention. It meant she had him at least wondering —*What was the defense up to?*

Maggie pushed through the waist-high gate that divided the gallery of the courtroom from the area where the lawyers worked. The simple barrier in the courtroom divided those members of the bar from the rest of the public. She still loved crossing that courtroom threshold—the chalk lines that meant she was back in the field of play.

"When are they bringing Charlotte out?" Cliff Acker asked from his seat next to Tim. "I got an email from her this morning that she wanted to—"

Tim nudged him, hard. "No email talk, Acker. You know the deal."

Cliff had been briefed on the special accommodations that were being made for his niece, but he was the only one that had expressed anger over the agreed-upon middle ground. He maintained that she should be released on bond, and nothing less would do.

"These people in the media should at least know the lengths this corrupt group will go to for—"

Tim knocked him again, this time harder than before. Maggie shook her head as she watched the two. She knew that Cliff's aggressive approach to Charlotte's release from jail had more to do with his own experience in federal prison. An experience he wanted his family as far away from as possible.

"Don't be sticking that elbow into me, Dawson," Cliff said, laughing as he nudged the investigator back. "I wish I'd have played ball against your ass back in the day. I'd bet—"

Tim was ready with his response. The two men had sparred over this scenario before. "You'd have been crying to the refs, Acker. We all know that's what would have happened."

"Easy, boys," Maggie said, pointing to one of the courtroom's side doors as it opened. They all turned as Charlotte stepped through it, her faded orange jumpsuit hanging loose on her runner's frame. "We have work to do."

"There she is," Cliff said, loud enough for all to hear in the room. His first reaction was to immediately start in on the deputy walking next to her. "I don't see why you can't take those shackles off her, man. What's she going to do? Run off down the road after the hearing?"

"Cliff," Maggie said in her best tone of warning. She felt like she was being forced to settle down an unruly little brother. "I'll handle taking care of your niece. We've talked about this. You're here for support, and that's it."

Charlotte stepped to the defense table. She smiled at her small entourage as the deputy removed the shackles from her ankles. She looked rested and healthy, prompting Maggie to make a mental note that she should take running back up once her work schedule allowed.

Maggie leaned in close to her client. "Listen, Charlotte, we don't have a lot of time, and—"

"All rise!" a deputy boomed from the courtroom's back wall. "This court is now in session. The Honorable Judge John Balk is now presiding."

Maggie glanced at her watch. The judge was taking the bench about five minutes early. She looked over at Hart. He too was checking the time on his wristwatch. They glanced at one another and exchanged their surprise. Although they were adversaries in the courtroom, there was always a bond shared between trial lawyers—the ones in the arena.

"Good morning to you all," Judge Balk said as he started to walk through his standard introductions to the parties, spectators, and members of the press. "I see that we have only one matter on this morning's calendar. It appears to be a rather unusual request from the defense that would require the State to expedite these proceedings."

"That's correct, Your Honor," Maggie replied, on her feet and moving to the lectern. "Would you like me to address the substance of our motion?"

"I've read your motion, counsel. I've also perused the rather large brief that accompanied your request. It's all very thorough."

Maggie stood tall at the podium. She gazed up at the judge, watching him as he considered the appropriate course of action. "Mr. Crane and I worked together on the brief, Your Honor. He is here today to answer any questions you may have on the caselaw we've included in support of our motion."

The judge nodded in the direction of Maggie's second chair, Lawton Crane. Criminal work wasn't usually handled by attorneys from large, corporate-like firms. Big firms had the resources to shell out massive briefs and memoranda that thoroughly argued every angle of the law, even in unwinnable cases. None of the local lawyers could afford to practice that way.

In fact, for most of the people that were accused of crimes in Blake County, there wasn't much of a discussion around even hiring a lawyer. It simply wasn't an option. Most had limited resources or were living beyond the edge of poverty. The ones that had enough money to hire an attorney usually retained one of the area's small-time lawyers that had too many cases and not enough time to assemble long-winded briefs in their defense. That wasn't the case for Charlotte Acker, though. She was a uniquely positioned criminal defendant. One that had highly skilled trial counsel, a brief writer with a big-law upbringing, a principled investigator, and plenty of funds to pay her legal bills. She was a dangerous defendant for any prosecutor to face in the courtroom.

Judge Balk glanced at the lead for the prosecution. "Do you oppose the timeline proposed in the defendant's motion, Mr. Hart?"

"This is a demand, Your Honor," Hart began as he rose from his seat. The tone in his voice made his position obvious. "The document is even captioned as *Defendant Charlotte E. Acker's Demand for Speedy Trial*."

It was unusual for any lawyer to correct—in open court, that is—the trial judge presiding over their case. Trial lawyers were instructed to choose their battles with the judge wisely. Especially in front of the public.

"Do you oppose the timeline, Mr. Hart?"

"Defendant Acker's speedy trial demand is premature, Your Honor."

"Then, you oppose the defense's motion," Judge Balk said, moving his gaze back to Maggie. "Counsel, if you would like to—"

"Judge, Defendant Acker hasn't even been indicted yet. How can we even argue about scheduling this matter for trial in a month? This is beyond what is acceptable procedure."

As ill-advised as it could be for a lawyer to correct a judge in open court, it was even more so for a lawyer to interrupt a judge mid-sentence.

"This is my courtroom, Mr. Hart." Judge Balk glowered from his bench. "I expect you take notice of this fact before you speak again. Is that clear?"

Hart paused for a long moment as he seemed to consider what level of rebellion he wanted to reach. "Of course, Your Honor."

Judge Balk's eyes moved back to Maggie. "Would the defense like to be heard?"

"We would, Your Honor."

"Very well, let's hear it."

Maggie started in on the relevant caselaw that surrounded a criminal defendant's right to a jury trial. "Once a person is accused of a crime, he or she has a constitutional right to a speedy trial. This right under the Sixth Amendment is attached either at the time of the person's arrest or at the time of their indictment, whichever occurs earlier." Maggie pointed over at Charlotte. She was seated at the defense table, looking very much the part of the accused. "As the court knows, my client has been in custody for almost three months now."

"Your client has yet to be indicted, though," the judge said, redirecting the argument to the portion he needed input on. "What authority does this court have to force the State to indict your client?"

In Georgia, serious offenses are typically brought before a grand jury for indictment. The grand jury is a group of sixteen to twenty-three jurors that are selected from the citizens of the county where the charges have been brought. Those jurors meet with prosecutors and investigators in private, behind closed doors. There, the jurors are asked to hear evidence in certain cases that the district attorney's office believes should proceed to indictment. The prosecution controls the grand jury—not the judge. If the grand jurors approve of the charges put forth by the prosecution, "true bill" will be stamped on the indictment. The indictments are then returned in open court, and those criminal cases can proceed to trial. No mechanism is available under Georgia law that allows an accused person to force their own indictment.

"My understanding is that the grand jurors of this court's most recent term have been excused." As Maggie said this, she turned to look at Hart. "The evidence was apparently available to the State, but they elected not to return an indictment against my client."

Hart patted his table as he stood. "There are important reasons why we are commanded to not disclose to anyone what happens while a grand jury is in session, Your Honor. The secrecy protects our witnesses from intimidation or tampering, it makes it difficult for witnesses to avoid subpoena, it ensures evidence isn't destroyed or hidden—"

"I know the policy reasons behind secrecy of grand jury proceedings, Mr. Hart," the judge said, rubbing his forehead as he looked at his wayward prosecutor. "You'll get your turn."

Maggie kept her eyes on the judge. "With that being said, Your Honor, we are not trying to invade upon the secrecy of the grand jury. We are trying to enable it to do its job."

"By paying the county for its expense in bringing in a special purpose grand jury?"

Maggie nodded. A special purpose grand jury was one impaneled at the request of the chief judge, the district attorney, or elected public official from the county where the grand jury sat. They were unusual, as the jurors were not tied to a particular term of court, and they often faced a specific investigative task in their service on the grand jury. "That's correct, Your Honor. My client is prepared to pay for the time, expense, and work involved in calling in a group of grand jurors to hear Mr. Hart's presentation of the evidence."

The judge glanced at the defendant, then back to Maggie. "And your client understands that this grand jury would be tasked with indicting her for the offense of malice murder?"

"Of course," Maggie replied, walking back to the defense table to place a hand on Charlotte's shoulder. She wanted the media to have a perfect shot of the two standing together, ready to take on the case. "My client is innocent. She just wants the world to see it."

"And I see that you have requested a trial date for next month in November?"

"Or sooner, if the court will allow it," Maggie said, glancing back over her shoulder at the line of reporters. She knew all eyes were on her as she motioned to the table where the prosecution sat. "This is if Mr. Hart over here can have his ducks in a row."

Hart stood from his chair, arms wide. "Your Honor, this whole discussion is preposterous. My office will indict the defendant in due time. She is throwing money at her lawyers, investigators, and now the State. I won't stand for this kind of—"

"When will the State be ready?" Judge Balk asked. "I respect that this decision is within the purview of your office, but I have a criminal defendant that remains in custody—at your insistence, I'll add."

Hart looked to his notepad on the table. "It'll most likely be another month or two before I present this matter to the grand jury."

Maggie folded her arms across her chest, shaking her head. "Judge, I'm not sure what the delay is here. Can we at least inquire as to *why* we need to wait so long?"

"Fair question," the judge said. "Mr. Hart?"

Prosecutors can usually fall back on delays in their state crime labs or the unavailability of witnesses that need to be interviewed. Hart couldn't do that in this case, though. He'd been public about his office's quick work on the case. To backpedal now would be a disaster.

"Well, you see—"

"Doesn't the senator want this case prosecuted, Mr. Hart?" Maggie asked. "I know he is in the middle of an election cycle and all, but—"

"Counsel, let's refrain from any such insinuations," the judge barked. He turned back to the prosecutor. "Mr. Hart, I'm waiting for an answer to my question."

"Our office has a schedule already in place," Hart managed after a short pause. "This delay has nothing to do with denying Defendant Acker her right to a speedy trial. We simply won't have our grand jury ready for another—"

"Get them ready, then," Judge Balk said, leaning back in his chair. "I agree with the spirit of the defense's motion. You maintain that you are ready, as do they. Let's have this trial next month."

Hart's shoulders slumped. "Your Honor, I'd like my objection noted on the record."

"So noted," the judge said, smiling at the parties. "Is there any other business that we need to discuss?"

Maggie looked at Charlotte and Lawton. They both shook their heads. "Nothing from the defense, Your Honor."

A briefcase snapped shut at the prosecution's table. "None from the State at this time, Your Honor."

"Very well," the judge said. "We'll look to a trial date in early November, then."

32

When Maggie pulled into her driveway, she found Eli waiting on the front steps. At the curb sat a well-worn Honda with Maya seated in the front passenger seat. Maggie offered a smile to Eli as she stepped out of her car, then waved over in the direction of the Honda.

· "This is a surprise," Maggie said as she walked toward the front porch. She was still running on the good energy from Charlotte's hearing that morning, finally starting to feel some momentum as the court shifted back in her favor. "I saw I missed a call from you earlier, Eli. I was stuck in court all morning and haven't been able to get back to you."

Eli nodded. "Yeah, I heard that the Acker girl had another hearing today. How'd it go?"

Maggie sensed some frustration in her client's voice. "Good, given the circumstances. The judge didn't grant our request outright, but the message was delivered to the other side."

Eli's eyes moved to his vehicle parked on the street. They seemed to rest on it as he considered his words. "Look, Maggie, I want you to know that we —Maya and I, that is—appreciate all that you've been doing for us. It's been a long summer for my family, and—"

"I know it has," Maggie said, glancing over her shoulder at the car.

Maya had her head down, probably fixed on a cell phone. "We have a long way to go, though."

Eli stood and walked down the few brick steps. He shoved his hands deep into his pockets, struggling to get through what he wanted to say. "I guess that's what I'm here about. We've talked about it, and we're going to make a change. It's just best for our family. Well, what's left of it."

"A change?"

"It's not anything against you, Maggie. It's just the way things need to be."

Maggie turned to the driveway and watched as Tim pulled in next to her vehicle. He, too, looked surprised to see Eli at the house. Maggie didn't take appointments at home with clients, so he'd understand this was an unannounced visit from the Jones family.

"Is this about Judge Balk hitting the pause button on the case, Eli?"

He looked away. "Man, the holdup in the case is my fault. I lost my cool on that lawyer. I shouldn't have let that happen."

Tim walked up and stood next to Maggie. "What's going on?"

"Eli and Maya are thinking about switching to another lawyer for their civil case against—"

"We aren't thinking about it," Eli said, some bass in his tone. "It's what we're doing. I just felt like I needed to tell you in person. They told me I could just send you a letter, but this felt right given everything."

In most situations, clients have the absolute right to fire the lawyer that is handling their case. It usually happens when a client disagrees with the strategy in their case. It can also occur when the client loses faith or trust in their lawyer, though. Maggie hoped it was not the latter.

"Why, Eli?"

"Yeah," Tim added. "We're all in for you and your family, Eli. I mean, look at us, we're standing in the front yard of a house we just bought in Blake County. We wouldn't be back here if it wasn't for you, for your case."

Eli shifted his eyes back to the Honda. He seemed to be grounded by the sight of his sister. "I talked to that lawyer you recommended, Maggie. The guy you told me would be able to help me out with my new criminal charges. He has a solution that will work for everyone."

Maggie nodded. To avoid any potential conflict, she'd recommended Eli speak with one of the local criminal defense attorneys about his new misdemeanor charges. The ones filed after the dust-up at the deposition. With the alleged victim being Gilbert Wesley, the prick that represented BTF Freight and Jimmy Benson, she didn't want to take on the criminal case. A move she now realized had been a mistake.

"What kind of solution?" she asked. "And who came up with it?"

"I'm not supposed to get into the details, but it's going to be handled. That Gil Wesley guy is going to drop the charges against me, and they are going to settle the case with us. Maya will get a little bit of money, and it'll help us get by."

Maggie felt the anger flash in her. "Who is going to rep—"

"Before you get upset with me," Eli said with a hand raised, "I talked to Jack Husto, and he told me you'd probably have some expenses that you put into the case. He's going to make sure that is taken care of."

Although clients have the absolute right to fire their lawyer, some attorney-client agreements provide for a lien against the client's case to recover the fair and reasonable value of the time and expenses the lawyer has spent on the case. Maggie had never been put in a position where she had to pursue such a remedy. She'd never been fired by a client.

"I don't care about the expenses," Maggie shot back. "I care about you and Maya."

"I know," Eli said as he started to turn back toward the Honda. "Caring about us isn't enough, though. Jack Husto told us that you've got to be committed to handling these injury cases to do it the right way. He told us it was an area for specialists and that you just hadn't gotten there yet. I get it, you have all the criminal type—"

"I'm committed!" Maggie shouted, angry now. "You called me this morning while I was in court. I can't step out and take every single phone call on the spot."

"I called you while I was in the meeting with Husto. He told me to call you. He wanted to make it fair."

"He knew I'd be in the hearing, Eli," she said as she shook her head. "He played you. Can't you see that?"

"Then he played you, too," Eli said, halfway to the Honda and not looking back. Maggie started to follow him.

"Give me a month," she said. "I'm going to get the Acker case tried next month, then we can get the stay lifted."

Maya opened the door to the Honda. She pulled her hoodie down to speak to her brother. "Can't we give her the time, E?"

Eli was opening the driver-side door to the vehicle now. "No, we can't wait any longer."

"It's just another month."

"We need the money, Maya," Eli said, leaning with his arms resting on the dented roof of the Honda. "You haven't been staring at all these bills coming in. Don't you know that a hundred thousand dollars will change everything for us?"

"Don't take the hundred," Maggie interjected, looking at Maya now. "Bet on me instead."

Eli rubbed his head, frustrated. "On you?"

"Better yet, I'll wager it all on me."

Eli considered her. "All right, bet. What are the terms?"

"I'll show you both I'm still a winner," Maggie said slowly. "If Charlotte is acquitted, you stay with me."

"They have that girl squared up, Maggie. Everybody knows that."

Maggie said it again. "If Charlotte is acquitted, you stay with me."

"And if they convict her?"

"You go with Husto. I won't go after a dime."

Eli considered this for a moment.

"Let's give her the month," Maya added, almost pleading. "We can wait it out."

Eli nodded to his sister, then to Maggie. "Deal."

33

After Columbus Day, campaign season started to hit its stride. It became difficult to turn on a television or log on to social media without being confronted by the political advertising funded by the big campaigns. Every candidate running for office claimed to hold the power to fix the economy, root out their version of injustice, and ensure freedom for all. Bold attack ads took snippets of quotes, then used them to support inflammatory conclusions as to the character of their opponents or the state of the country. The politicians could be seen up close, attending events of all kinds as they stumped at community organizations, churches, and clubs they wouldn't return to again until another election year. Every candidate needed more votes, more donations—a nudge in the polls. Most of all, though, they needed some dirt on their opponents. Enough for a nice little October surprise.

"Y'all can follow me," Sheriff Clay said, leading Maggie, Tim, Lawton, and Charlotte down the back hallway of the Blake County Sheriff's Office. A deputy covered the rear of the defense team as they walked in a small phalanx. "Most everyone is gone for the day, so you should have some peace and quiet."

"We appreciate this," Tim said, patting the sheriff on the back. "I know having some space to work in will help us immensely."

"Don't mention it."

"He really means that," Maggie said with a grin. "The last thing his campaign needs is some story about being in cahoots with the evil defense lawyers."

"I prefer *slimy* defense lawyers," the sheriff said, holding the conference room door with a smile. "So do most of my constituents."

"Of course."

"I'll keep my deputy by the door," the sheriff said with a nod. "When you're finished, he'll walk Ms. Acker back to her cell. Take as long as you need."

Tim pointed to the sheriff's dress shoes, his blazer over a dress shirt. "You and Mrs. Clay hitting the town tonight?"

"I wish, Dawson. I'm off to do some campaign work. The Blake County Young Farmers Club and the local Scouts are doing a combined event tonight. They invited me out."

"Those kids can't even vote, Charlie."

"You're right," the sheriff said with a laugh. "Their parents can, though."

"Spoken like a *slimy* politician," Maggie chided.

"One that's ready for this election year to be over."

They all thanked the sheriff again as he pulled the door closed. They had just under three weeks to spare before the opening statements were presented in *State v. Acker*. The short window of time would force the State to present their case during the first week of November. A tactic that was carefully planned and at the core of the message from the defense. The juxtaposition between two stories. The most important week for Bill Collins's campaign. The most important week in Charlotte's life.

"Let's talk about the evidence," Maggie said, taking a seat at the head of the long conference table. While she assembled her thoughts, Lawton passed around large binders to everyone. She could smell the faint odor of beer coming from her co-counsel as he dropped a binder near her. "Does it look to everyone like we have the entire discovery packet?"

Each flipped the front cover on their binder, diving in. After indictment, and once a criminal defendant is formally arraigned, they are entitled to a copy of the discovery. A modern discovery packet usually included digital evidence, like recordings, or video from interviews, dash cameras, or body cameras. It also contained all the reports, photographs, and test results that were tied to an investigation. This information could be crucial to the defense, and the prosecution was required to turn over all their evidence—especially evidence that could exonerate the defendant or could be favorable as to the issues of innocence and punishment. If any discovery was withheld—especially discovery that was material to the accused's case—the defendant could cry foul. In a murder case, though, half the battle was knowing where to look, and that's where Tim shined.

"It looks like it," Tim replied from his end of the table. "I've cataloged all the narratives, witness statements, photographs, and reports. All in chronological order. They pretty much had Charlotte pegged as their main suspect within eight hours of the victim's death. Never had a reason to look anywhere else."

The group stayed quiet for a moment as they flipped through the thick stack of information. They'd made a deal with the judge to expedite the trial. The defense wouldn't file any written motions to challenge the evidence collected in the investigation. They'd get their trial the first week of November—they'd just have to walk in blind.

"Shouldn't we at least discuss hiring an expert to refute some of these reports?" Lawton asked. "I feel like it couldn't hurt to bring in our own crime scene investigator."

"We have one," Maggie said, pointing to the other end of the table. "Tim is going to be as good as anyone out there on the expert circuit. Plus, he knows the players around here."

"I agree," Charlotte added. "Tim told me last week while we were running that there wouldn't be a lot to go on anyway. That the scene is close to textbook."

"The crime scene is damn near perfect," Tim added. "It's an investigator's dream. The whole deal reminds me of the examples from my days in the basic agent course. New recruits may even study this case one day."

Charlotte smiled. "I've always been an overachiever."

"You joke," Tim said, "but when I was a fresh-faced agent, I thought a lot of my homicide investigations were going to be this easy. I figured they'd all have clean prints, clear foot impressions, gunshot residue, and sprinkles of DNA everywhere."

Lawton burped into his hand, wafting a boozy smell over the table. "I guess that's not how it goes down out there in the real world?"

"Heck no," Tim exclaimed. "You're lucky if you get much outside of an eyewitness in a lot of these murders that investigators work on. When they do make an arrest, it's usually because the shooter wasn't too bright or forgot to ditch the firearm. It's really a miracle anyone gets convicted."

"There isn't a gun in this case, though."

"That's true," Maggie said as she stood from her chair. She made her way over to a large whiteboard. "And that's where we make some waves at trial."

"That's right," Tim added. "There is something interesting about these bullet casings that are included in evidence, too. They should tell the jury something about the killer."

Lawton flipped through the pages in his copy of the discovery. "Bullet jacket items one through three, consistent with being ejected from a firearm that had the capacity to fire a nine-millimeter round. That's the gist of the report, right?"

Maggie started writing on the board. "That doesn't narrow it down by much, but the manufacturer of the three rounds might."

"What do you mean?" Lawton asked, leaning back in his chair.

"I mean whoever fired these rounds, they sure waited a long time to do so."

"They are old," Tim added with some excitement. "And I mean *really* old."

"That's right," Maggie said, talking as she scribbled on the board. "It has been nearly fifty years since this particular manufacturer has produced the kind of rounds found at the scene."

"Okay," Lawton replied, squinting his eyes at the photograph in hand. "Who's the manufacturer?"

"A Czech company that stopped producing this cartridge in the seventies."

Lawton shrugged. "I bet there are lots of houses with old ammo packed away around here. Why is the jury going to find old nine-millimeter rounds all that unusual?"

"Tell them what you found out, Tim."

"As you would expect, the nine-millimeter round has been modernized over time," he said, taking the handoff. "I spoke with a historian over the phone last week, and he gave me the rundown. He told me that the nine-by-nineteen-millimeter Parabellum and nine-millimeter Luger have been around a good while because they were originally developed in the early nineteen hundreds. Apparently, they were used extensively around the time of—"

"Aren't they common today, though?" Lawton asked. "I see them mentioned all the time in the news."

"Hold your horses," Tim said with a hand up. "Yes, they are common today all over the world, but initially, it was the Germans that started using them during World War I. After that, they started to spread rapidly throughout Europe and the US. By World War II, pistols and other arms chambered for these cartridges were in a number of countries, like Belgium, Bulgaria, Czechoslovakia, Finland, Poland, Sweden, Switzerland, and—"

"What about Spain?" Charlotte asked, looking up from her discovery binder. She'd been quiet in her seat, absorbing the discussion around her.

"Bingo," Tim said with a smile. "They were especially popular with the manufacturers in the northern part of Spain."

"So, maybe it was fired by someone who was a collector of Spanish pistols?"

"Maybe," Tim said, looking over at Charlotte. "Maggie and I have a little theory, though. You've had at least one unusual visitor come to see you here in jail, and we—"

"What unusual visitor?" Crane asked pathetically. "I mean, are we talking about someone from around here that is—"

Charlotte put a hand on Lawton's shoulder to stop him from rambling. Maggie noticed the placement of the hand, the way it lingered on his shoulder in a more intimate manner.

"Charlotte hasn't had a lot of visitors at the jail," Tim said, pushing on. "Mostly us, family, and a few friends."

"Almost no friends," Charlotte said with a laugh. "No offense."

"She did have an interesting guy come see her a couple of months ago, though. A man by the name of Fernando Lazkano."

Maggie added the name to her diagram on the whiteboard, circling it in a sweeping motion. She looked back to Tim. He sat leaned back in his chair, speaking with his hands as he pitched his idea. He loved playing the role of lead investigator.

"See, Fernando, along with his brother, Juan, are third-generation owners of a family-owned Spanish weapons manufacturer. This is a little company based out of a town called Eibar. The family has been producing small arms since the beginning of the last century, right there in the Basque Country, a region in northern Spain."

"And their company built a manufacturing facility right here in Blake County," Charlotte added. "It opened just last year. The brothers told me all about it. It's their first plant here in the US."

Tim nodded. "Well, the brothers apparently thought they could leverage the Blake County connection, so they scheduled a meeting with the senator's office on Capitol Hill this past summer. Bill Collins supposedly stiffed the young guys. They had to meet with Charlotte and another lead from Collins's camp instead."

"George Dell was there with me. The brothers wanted to talk about getting a prime spot at a big conference set to take place in Bilbao. They wanted the senator to support a discussion around ways to expand partnerships in the gun industry."

"Okay," Lawton said slowly. "You're not suggesting these guys put a hit out on the senator's wife just because he dodged a meeting?"

"Of course not," Maggie said, still standing by the board. She capped her dry-erase marker and started to walk the room. "We don't care whether they did it, Lawton. What we care about is *could* they be considered suspects."

"They're not suspects, though."

Maggie continued to pace the room. "You're missing the point. I just need a reason—one that is at least arguably tied to the evidence—to put this Lazkano brother on the stand. I need an opening for the jury to hear him speak."

"We don't know what he'll say, Maggie. He's going to raise hell over the accusation that he—"

"I don't really care about that," she said, lifting a hand, "and I'm not necessarily making accusations. I'm trying to create reasonable doubt."

"How?"

"By asking him why he walked into the county jail and told our client that Bill Collins set her up."

"And you think he's going to testify to that?" Lawton said, shaking his head. "You've been off the playing field too long, then. Let's just bring in every crackpot conspiracy theorist and line them up at the witness stand. The judge will love that."

"Tell me how your last criminal trial went," Maggie shot back. "Actually, let's go have a few more drinks and you tell me all about your theories on how to defend a murder case."

Lawton stood. "At least I know how to take a case the distance. I'm sure those Jones kids would love a lawyer that—"

"Whoa!" Tim interjected. "Let's take it down a notch."

The deputy standing guard outside stuck his head in the conference room. Maggie turned to him and assured the young deputy that everything was fine. She asked him to shut the door.

"I apologize, Lawton," Maggie said, quick to be the bigger person. "We need to discuss the evidence in *this* case. Not insult one another. That's my mistake."

"Mine, too," Lawton murmured. "I just think that—"

Tim stopped him. "Look, Maggie is going to get into evidence the fact that those rounds are unique to this area and almost impossible to find."

"But what does that do for us?"

"I'm glad you asked," Tim replied with a smile. "Like I said, Maggie is going to set the stage for the discussion on the origins of the rounds. Then, we are going to walk right into why the prints are so clean on these weird casings that are in evidence."

Lawton nodded, listening.

"Every investigator knows that with the heat, gas, and friction that comes with firing a weapon, it's damn near impossible to lift a latent off a spent casing. Not one that is as clear as those in evidence."

"You think someone applied my prints to the rounds after the murder?"

Charlotte asked, running a hand through her hair. "I don't know, it all sounds—"

"What's the connection with that to the Lazkano brothers?" Lawton asked.

"I'm not sure," Maggie said, walking the room again. "Something's there, though."

Charlotte leaned over the table. "Fernando told me he's never met the senator. He said he only dealt with Lucy Collins and her team."

"That still could mean he was involved."

"Bill told me he wasn't doing any work with her anymore, though."

Maggie returned to her board, staring at her handiwork. She wanted Charlotte's sharp mind to keep working in the silence.

"Fernando never told me why he believed what he believed."

"You told me Fernando wrote the statement about Collins setting you up on a piece of paper," Maggie said, prodding her along. "Think about what he *did* tell you."

"He told me about the conference. He said he'd spent time with Bill's old lackey, John Deese."

Maggie added Deese's name to the board. "I thought you told me Deese was excommunicated along with Lucy."

"I thought he was, too," Charlotte said. "I mean, maybe he was working behind the scenes, but I never heard Deese mentioned in any of my time around the senator."

Maggie spun the marker in her hand as she waited. Charlotte continued.

"I mean, the senator was privately distancing himself from all his old political operatives and causes. He was still publicly courting endorsements from his old cronies, but he was planning to pivot after the election. I assume he still will."

"Where was he on gun legislation?" Maggie asked.

"Privately, he was undecided."

"Publicly?"

"He toed the party line."

Maggie nodded as she taped a picture of one of the casings on the whiteboard.

"Tim, what was that phrase you said had something to do with the naming of the nine-by-nineteen-millimeter Parabellum?"

"*Si vis pacem, para bellum.*"

Lawton, eager to show he was the best educated in the room, spoke up first with his interpretation. "If you want peace, prepare for war."

They all stared at the picture on the board.

Lawton stated the obvious. "Bill Collins was on a stage giving a campaign speech when his wife was murdered. He couldn't have pulled the trigger."

Tim folded his arms across his chest. "That doesn't mean he didn't have someone do it for him."

"That's why I need to get Fernando Lazkano in front of the jury," Maggie said. "Even if it's just to ask him a few simple questions."

"He isn't going to know a thing," Lawton said. "I'm telling you, Maggie."

"He might know where the killer could find an old casing like the one in this picture, though."

34

Maggie sat at the only coffee shop in downtown Blakeston. She had her laptop open, earbuds in. She was still in the market for office space, but her future in Blake County had suddenly started riding on a respectable outcome in *State v. Acker*. *The life of a trial lawyer*, she told herself. *When you're winning, everyone loves you. When you're down, you need to keep the faith, keep betting on yourself. Even if no one else will.*

An older woman tapped her on the shoulder and pointed to the coffee bar. Maggie pulled an earbud from her ear and looked in the direction of the barista. "Double americano, room," he said, making no attempt to hide his frustration. He pointed with a thumb toward the takeout counter. "Bagel is at the window, too."

Maggie thanked the woman as she stood, her mind still drifting with thoughts around the upcoming trial.

"It's not a problem, Maggie. I know you have a lot on your mind."

The woman turned before Maggie could say something, so she just watched the kind stranger as she made her way toward the door. Maggie didn't recognize her. A fact that troubled her. They would start selecting a jury in a week and a half at the Blake County Courthouse, and Maggie felt more like a stranger than ever before in Blakeston.

"Do you know who that woman was?" Maggie asked the barista as she collected her cup from the bar. "The silver-haired woman that just walked out the door."

The barista looked up at her from under the bill of his retro cap. He had a machine whistling and spitting in front of him. Two shots of espresso filled small glass cups with black liquid. "I'm not sure of her first name. I know her husband is a judge around here. Last name is Balk or something."

As Maggie returned to her small table in the corner, she analyzed the brief interaction. What could she glean from those few words? *Some sympathy*, she told herself. *Some compassion for me, maybe even for Charlotte.* Maggie wondered if that same sentiment might be something felt by a wider slice of the Blake County population. If so, then that meant they had a shot in front of a jury of Charlotte's peers.

Maggie was reading an email on her cell phone when the call came in. The screen on the device flashed with the name of the last person she wanted to see calling—Jack Husto. *Wonderful*, she thought. *Remember, just don't cuss him out.*

"Hello, Jack," she said through gritted teeth. "To what do I owe the pleasure?"

"Afternoon, Maggie. Oh, you know, just catching up. How're you on this fine October day?"

"Well, I'd be a lot better if I didn't have other lawyers trying to poach my clients. What the hell, Jack?"

"Listen, I didn't call to—"

"I know you probably forgot what it was like to care about anything other than the numbers on your settlement checks, but you aren't taking Eli and Maya Jones from my firm. I've already—"

"Your firm?" Jack laughed into the phone. "You mean your little one-woman band you're running up there in South Georgia. Stop it, Maggie. Let's be practical here."

"I still haven't decided if I'm reporting you to the bar, Jack, but go ahead and tell me how practical we all need to be."

The line went silent for a moment. The wheels in the slick salesman's brain were obviously turning.

"I talked to Eli Jones this morning," he said. His tone was far from contrite. "He told me that he and Maya have decided to wait to sign with my firm. Something about wanting to see how that trial you have going on up there turns out. The one involving the murder of the senator's wife."

"Good," she said, relieved. "That's what he and I agreed to—"

"That's ridiculous, though. You know there isn't any reason for them to push that lawsuit forward. Their mother caused that wreck. I'm offering them a way to get some money now. It's win-win, young lady."

"One hundred grand for the loss of their mother and brother?" Maggie snorted. "That's a fraction of what they deserve, and you know it."

"It's better than nothing. Which is what they'll have if they wait for you."

"Look, I don't want to argue about this. I'm busy, and the Joneses have made their decision."

"Have you seen the discovery that the trucking company provided?" Jack asked, still the tone of a gentleman. "Their case is going to be strong against—"

"What discovery?"

"The documents and responses to our interrogatories that were provided last week by BTF Freight," he said slowly. "Gil Wesley's office sent them by mail."

"What about the judge's order that stayed the case?"

"I know those Atlanta boys well. They understand the position I'm in—*we're* in, Maggie—so they sent their responses over as a courtesy."

Maggie knew the fix was in. No insurance defense lawyer would voluntarily provide discovery while they had a judge's finger on the pause button. Husto and the other lawyers had to be back-channeling, trying to get the case settled without Maggie's involvement.

"I didn't get them, Jack."

"I'll send you a copy of mine, then. Look at the responses and get back to me. That's all I'm asking."

She considered telling him to kick rocks. She never turned down an opportunity to get more information that might help a client's case, though. She owed that to Eli and Maya.

"Send them to me."

"I'll have my girl, Melissa, send it over to you."

She disliked so much about him. "Sure."

"How's the trial looking, by the way?"

"It's coming together."

"Evidence sounds pretty damning, from what I hear. You'll need to pull a rabbit out of a hat to get your client home."

"That's why the Ackers hired me."

"Magic, Maggie," Husto said with a laugh. "Well, good luck up there."

She hung up the phone and tossed it aside. She wanted to scream. *Maybe he's right*, she thought. *Some money is certainly better than no money. Maybe settling is the best deal for Eli and Maya.* Maggie thought about this as she weighed her options. She was determined to not let her ego get in the way of doing what was right for her clients. She decided that she would review the discovery sent over by Husto's office, then make her decision. She wanted what was best for her clients.

―――――――――

As Tim pushed through the front door to the house, he held a stack of documents in one hand, his running shoes in the other. It was late, and he was worn out from the long run with Charlotte that night. Not only was she fifteen years younger than he was, but a top-level athlete that stayed locked in a cell twenty-two hours a day. The combination of the two factors had created a machine he couldn't compete with. When it came time for their late-night runs, she brought it every time. He just had to hang in there and survive.

"You look like you had a long day," Maggie said as Tim plopped down on the couch next to her. "Charlotte still kicking your butt out there, old man?"

"I'm pretty sure I know how John Henry felt when he got home from driving steel every day."

"It can't be *that* bad?"

"Oh yeah?" he said with a laugh. "I've been running with her the last month and a half. I'm in better shape right now than I've been in years. I still can't keep up."

"They say that girl was the real deal in college. Borderline Olympian if she'd opted not to attend law school."

"She probably still could try to qualify for Paris. Will they let her compete in the Olympics on loan from the Georgia Department of Corrections? Some kind of *Longest Yard* deal where the guards deliver her to the stadium for the races."

Maggie laughed. "Don't tell me you're losing faith in me, too."

"Nah," Tim said, struggling to get his tired legs into a comfortable position. "You know I'm just being realistic. I think the girl got set up, but it was a flawless frame job."

"I know," Maggie said. "And if she did do it, she has us both fooled."

Tim nodded.

"What's that you have there?" Maggie asked, pointing to the stack of paperwork.

"I picked the jury list up this afternoon," he said, handing the packet over. "I've not flipped through it yet, but I thought we could get a jump on researching some of the potential jurors."

"Did you send one over to Lawton?"

"I called him on my way home to tell him I dropped it to him by email. He picked up. Sounded like he was hammered, hopefully at a bar somewhere."

"Is he in town still?"

Tim smiled. "Yeah, he's staying out at the Holiday Inn by the bowling alley. I guess he's planning to stick around until the trial."

"What has he been doing?"

"I think he just goes to see Charlotte at the jail, then hangs around town at night. He told me he was out doing 'jury research' this evening. I told him I'd give him a ride back to his hotel if his research got too in-depth."

They laughed together at the thought of Lawton hanging out in the smoky barroom of the bowling alley. It was a long way away from Washington's Michelin-starred restaurants and swanky bars.

"Speak of the devil," Tim said, pointing to his cell phone. He picked it up and pressed speaker as he answered the call. "Hey there, buddy. How's the work coming along?"

Music blared through the phone, a 90s country song that had endured as a jukebox favorite. Loud voices in the background shouted until the caller could be heard taking the phone into a quieter space. A woman began on the other side of the line.

"I've been hanging out with a guy by the name of Lawton Crane here at Decker's," she said, a slight thickness in her tongue. "He's about to leave, and I think somebody should give him a ride home. I asked him for his phone, and he told me to call you, Tim."

One of Blake County's best-known honky-tonks was a shady spot on the south side of the county. The place was owned by Billy Ray Decker, an aging redneck party-boy. He appropriately named the place *Decker's* in an attempt to meet as many women as possible that walked through the doors of his establishment. The place rocked Thursday through Saturday night, and the local law enforcement knew the regulars well.

"Yeah, I know him," Tim said, grinning at the thought of Lawton two-stepping on the dance floor or shooting pool at Decker's. "I'll come by and get him in about fifteen minutes. Billy Ray's place isn't too far away from me."

"Okay," the woman said. "He's been stumbling around the place for the last thirty minutes, flashing cash at the bar and talking too much. You may want to hurry."

"Keep him busy. I'll be there soon."

35

Tim pulled into the parking lot of Decker's and saw a BCSO Dodge Charger parked near the front entrance. The lights were off on the vehicle, but Tim could make out Lawton as he stood out front talking to a deputy. A redhead in tight pants and a flowy top stood nearby. From where Tim parked, he could see Lawton's disheveled clothing, the stream of blood coming from his nose. Tim stepped out of his vehicle and hustled over to the front steps of the bar.

The deputy recognized Tim as he passed under the bright lights of the bar's neon sign. "What's going on, Dawson?" he said with a wide grin. "You here for this guy?"

"That depends," Tim replied, extending a hand to the khaki-uniformed deputy. They shook hands like two men on the same side of a problem. "You aren't taking him downtown, are you?"

"Tim!" Crane yelled from their close distance. He'd finally recognized the face of someone he knew. It wasn't hard, since Tim stuck out as the only Black man at the rural watering hole. "I've been—I've been trying to tell these people—or *these folks*, I guess you people say—that I just don't see why—"

"Please, Lawton, let's just get you back to your hotel," Tim said, glaring at the drunk lawyer. "I'm sure you'll tell me all about it while—"

"I just want to tell you—"

"No," Tim said firmly. He glanced over at the deputy. "As long as our friend here is going to allow you to go back to your hotel, that's what we're going to do."

The deputy shrugged. "He's just my victim in a little barroom tussle. A couple of boys smacked him around a little bit. They said he was talking to their girlfriends or something. Trying to buy them all drinks. You know how these things go."

"Well," Tim said, putting an arm around Lawton. "My man here isn't going to want to prosecute. He probably wasn't exactly an innocent party in all this."

The redhead wanted to add her two cents. "They just didn't like him trying to buy everyone drinks. He was going around all night buying beers and seltzers for everybody. Talking about how cheap everything was down here and all."

"People don't like when you try to give them handouts, Lawton," Tim said, squeezing the lawyer's shoulders as he pulled him away from the redhead. "I'll talk to you about those manners tomorrow."

"I'm just trying to talk to people, Tim—to ask them what the deal is with all—"

"Is he good to go?" Tim said in the direction of the deputy. "I'm going to get him out of here, if that's all right with you."

"Go ahead," he replied with a laugh. "Billy Ray told me he didn't want him back anytime soon, though."

"We can manage that."

———

Tim kept Lawton upright as they made their way through the lobby of the Holiday Inn. A burned-out clerk looked over from the front desk, staring a moment at the odd pair as they stumbled through on the otherwise quiet Thursday night. Lawton tried to say something to the clerk, but Tim moved him along, trying to avoid any further embarrassment for the lawyer that would soon stand as an advocate in one of Blake County's highest-profile trials.

They found Lawton's room and pushed through the heavy hotel door. Tim had planned to leave the lawyer in the entryway to his room, but he stopped short when he saw the condition of the man's living quarters.

"What in the world, Lawton," Tim said as he caught his first glimpse of the inside. "Look at this place."

There were beer bottles cluttered around the television that sat on the room's main dresser. Another two empty vodka bottles were visible from the doorway. Tim pushed his way deeper into the room, and Lawton stumbled in behind him. As he did, Lawton picked up a half-empty bottle of beer from the counter inside the bathroom. He started drinking from it with a glassy-eyed smile.

"There should be some cold beer in the mini fridge, Timbo," he said. "Sit down—sit down and stay awhile."

"This place is a mess," Tim replied, rubbing his neck with one hand. He kept an eye on the lawyer as he ambled across the room. "You're a mess, man."

Lawton fell into the open chair that sat in the corner of the hotel room. A glass with some kind of clear liquid in it sat on the nearby end table. Lawton picked it up with his free hand, sniffed it, then knocked it back.

He smacked his lips. "Maybe I'm just having a long week."

Tim shook his head. Even when the guy was sauced out of his mind, he was able to pull pieces together for an argument in his defense.

"Where's your cell phone?" Tim asked. "I left mine in the car, and I need to call Maggie."

"Are you going to get me—are you trying to get me in trouble or something?"

Tim grabbed the phone without a word. Lawton struggled to remember his passcode but finally provided it on the third try to allow access to the phone. There were five missed calls, along with a few unread text messages. Tim figured at least one missed call was from Maggie, so he opened the call log. All were from a contact labeled *J.D.*

"We need to get you some help," Tim said after dialing Maggie's number. "I'll see what Maggie wants to do, though."

The phone rang until it went to voicemail, so Tim left a message for her to call him back. He pocketed the phone and took in the rest of the destruction in the room. There was an empty pizza box, two empty beer boxes, at least three spent liquor bottles, and countless other wrappers from chip bags and snacks. It looked like a frat party had gone down in the room, not a one-man bender.

"I know I need some help," Lawton finally said in a low voice. He'd found another beer and cracked it as he spoke. He spilled some of it on his shirt as he took the first sip. "I'm just trying to get to the other side of this—of this trial down here for my girl. I hate to see her like this."

Tim nodded, listening. Maggie had mentioned to him that she thought something unusual was going on between Charlotte and Lawton. He wanted confirmation.

"I know what I have to do," he said. "I just don't want to do it. I'm too—"

The phone rang in Tim's pocket. It was the same contact that had already called multiple times that night. Tim answered it.

"I told you that I needed an update every night on what was going on," the voice hissed. "Now, get your drunk ass together, or I'm going to be noti-fying a little friend of mine over at the bar."

Tim kept his ear to the phone, hoping the voice would say more.

"Crane?" the man said. "Did you hear me, dammit?"

"Who is this?"

The line went dead.

36

Maggie mashed the intercom button at the entrance to the county jail. The late October evening air felt cool on her face. She pulled her light peacoat tight around her body, waiting for a response from inside.

"Another late-night visit with Ms. Acker?" the familiar voice asked through the intercom.

"That's right," Maggie replied, leaning close to the intercom. "I shouldn't be long."

"It just you coming in?"

"It's just me, Elroy."

"Good," he said. "I told the other lawyer he can't come back anymore."

The metal door buzzed, and Maggie pressed against it to enter the jail. Although it was close to midnight, she needed to speak with her client. Tim's findings from earlier that evening had left them with too many questions.

"What's this you said about the other lawyer?" Maggie asked as she entered the intake area. "Are you talking about my co-counsel, Lawton Crane?"

The night manager nodded, a strange look of frustration on his face. "I don't want him back up here visiting with Ms. Acker. I've already told the sheriff about it. He'll be banned from entering the jail from here on out. Unless we pick him up for something here in town."

"Okay. What happened?"

The door to Charlotte's little private cell was ajar. She pushed it open and stepped out into the bright fluorescent lighting.

"I asked Mr. Monroe here to ban him," Charlotte said, a grogginess in her voice. She looked like she'd just woken up. "That's what happened."

"He was coming up here drunk the last few days, Maggie," Elroy added, more concerned than angry. "I can't have that in my jail. He was buzzing the intercom at night and trying to come in here to see Ms. Acker. It wasn't right."

"Why haven't I heard about this?"

"I was going to tell you next time I saw you, Maggie."

Maggie pointed to the open door of the private cell. "Well, I'm here now. Let's go talk."

Maggie leaned against the cell's concrete wall, taking in the scene. The small quarters remained unchanged from her last visit. Although Charlotte was receiving special treatment as an inmate at the county jail, she was still an inmate. Maggie was in her space, though. She'd wait for Charlotte to speak first.

In the silence, Maggie surveyed the few belongings in the room. The small stacks of paperwork. A box of letters. The laptop and binder full of discovery. Her running gear drying on a hanger. The pair of running shoes in a corner.

"I wanted to tell you earlier," Charlotte said in a soft voice. "I just didn't know how."

Maggie stared down at her. Charlotte sat at the edge of her bed, her feet on the ground. She leaned forward with her elbows on her knees, eyes fixed on the jail floor between her sandaled feet. Maggie couldn't ever remember seeing an Acker appear meek. There was something wrong, and she wanted to hear it all.

"I'm going to need you to tell me exactly what's going on, Charlotte. *All of it.*"

Maggie had her in a corner, a position that wasn't necessarily uncomfortable for an Acker. Charlotte nodded in response to the demand, though, slowly starting in on her narrative. "I can't put my finger on exactly when it all started," she said, "but it's been going on for a few months now." She described first their relationship as student and professor. She respected his approach to teaching, and the students in his classes had no doubt that he understood the ins and outs of high-stakes litigation. "He was well prepared for every lecture. The classroom discussions were dynamic, even lively at times. I loved learning from him."

Maggie nodded. She remembered taking courses from talented professors in law school. People that made the profession feel both exciting and honorable at the same time.

"He was the best-looking professor at our school, too," she said with a sad smile. "It added to his intrigue."

Charlotte recounted how her last semester at Georgetown ended with the visit from the senator. "It happened during Lawton's last class of the year," she said, "and I was beyond angry that my professor—especially my favorite professor—would allow such a move."

"Was he part of the plan to bring the senator to class that last day?" Maggie asked. "Did you ever press him on that question?"

"Of course," Charlotte said, looking up at Maggie. "I've been seeing him for months now. I asked him the first night we spent time together away from campus."

"What did he—"

"He swore he didn't know Bill was going to visit until the morning of. I believed him, too."

Charlotte then described how the two ran into each other the last night of final exams. How they stayed and talked at the bar until they closed the place down. She described Lawton as a smart, witty conversationalist. One that cared deeply about his chosen vocation.

"Then he should know that he is violating our code of ethics by engaging in a sexual relationship with a client."

"I thought that there was an exception to the rule if the relationship was already going on," Charlotte replied defensively. "I know that is the case in a lot of states."

Most states prohibit lawyers from being in a sexual relationship with their clients. The prohibition is largely intended to prevent a client from feeling coerced when making decisions in their case. Clients that engage in sexual relationships with their attorney often develop a different kind of trust with their lawyer—the kind that can be easy to manipulate.

"It was dumb, Charlotte. I shouldn't have to tell you that."

She nodded. "It's over, though. I broke it off with him a few days ago."

That might explain the bender, Maggie thought. *It doesn't explain the strange call that Tim picked up on, though.*

"Have you been hooking up with him in here?"

"Not a lot."

"Are you fu—"

"Look, Maggie, you're giving me my lecture. I know it was a stupid, stupid decision. Let's move past it, *please*."

Maggie liked to walk and think. The seven-by-twelve didn't give her a lot of room to pace, though, so she looked up at the ceiling instead. The trial was just around the corner, and they had a spy in their camp.

"We may have bigger problems, Charlotte."

"Bigger problems than me just breaking up with one of my lawyers less than two weeks before trial?"

Maggie nodded. "I'd say so."

"What?" Charlotte asked, pulling her feet up into a crisscross position on her bed. She made space next to her on the thin mattress, patting an open spot for Maggie to sit in.

"Did Lawton ever talk to you about a friend of his by the name of J.D. being involved in any kind of investigation with him?"

Charlotte shook her head. "No, I never really met any of his friends. I wasn't aware of anyone working for him."

"From some messages Tim found in Lawton's phone, it looks like he's been telling J.D. everything about our strategy in your case."

Charlotte thought a moment. "Could it be John Deese?"

Smart girl, Maggie thought. *Maybe she'll be able to give us some more help now.*

"That's what we think."

"And you think he's been feeding updates to him about my defense?"

Maggie nodded. "Daily updates."

"Is this something we can use to get me out of having to go on trial for this murder?"

"I'm not sure about all that," Maggie said after a long moment. "I was thinking more like we use it *when* you go on trial for this murder."

37

The Thursday morning before the week of trial, Judge Balk summoned the lawyers to his chambers for an informal meeting. He wanted to discuss the trial one last time before they all broke camp for the weekend. *State v. Acker* had been specially set, so no other cases would be presented to a jury that following week. Maggie suspected the judge wanted to make sure the defense team hadn't been bluffing when they demanded such a speedy trial of their case. She also suspected that the old judge wanted to give her one last chance to ask for a continuance. A move that would allow her more time to prepare for what they all expected to be a career-defining affair.

Michael Hart sat alone on his side of the table, his two support lawyers off handling routine matters that had to be processed through the district attorney's office. From where Maggie was sitting, she could see the subtle bags under the lead prosecutor's eyes. Like Maggie, he'd probably been burning the midnight oil in preparation for the week ahead. Hart had to present his case first at trial—she knew he'd be prepared.

Maggie and Lawton sat on the other side of the table. Lawton sipped coffee and chatted aimlessly with Hart about the implications of the upcoming election cycle. The DC lawyer looked rested and relaxed. Better than he had in weeks. All the product of his decision to move into the guest room at Tim and Maggie's place. He'd been getting quality sleep, eating healthy food, and staying out of the bottle. In his current state, Maggie caught glimpses of the intelligent trial lawyer that had once been. The one with a large bank account and a stellar reputation in the mid-Atlantic states. That man was gone, though. She knew the truth about him now. He'd violated his oath—no client could ever trust him.

"Good morning, everyone," Judge Balk said as he entered the room. He didn't wait for a response from those seated. "I have a calendar full of domestic matters set to begin in about thirty minutes, so I'll be quick."

Placed on the table for the judge to review were the witness lists from both parties, along with a line-by-line work-up of proposed stipulations. The judge had requested that the parties come to an agreement on as many issues as possible to ensure the trial moved along in an efficient manner. The request was a common one for judges, a breed of lawyer that had conveniently forgotten the pesky little problem of having to represent the client's interests to the fullest.

The judge frowned as he looked at the stipulations. "Is there not more we all can agree to?"

Maggie buzzed in first. "My client doesn't have the burden, Your Honor. We can't just allow every piece of incriminating evidence to walk in without resistance."

"You're the one that decided to forgo the opportunity to examine the State's witnesses and evidence in a pre-trial hearing," the judge said, his brow furrowed. "Is that not so?"

Maggie knew the judge's bark was always worse than his bite. "I don't plan to make frivolous challenges to the evidence at trial, Judge. I just can't take—"

"I'd like that memorialized on the record," Hart said from his seat, an attempt at humor. "Defense counsel has assured us there will be no frivolous attacks on the—"

"Let's not interrupt one another," the judge grumbled. "And there is no record here. Save it all for the courtroom if you must."

Maggie watched the judge as his eyes moved to the list of witnesses. In the past, her tactic was to provide a long list of names to the State. She'd bury a few key witnesses in the bunch, hoping the prosecutors would have to spend precious time chasing their tails.

"I see you have a rather thin witness list, counsel," Judge Balk said as he looked over at Maggie. He waved the single piece of paper over the table. "Just five potential witnesses?"

Maggie nodded as she picked up her copy of the list. "Bill Collins, Pete Baggett, June Moray, Fernando Lazkano, and John Deese. My client, of course, may also testify."

Hart seemed frustrated as he reached across the table to take a copy of the same witness list. He stared at it a moment more, rubbing his chin.

"Is anything wrong, Mr. Hart?" the judge asked, appearing surprised at the prosecutor's reaction. Fewer witnesses from the defense meant more time to prepare the State's case.

"I've been provided only the barest amount of information about three of the witnesses included," Hart said, somewhat pleading. "Moray, Lazkano, and Deese."

Judge Balk turned back to Maggie. "Do you have anything more that is discoverable to provide to the State?"

Maggie paused a moment. She'd learned in her first year as an attorney that there was a clear difference between misrepresentation and gamesmanship. Although the two were related, they dovetailed when it came to the lawyer's frame of mind. Maggie wanted to stay above misrepresenting her intentions to the court, so she did what every lawyer did when they engaged in gamesmanship—she relied on certain technicalities.

"I believe we've provided the basic information about Ms. Moray, Mr. Lazkano, and Mr. Deese. I've been told we are still trying to serve a subpoena on Deese, but we have Lazkano and Moray set to appear near the end of next week."

Judge Balk frowned some more. "None of these people are experts, right?"

Formal disclosures were required when an expert witness planned to be involved in a trial. That wasn't the case with the average lay witness.

"No, Your Honor. They are fact witnesses."

"Right," Hart said, not trying to hide his frustration. "What are they going to say about the *facts* in the case, though?"

"You'll need to call them and ask, Mike."

"Counsel," the judge said with a slight groan. "Give us the brief summary of what you expect they'll say."

As if on cue, Maggie took on the role of technician and pointed to Lawton. He pulled a legal pad from under a folder and flipped a few pages to the information he needed. "Moray and the defendant are friends," he said, his voice near radio quality. "She attended law school with the defendant during the last year. They were in contact with one another around the time of the murder. She is familiar with the defendant's state of mind the night of the murder."

Hart shook his head. "Are there cell phone records that back this call up?"

"There are not," Maggie said without concern. "Not that we have, at least."

Lawton continued. "Lazkano met with the defendant this past summer in the course of the defendant's internship on Capitol Hill. He made threats about the senator and may be an alternate suspect. Lazkano is also a part owner of a local business in Blake County, Borroka S.A."

"The Spanish gun company?" Hart asked.

Maggie nodded.

"Okay, well, do you know if Fernando Lazkano was in the country when this happened?"

"We think so," Maggie added. She nudged Lawton. "Tell him about Deese."

"Wait," Hart said with a hand up. "You're not using plane tickets or something as documentary evidence?"

"Nope. We'll rely on what's going into evidence in your part of the case."

"Shall I move on to Deese?" Lawton asked.

Hart shrugged, confused by the information. "Go ahead."

Lawton flipped to the next page in his legal. "We don't really know much about Deese. He won't return our phone calls. He is a career political operative. It appears he might still be affiliated with Bill Collins's activities."

The prosecutor wrote a note on his own pad.

"Do you know who he is?" Maggie asked, eyeing the prosecutor as he scribbled.

"I know of him," Hart said, choosing not to look up at her as he spoke. "I don't believe he would know me, though."

"Very well," the judge said. "It sounds like the defense is going to have to come together as the trial proceeds along."

The prosecutor looked up from his pad. "Isn't your husband involved as your investigator?"

If Maggie had decided to identify Tim as an expert witness at trial, one qualified in crime scene investigation or police practices, she'd be forced to turn over some of his findings in the investigation of the case. Even if they'd decided not to put anything in writing while Tim investigated the case, she'd still be required to reduce all the relevant and material portions of Tim's expert opinion into a report and provide it to Hart no later than five days prior to trial. By making the decision to not call Tim as a witness at trial, Maggie wasn't required to provide that information to Hart. He was her investigator, so technically, all his opinions were not discoverable—they were attorney work product.

"That's right. Tim is employed as my investigator."

"Excuse me for asking this," Hart said after a moment. "But why aren't you calling him as an expert, Maggie? Don't you need him to offer a competing opinion on the scene?"

"We considered doing that," she said, her words careful as she gamely tiptoed around her strategy. "We're going to rely on what you put into evidence."

Hart stared across the table at her, stuck on this point. "But how? I mean, my investigator's evidence is—"

"I need to wrap this up," Judge Balk said, cutting the prosecutor off. "Is there anything else we need to discuss before Monday?"

"I don't believe so," Maggie said, smiling.

"Mr. Hart? Mr. Crane?"

Both men shook their heads.

"No motions of any kind?"

"None."

The judge nodded. "The jurors will arrive on Monday morning at nine. You're all dismissed."

38

Lawton placed the call as he pulled out of his parking space in front of the Blake County Courthouse. As the dial tone sounded through the speakers of his rental car, the rumbling of tires invaded the interior of the vehicle. The base-model sedan bobbed up and down as it rolled through downtown Blakeston, a collection of a few streets covered in uneven bricks. As he drove, he waved to pedestrians like a local, eying the small shops and offices that ran along both sides of the street. He told himself that he liked it in Blakeston, as much as one could like life in a small town. It wasn't for him, though, there was no sense in pretending. As Lawton turned off the main drag, the call connected.

"Good morning, Professor."

"I hate that you call me that," Lawton said, his clear eyes focused on the road ahead. His mind felt better than it had in months. He reminded himself that it needed to stay that way if he wanted to get out of this mess unscathed. "I'm calling with your update."

"Did you move out of your hotel?"

"Yes," Lawton replied, not surprised by the fact that tabs were being kept on his whereabouts. "I moved in with Maggie and Tim for the rest of my time here in Blake County. It helps us work on the case and—"

"And keeps you off the sauce."

Lawton gritted his teeth. "Do you want your update or not?"

"Let's hear it."

Lawton took in a deep breath. "The trial is still set to move forward on Monday."

"Good. Any idea what the prosecutor has planned?"

"It doesn't sound like it'll be too creative," he replied, trying to be as brief as possible. "Hart doesn't really have to be, though. I expect the evidence will be put on in chronological order. No surprises as far as potential witnesses."

"What about Maggie? What does she have planned?"

"I'm not really all that sure," Lawton said slowly. "She is trying to serve you with a subpoena, though."

For a moment, silence filled the other side of the line. "You don't say?"

"Yep," Lawton said with a laugh. "And I bet she'd rip your ass to pieces if she ever got you on the stand."

"Well, we know there won't be any of that. You're going to be a good little boy and not tell her where I am."

"Honestly," Lawton said, his car reaching the outskirts of Blakeston's city limits, "I haven't decided yet. I might enjoy seeing them drag you into a courtroom."

Lawton knew that his threats would be perceived as nothing more than words. Empty promises that wouldn't be followed by action. They had him in their trap. If he tried to take them down, he'd be sucked under with the wreckage.

"You don't have the balls, *Professor*. If you did, you wouldn't be where you are now."

"I think you forgot that the little conspiracy between you and the senator trumps anything I've ever done."

Lawton waited for a response, but there was no reply. That's how it always was with Deese. Admit nothing. Deny everything. Keep on moving.

"I won't talk to you again until next week," Lawton finally said, wanting to end the conversation. "I'll call you once the jury is picked."

"I'll need to see you before then."

"For what?"

The same silence filled the line again. Lawton knew a response wasn't coming.

"Just send me the information, Deese."

"That's a good boy."

As Lawton ended the call, he beat one fist on the steering wheel, yelling as loud as he could into the otherwise empty interior of the vehicle. He fought back tears as he turned onto a thin gravel road just off the two-lane highway. He needed a place to stop. A place to gather his thoughts. Up ahead, he saw an unassuming wooden sign next to the road. In faded letters, it read: The Sandbar.

"That didn't take too long," Tim said, handing his phone over to Maggie. "At least our guy is reliable, though."

Maggie smiled as she glanced down at the screen. A small dot that represented Lawton's location sat squarely in the parking lot of her favorite dive bar in Blake County. Her co-counsel's real-time location was being provided courtesy of an app that had been added to his cell phone a week earlier. All thanks to a quick decision on Tim's part while the law professor sat slumped in a chair, passed out. The app was a complete invasion of privacy, but it was one that allowed them to track Lawton's location and listen in on his conversations. Lawton was the trojan horse. Now, they just needed him to roll inside the city's gates.

"You think they're planning to meet there?"

"I doubt it."

"They could be," Maggie said, pushing back. "I mean, we know Deese must be somewhere here in the area."

Tim put an arm around her shoulders. "What makes you believe that Deese is even here in Blake County?"

The two sat together in the quiet for a moment, thinking. From their bench that fronted the downtown's main square, they could look out on the Blake County Courthouse. Maggie liked the spot. It allowed her to admire the architecture of the old judicial building. She loved its porticoed entryways, its fundamentally Georgian silhouette. It was her training ground, and future arena. The place where it all began. The place where it all might end.

"He must be here," she said after a moment. "Where else would he be?"

"That little devil probably couldn't stay away if he wanted to."

Maggie smiled. "Little devil?"

"You heard me," Tim said, grinning.

They turned and laughed together. A rarity given the stress of the last few days. They had roughly seventy-two hours before Maggie had to be ready to stand before a whole panel of potential jurors. They needed to stay loose.

"Collins is going to want his people nearby to see the trial through," Maggie said, her eyes back on the courthouse. "Deese is family, and he's as loyal as they come. I can't imagine the senator would trust anyone else with something like this."

"Plus, he's running out of family members *to* trust."

"That's why he made a mistake this time," she said. "He brought in someone from outside the family."

Tim nodded. "Maybe so."

"Let's run the theory again," she said, ready to get back to work. "I need to hear it out loud."

Tim stood from the bench and handed Maggie his cell phone. The investigator liked to talk with his hands as he worked through his thoughts. "Well, we have the Lazkano connection. We know he can open the discussion up about the shell casings and the smoke around Collins. Then, we have Lawton and his—"

Maggie looked down at the cell phone. It vibrated as a notification appeared on the screen. The dot was moving.

"What's up?" Tim said, moving closer to see the screen.

"He's on the move."

Maggie and Tim sat parked on the roadway. Tim had a cell phone to his ear, talking quietly with a deputy on the way. From their position, they could see the gated entryway to an old trail that ran along the back side of

Kelley Hill Plantation. The large swath of private land had been held in a trust for the benefit of generations of Kelleys, now Collinses. Lawton's last known location had been about two hundred yards up the trail.

"I hope he didn't go in there to kill himself," Tim said as he hung up the phone. "Then Charlotte would really be screwed."

"She's screwed already," Maggie said, eyes fixed on the gated trail. "Even if Charlotte gets convicted, I'd still like to get Deese on the stand to rough him up."

"He'll never point the finger at Collins."

"Maybe not," Maggie said, turning back to Tim. "I have to at least try, though."

A deputy from the BCSO pulled up behind them. Another unmarked SUV followed closely behind. Tim adjusted the rearview mirror to see both men as they exited their vehicles, waving them over with his free hand that hung out the window.

"Looks like Charlie decided to come out here and check up on us," Tim murmured as the men approached the vehicle from the rear. "I wouldn't say anything about the app we used to get out here, by the way."

Maggie whispered, "Don't worry, I'll come bond you out."

"It's been a while since I've had to bust a couple hanging out here alone in the woods," the sheriff said as he leaned down to the window of the vehicle. "Especially out here in broad daylight."

"Our therapist told us to spice things up."

"What about your pastor?"

"There's a thought," Maggie said, leaning over to say hello to the sheriff. "We still haven't found the right church, though."

Sheriff Clay laughed and moved on with his business. "What's this you're calling my deputy out here to do, Dawson?"

"I need him to serve someone for us. A witness for the defense next week."

"Name?"

"John Deese. I think he also goes by Prickhead."

"Is this Mr. Prickhead's last known address?"

Tim nodded. "Something like that."

The sheriff shook his head, squinting as he stared over at the old plantation gate that sat closed. He knew, along with everyone else in Blake County, who owned this land. Still, he turned to his deputy and motioned for him to walk over toward the gate to check it out.

Once the deputy was far enough away, the sheriff leaned in close to Tim. "I don't like what's going on here," he said, his voice low. "If any of this isn't above board, I'll have to come see you about it. I don't want to have to put you in the holding area, too."

"We're playing by the rules," Maggie said from the passenger seat. "We just need a little help."

"I'm not trying to—"

"I'll worry about what gets in the courtroom, Sheriff. I just need that subpoena served."

Tim nodded. "I'd take care of it myself if I were one of your deputies."

"The offer still stands."

Maggie leaned over the center console. "What offer?"

"Get out of here," the sheriff said, smiling as he patted the hood of the car. "We'll get our job done."

39

A mentor once told Maggie that she never had to speak in a courtroom until *she* was ready. Judges could demand an answer to their questions. Opposing counsel could offer objections from their position across the aisle. A witness on the stand could even wait expectantly for the next pointed question. That didn't mean Maggie had to oblige, though, at least not immediately. For it was often overlooked that a well-placed pause—or a moment to collect one's thoughts—looked the same to the common observer. Maggie reminded herself of this simple truth each time she prepared for an appearance in front of a jury. The people were the audience that mattered. *They held the power.*

"We the jury," Maggie said, rising from her seat at the defense table. Her words echoed throughout the large, wood-paneled courtroom. Placing a hand on Charlotte's shoulder, she said: "We, the jury, find the defendant Charlotte E. Acker *not guilty.*"

Charlotte placed a hand of her own on top of Maggie's. She squeezed it as she looked out on the mass of faces seated in the courtroom. The local faces sat shoulder to shoulder, numbers pinned on their chests to help with *voir dire*—the jury selection process.

"Does anyone in this room feel that they can't say those words at this moment?" Maggie asked, carefully moving her gaze across the faces in the first few rows. She expected no response from the group, so she pressed on. "Does anyone here this morning look at Charlotte and see anything other than an innocent woman?"

Maggie loved *voir dire*, the initial phase of the jury trial. It was an opportunity to speak with the men and women that would decide the case. Her strategy in *voir dire* was to appear casual, curious. The truth was, though, it was the phase of trial she planned the most for.

"Anyone?"

A single hand raised near the middle of the courtroom. Maggie pointed to it.

"I see a little girl I taught in first grade," a voice said, hidden behind two large men. "I see the—"

"Please stand and identify yourself with your name and juror number," Judge Balk bellowed from his seat on the bench. They'd been over this routine already in the prosecution's portion of jury selection. The judge made no effort to hide his frustration with the need to remind the woman. "That goes for each of you."

As Maggie had been taught in seminars on jury selection, she simply smiled at her potential juror as the judge's rebuke oscillated about the room. She needed to appear in control of the process.

"Martha McNeal," the woman said, barely cresting five feet as she rose to a standing position. "Number thirty-seven." She eyed the judge with a schoolteacher's glare. "*I said*, I see more than an innocent woman. I see the little girl I taught in school. The young woman I cheered for as she excelled and competed. I see more than what we have here today."

"Thank you, ma'am," Maggie said. She noticed a few heads nodding along with the heartfelt response. "What about anyone else?"

"I see Lee's little girl," another man said as he stood from his seat. "Kyle Bannister." He fumbled for the number on his chest, glancing down at it as he spoke. "Number forty-three." He looked back up at Maggie. "I see my high school buddy's face when I see her. And when she competed, like Ms. McNeal said, I could see that same fire he had."

"She isn't his daughter," another woman said, the response barely audible, as it wasn't meant to be heard by the parties.

As could be expected, there were several formal rules that lawyers were required to follow in *voir dire*. The parties were allowed to challenge potential jurors "for cause," or they could exercise peremptory strikes. Once the parties exhausted their challenges, they could whittle down a *venire*—the panel from which the jurors are chosen—into a collection of twelve.

Aside from the formal rules of *voir dire*, there were informal rules that attorneys avoided violating as often as they could. One of the cardinal rules, of the informal variety, was the directive that a lawyer never confronts a potential juror over his or her answers in the selection process. To do so could spell defeat before the trial even began.

"I don't believe I heard that," Maggie said, stepping over the line. She knew not to single out a juror in front of the panel. "You mentioned something after Mr. Bannister's comment."

"I don't think I—"

"Yes, you did," Maggie said, a smile on her face. "And remember, you're under oath."

"Karen Tillman," the woman said as she stood. Her face was red from embarrassment. "Number seventeen."

Maggie nodded, waiting for more.

Potential juror seventeen averted Maggie's eyes as she spoke. "I said that I don't believe Charlotte was Lee's daughter. Not his biological daughter, at least."

Maggie had hoped for some friction. She leaned into it. "So, what do you see when you look at her, Ms. Tillman?"

"I see a young woman that is probably confused," Tillman replied with a shrug. "I think everyone in this room knows that her daddy wasn't Lee Acker. That's probably hard to deal with."

"Do you see a Collins seated next to me?" Maggie asked, her eyes squarely on the woman. "Do you see Lucy Collins's illegitimate grand-daughter?"

The woman looked at those seated around her, hoping for some help. Maggie wanted the potential jurors to see the different layers to Charlotte. She wanted them to think about the blending of the two local families, the implications of accusing someone of murdering their own.

Judge Balk offered a lifeline to the woman. "Ma'am, you're always welcome to answer the questions from the lawyers with a simple, 'I don't know.'"

"I'm honestly not sure," the woman said, grateful for the answer fed to her from the bench. "I don't know."

"You do see something, right?"

The woman nodded. "I guess I just see a murder suspect when I look at her."

Maggie thanked the woman for her candor and took the opportunity to turn to her table. Lawton and Charlotte sat on opposite ends of the table. He had his head down, scribbling notes on his legal pad. She sat up straight in her chair, eyes focused on Maggie. They exchanged another glance before Maggie moved on.

"Who in here has already voted?" Maggie said, raising her own hand to spur participation. She hadn't voted yet, but that was something rather private.

Michael Hart looked over at Maggie with a face meant to communicate his frustration. He'd already made stern objections to the judge about discussing the upcoming election with the potential jurors. The judge had ordered her to limit her questions to general matters about the various contests across the country. She had a plan that might allow her to tiptoe around the judge's instruction, though. She just needed someone to open the door.

"I see Mr. Hart over here doesn't have a hand raised," she added, smiling at her opponent. "I guess he is just a—"

"I've voted," Hart replied quickly. "I just believe that voting is a personal matter."

"Who agrees with Mr. Hart?" Maggie said to the group. She did so before the prosecutor could catch the implications of his statement. "He says that who you vote for should be a personal matter."

"I disagree," a man in the front row barked. "Tremaine Dillon. Number eight." The man stood and leaned on the barrier that divided the gallery from the front of the courtroom. "People shouldn't feel ashamed with who they vote for. We need to all be able to respect our neighbors enough to not get mad about who they voted for. I voted for Bill Collins, and I'm proud of that. I didn't vote for Sheriff Clay, and I'm proud of that, too."

Several heads started murmuring and nodding in the gallery, enough so that it prompted the judge to hammer his gavel. "Let's have order," he grumbled. "Counsel, I'd like to move on from the election talk. I don't see why these people must tell us who they voted for to sit on this jury."

Maggie disagreed, but she hadn't asked who the potential jurors voted for. She didn't need to. As she turned to walk back toward the defense table to collect her list of questions for use in the rest of the session, her eyes were on Charlotte. Her sharp client had already noted the problem jurors. The ones that were brazen enough to make their loyalties known in this setting. That's where they would start with their challenges.

40

At 9:00 a.m. the next morning, Judge Balk assumed the bench at the head of his courtroom. As a superior court judge, he'd presided over almost every serious criminal trial that had taken place in Blake County during the last twenty-one years. He'd watched drug dealers, murderers, rapists, and molesters tell their lies and half-truths from his witness stand. He'd refereed many a competent lawyer as they worked in his rural courtroom, and he'd chastised the inept. He believed, unfortunately, that he'd seen much of what there was to see in the practice of small-town law. He hadn't yet seen a defendant as favored as the one that was about to stand trial, though. For the first time in Judge Balk's career—though he'd never admit it—he was just as enthralled as those spectators in his own courtroom.

"Good morning, everyone," he said as he looked out on the packed gallery. The pews were jammed with locals and the back row lined with members of the media. "We will bring the jury into the courtroom in just a few moments, but I'd like to first address some people that shouldn't be overlooked in all this—the members of the Acker family."

The judge pointed to the front row directly behind the defense table. He saw the surprised faces of the defense team as he did this. Grace Acker sat next to her brother-in-law, Cliff. She mouthed her thanks as she nodded back at him.

"I've watched you raise this young lady that sits before us today," he said. "And while she is on trial for what we all know is a serious crime, that doesn't mean your family isn't a part of this community."

Murmurs could be heard across the courtroom, people reacting to the unprecedented introduction from the judge.

"Regardless of what happens here this week, that won't change."

With that, the judge turned his attention to the remaining members in the gallery. He offered his standard remarks to the members of the media, along with his admonishments to those seeking some level of entertainment that day. He felt a solemness in his words as he wondered how many more trials he would handle from his post.

"Anything else?" the judge asked, checking with the lawyers for both parties.

Each nodded, indicating they were ready to proceed.

"All right," the judge said, turning to his head bailiff. "Let's bring in the jury."

Michael Hart stood from his seat at the prosecution's table and walked to the center of the jury box. He stood calmly in front of the twelve faces. He knew that his straightforward, methodical approach to presenting a case was a luxury of those that prosecuted people on behalf of the State. He had a job to do, though. An honest calling that bestowed on him the responsibility of bringing wrongdoers to the courtroom for their day of judgment. He had no other option but to present his case with a well-refined order of proof. An approach that would push the jurors to understand the elements of the offense and arrive at the right conclusion. The conclusion that produced a verdict form with only one word at the bottom—*Guilty*.

"I've always enjoyed the discussion around right and wrong," Hart said, scanning his small audience. "We *know* what is right, don't we?" Hart nodded his head as he spoke. "And we *know* what is wrong, too."

A few of the jurors nodded in response. Hart knew that the first few minutes of the opening statement were crucial. He needed to hold their attention, get them thinking about what had to be done.

"I like the discussion because I find it interesting to watch others as they tie themselves into knots, trying to justify what they know is wrong. Twisting and contorting their views to convince all that will listen that wrong can somehow be right."

Hart stuck both hands in his pockets. He slumped his shoulders and frowned, walking along the edge of the jury box as if he were struggling with the idea. He stopped at the end of the box closest to the gallery, his back to the jury.

"Someone has to be the voice of reason, though."

Hart let his statement hang in the air before he turned back to the twelve.

"I mean, I understand people make mistakes. I get it. We've all made mistakes, right?"

More heads nodded in the jury box. They were with him.

"But doing something wrong—even if you believe it's for the right reasons—doesn't make it okay." Hart pointed to the floor at his feet. "Especially not in here. Not in this place where matters of justice are handled by the people."

A screen on a large television turned on at the other end of the jury box, drawing the eyes of the jurors to the first slide of the prosecution's presentation.

"Now, at the end of this trial, I'm going to ask you to find Charlotte Acker guilty of murder," Hart said, adding as much theater to his voice as he could muster. He pointed to the first slide on the nearby screen. "First, though, I'm going to show you the evidence. I'm going to tell you what you will hear. I'm going to tell you what you will see."

A photo of the crime scene, shot from a distance, appeared on the screen. A morning haze hung over the bloodied slice of Kelley Hill Plantation.

"Then, after you've seen and heard all of the evidence, I'm going to plead with you to do what is *right*."

After the prosecution's forty-five-minute opening statement, Maggie stood to address the twelve. As she made her way to the same place that the prosecutor stood only moments earlier, she saw annoyance creeping into the faces of some of the jurors. The judge had offered them the opportunity to recess for fifteen minutes. A "stretch break," as he liked to call it. Maggie assured him that she would be brief, though. A promise she intended to make good on.

"You're going to hear a lot from me during this trial," Maggie said with a smile. She stood with her hands clasped at her waist. A proper stance. "And I ask that you listen carefully."

An unfavorable juror in the front row sighed at this.

"I ask this of you all, ladies and gentlemen, because I know the *truth*."

She let the word hang in the air, drifting above them like a balloon running low on helium. Maggie had never invoked the truth in her opening statement. Never.

"The State wants to knock around the concepts of right and wrong." Maggie said this without looking over at Hart's table. "But what about the truth?"

Criminal defense lawyers lived by one rule. It was the proof that mattered—not the truth. Charlotte's case had flipped the rule on its ear, though. The State's proof was there—it just wasn't the truth.

"What is a defense lawyer, anyway?" Maggie said, her hand on her chin. Her gaze drifted over to her co-counsel, Lawton. She locked eyes with him, then invited him to stand. He obliged, standing awkwardly in a moment that he'd obviously not prepared for. She watched as the twelve pairs of eyes moved back and forth between the two defense attorneys. "*I* stand in defense of Charlotte, in defense of the truth."

Lawton slowly returned to his seat when Maggie started listing off the names of the State's witnesses. She knew them all by memory. After each name, she used the same phrase: *Do they know the truth?* The repetition in her presentation seemed to beat on everyone in the room. Maggie wanted them to hear the word. She needed them to want the truth.

"Charlotte," Maggie said, pointing over to her client. They'd selected a smart, knee-high skirt and a neutral blazer for her first day of trial. "Can you stand up, please?"

Maggie then pointed in the direction of the prosecution. Her voice was clear, forceful. The presentation was as much for her client as it was for the jury. "They don't know the truth."

One juror, an older woman that sat in the back row of the box, nodded along as Maggie spoke. The connection between lawyer and client was not lost on her. Maggie held the juror's eyes for a moment, then pointed back to Charlotte.

"*She* knows the truth."

41

The State came out of the gate strong with its first witness. Hart dove right into the story with the testimony of the first deputy that arrived on scene. The young lawman took the witness stand in his standard uniform. As he leaned into the microphone, he readjusted his armored vest that was tucked snugly under his shirt.

"Deputy Kelvin Ramirez. I'm employed by the Blake County Sheriff's Office."

In Ramirez, the prosecution had an intense, fresh-faced deputy that had arrived at the crime scene within minutes of the 911 call.

"What did you see when you arrived at the home of Lucy Collins?"

With Hart's careful direction, Ramirez walked the jury through his first moments on scene. He explained to the twelve that at the time of the murder, he'd only been with the BCSO for a few months. Responding to the scene at Kelley Hill Plantation was his first experience attending to a victim at a real-life murder scene.

"I won't ever forget that day," Ramirez said, an earnest expression plastered on his face. "As soon as I pulled up, the housekeeper came running to me, crying hysterically. She took me straight to the body."

Hart handed the deputy a grisly photograph of Lucy Collins on the ground outside her home. Maggie stood and started in on an objection to the photograph being offered. Under the rules of evidence, she could object to photographs at the crime scene for various reasons. Her main argument centered on the goriness of the photos and the risk of unfair prejudice if admitted into evidence.

"The photographs from the scene, Your Honor, they elicit a strong emotion and might confuse the issues in this—"

Judge Balk overruled the objection without further discussion. "Proceed, Mr. Hart."

The first photo of the victim appeared on the large courtroom monitor. The photos looked worse in high-def, blown up in a circus-like manner that made a few of the jurors shut their eyes.

"Was the victim conscious when you arrived?"

Ramirez shook his head, pointing to the bloody photograph. "When I arrived, Mrs. Collins looked almost exactly like what you see on the screen. I checked her pulse and got nothing."

Maggie ignored the deputy as he testified. She watched the faces of the jurors instead. They were locked in and hanging on every word.

"Does the defense have any questions for the witness?" Judge Balk asked once the prosecutor finished his direct examination.

Maggie heard the question from the judge, but she kept her eyes on the jury box. When no response was given to the question from the bench, the twelve turned their attention to the defense. She took a deep breath, thinking about whether there were any points to be earned on cross-examination.

"Counsel," the judge said after another moment. "Any questions for this witness?"

Maggie stood. "Yes, Your Honor."

She grabbed her legal pad from the table and walked past the lectern. She walked to within four or five feet of the deputy. Ramirez leaned back in his chair, distancing himself slightly from his interrogator. Maggie hoped the jurors noticed the young bull's reaction to her stepping into his space.

"Did you see anyone running through the woods as you drove onto the property of Kelley Hill Plantation?"

"No, ma'am. I saw a few good-looking deer, but no one out running."

"No one out for a jog?"

"No, ma'am. There aren't very many houses in that part of the county. No sidewalks for people to run on, either."

Maggie smiled. "And a good-looking runner out jogging along the side of the road is something you would notice, right?"

"Well," Ramirez said, a slight redness entering his face. "I'm just saying that—well, you know how—"

"Especially one that looked like my client?"

"Yes," Ramirez sputtered. "I mean, not that—"

"I think we know what you mean," Maggie said, winking over toward the jury as they laughed at the rookie's expense. "And you told Mr. Hart earlier that the State's Exhibit 1—this awful photo of Mrs. Collins—is almost exactly how she looked when you arrived?"

Ramirez nodded, not thinking before he reacted. "Yes, ma'am."

Maggie pointed to the photo. "Is this dried blood here on the clay beneath her body?"

The deputy leaned closer to the picture, as did the jurors.

"I think so."

"You think so? Weren't you there?"

"Yes, ma'am, but I didn't touch the blood. I didn't touch anything but the victim's neck and left wrist."

"What about the victim's coloring? Is this how she looked when you arrived?"

The deputy and jury repeated their closer examination of the gory photo.

"I'm not sure, ma'am."

"Didn't you just tell Mr. Hart all about how this was your first response to a murder scene, and you'd never forget it for the rest of your life?"

"I meant the whole incident in general, ma'am. It was a bad scene out there."

"It's just a few of the small details you're unsure on?"

"Well—"

"Like the blood?"

He nodded. "Right."

"And the victim's appearance?"

"Yes, ma'am."

"But you're damn sure you didn't see a pretty girl running through the woods, right?"

The jury chuckled again as the judge scolded Maggie for the use of language. The deputy didn't answer, but she had what she needed as she turned to walk back toward the defense table.

"No further questions."

The defense ate lunch together in the courthouse's law library. A BCSO deputy stood by the door, keeping watch on the hallway. He appeared more concerned with keeping people out of the library than keeping Charlotte in it. Still, they sat around the table chewing on their sandwiches from the downtown deli and discussing the afternoon ahead in court.

"I think we need to keep discussing this strategy on the back half of the case," Lawton said as he popped a bag of chips. "Maggie had a good run at that first witness this morning. There might be more points to get there."

"Are you saying we need to rethink the strategy?" Tim asked. "What part of it?"

"I don't know," Lawton said with a shrug. "I feel like the whole conspiracy angle is going to confuse the jury. It might even turn them against us."

"No way," Maggie said, shaking her head. "We were able to get John Deese served by a stroke of luck. He's the key to that theory. I'm not releasing anyone under subpoena."

"Pretty wild that deputy just happened to come across Deese the other day," Tim said, leaning back in his chair. "Seems like fate to me."

"I just don't like the theory," Lawton said, turning to Charlotte to work on her. "We're running the risk of putting on some bogus defense theory that the jury rejects outright. They might hammer you for thinking they're stupid."

Charlotte didn't offer a response. She just shook her head and continued reading through the reports put together by the crime scene technicians that would testify that afternoon. They only had thirty minutes until the court session resumed. She was focused on the task ahead.

"I'm going to run an errand," Lawton said after another couple of minutes of the silent treatment. "Does anyone need anything?"

"Come back with your head on straight," Maggie replied, not looking up from a report of her own. "I need your help out there."

Lawton walked out the door.

By the end of the first day of trial, the State was moving well ahead of schedule. Many appeared surprised—including Michael Hart—as the defense offered almost no resistance to the large amount of incriminating evidence that poured into the record that afternoon. One witness after another testified about the evidence collected from the crime scene. The State entered their findings as to the fingerprints, footprints, strands of hair, and other unusual debris found at the scene. Maggie offered an objection when a witnesses ventured into territory outside their expertise, but she didn't challenge the results from the tests themselves. They all pointed to Charlotte.

"Is there anything else the parties need to address before we adjourn for the day?" the judge asked once the jury exited the courtroom.

Maggie looked over at Hart. He was conferring with his sidekicks before responding. "Judge, we're going to have to move a few things forward on our end. I expected the witnesses from this afternoon to take at least two full days to get through."

The judge watched as several people in the courtroom started to make their way toward the exit. They'd attended for the thrill of the trial. Not the housekeeping discussion between lawyers.

"When do you expect the State to conclude its case?"

"At this rate, Your Honor, it may be at the end of the day tomorrow."

Judge Balk nodded, pleased by the news.

"Barring any delays, will the defense be prepared to move forward Thursday with its evidence?"

"We'll be ready, Your Honor."

42

Kevin Bond took the witness stand in a slightly oversized navy-blue suit. His face was clean-shaven, haircut high and tight. On the lapel of his suit, he'd pinned a small American flag. It glinted from time to time as it caught one of the beams of morning light that cut in from the high windows in the courtroom. His lips curled as he offered a phony smile to the twelve seated in the box. A few nodded, absorbing the lawman's unusual gaze.

"Good morning, Investigator Bond," Hart said as he made his way to the lectern. Although most of the State's exhibits were available in digital format, the prosecutor still carried with him a large binder. He dropped it onto the wooden surface of the lectern with a thud. The sound from the weight of the evidence startled those seated in the courtroom. "Although most of these fine people probably already know you, go ahead and introduce yourself to the jury."

Kevin Bond turned back to the box, introducing himself with the same curled-lip smile and phony affect. At forty-seven, the investigator had almost twenty-five years of experience in law enforcement. There was no question that he was one of the most experienced investigators in the employ of the BCSO. Over the years, under the regimes of several different sheriffs, Bond had worked as the lead on about every kind of criminal investigation that might happen in a small town. He'd trained young deputies just joining the profession and cooperated with those at the highest levels of statewide law enforcement, working hard with task forces meant to address large drug conspiracies, multilayered theft rings, and human trafficking. He was experienced, and that experience was at the core of his campaign for sheriff.

"Now, you're currently on leave from your duties with the BCSO?" Hart asked.

Bond nodded. "That's right. When someone is running for sheriff, it's common to go on some temporary leave from the office, since you're working for the person you're running against and all."

As Maggie left her house for the courthouse that morning, she noticed a *Blake County Needs Bond!* sign sticking in her next-door neighbor's yard. Countless others littered the sides of the roads and highways around the county. The largest sign she'd seen for Bond's campaign was a double billboard out on the bypass. In red, white, and blue letters, it read: *Experience Matters, Vote Sheriff Clay Out!*

"Now, when did you go on leave?"

"About a month after this happened. Right at the end of the summer."

"By *this*, you mean the murder of Lucy Kelley Collins."

The investigator looked over at the defense table for a moment, then responded to the prosecutor. "Yes, sir, and the investigation into Charlotte Acker."

Hart cracked open the thick binder at his lectern and started reviewing the chronology of Bond's investigation. Prosecutors were afflicted by the impulse to continually reiterate the timeline of the alleged crime. After only one day of trial, the jurors had already heard almost the entire chronology three separate times.

Maggie stood and offered a smile to the judge. "We'd stipulate as to the order of arrival for the various BCSO personnel that appeared on scene, Your Honor. Also, the manner in which the evidence was collected. We heard that testimony yesterday afternoon."

Hart turned at the mention of the stipulation. His face reported his surprise for a moment. The judge also seemed to consider the statement before he responded.

"Let's see the lawyers at the bench," the judge said, staring at Maggie.

He pressed a button by his microphone, engaging a set of speakers in the
area around the jury box. A distorted white noise filled the courtroom as
the parties made their way to the bench.

"Yes, sir?" Maggie asked, arriving first at the space just in front of the
judge's elevated desk. "Is there a problem?"

Bench conferences were common during a jury trial. They involved the
lawyers huddling around the judge, speaking to one another in low voices
that were meant to go unheard by the jury. Oftentimes, though, bench
conferences were the moments during a trial when the jurors watched the
lawyers the closest.

"This is the State's lead witness," the judge said, stating the obvious.
"Isn't there some concern that you're being ineffective by stipulating to a
large part of his testimony?"

Lawton stood over her right shoulder, relegated to the second layer of
lawyers participating in the conference. She could smell the sharp odor of
wintergreen mints, but the breath freshener couldn't completely conceal
the smell of booze on his breath. "I think we could probably ask a few questions about those matters for the sake of the record, Your Honor."

"No," Maggie said, mindful of her facial expression. The twelve seated
nearby would make assumptions about the winners and losers of the
bench conference based on the body language of the parties. "This
evidence is in, Your Honor. This witness doesn't add anything new for the
jury to weigh in their determination of this case."

Hart shrugged. "I'm a little confused, Your Honor, but if the defense
wants to stipulate to these matters, I'm not going to argue with them."

"I can't believe I'm saying this," the judge whispered, mainly in the
direction of Maggie. "But this is a murder case, counsel. Your client is facing
life in prison, without parole. There are certain things I would expect to see
in an effective defense."

Maggie smiled, hoping the jury might see. "Of course, Judge."

Maggie pointed a remote at the large screen in the courtroom. She tested
the laser pointer on the remote as she waited for the monitor to boot up.

Tim sat at the defense table with a laptop at the ready. He'd control the slides on the screen as she worked through her questions with the investigator.

"How's the campaign going?" Maggie asked as she waited on the courtroom technology.

"It's going well," he replied. "I hope that everybody gets out to—"

The judge interjected. "Let's not get into anything on the election for sheriff."

Maggie only smiled.

"It's ready," Tim said from across the way. "Exhibit 4 should be up."

Maggie pressed a button on the remote, bringing a large photograph into view. The picture was an overhead shot of a well-defined shoe impression.

"Investigator Bond, can you tell me what you see in this photo?"

"It's one of the footwear impressions that we found near the victim's body."

Maggie nodded. "I believe you testified earlier that the outsole designs on Ms. Acker's running shoes appeared to match this impression?"

"That's right," Bond said. "When the conditions are right, footprints can sometimes be found at our wooded crime scenes. We believe this image on the screen is an impression left by the defendant while committing this crime."

"Would you agree that the quality of shoe impressions can vary greatly from one scene to another?"

"Yes, ma'am," Bond said. "They usually vary quite a bit at specific crime scenes, too. It depends on a lot of factors."

Usually, Maggie pressed an investigator on their "factors" and use of investigative terms during a cross-examination. She wanted this investigator to remain credible, though.

"And you've investigated a lot of crime scenes?"

"Correct."

"Seen a lot of evidence like this?"

He nodded. "I've handled quite a few cases where we collected evidence around a defendant's footwear."

Maggie stared over at the screen. It was a perfect imprint of Charlotte's running shoe. You could even make out the logo from the manufacturer.

"This one is a really clean impression, right?" Maggie smiled as she said this.

He responded with a smile of his own, confused by the back-and-forth. "Honestly, it's probably one of the best I've ever found."

"Yeah, it is," Maggie added. "I've not been involved in criminal work for as long as you have, but I've not seen another investigator bring in something like this."

Bond seemed to appreciate the unexpected praise, so he rewarded her with a detailed explanation around the difficulties of collecting evidence like the footwear impressions in the photograph. Partials were common, but the analysis was so time-consuming and difficult that they usually abandoned use of the impressions.

"Let's look at the strands of hair you found at the scene."

"Okay," the investigator replied. He'd located multiple strands of the defendant's hair on the victim's body. "We found five strands of hair that were a match for the defendant."

"And where were they, Investigator Bond?"

"On the victim."

"Right," Maggie said with a smile. "But where, exactly?"

They both looked at the large screen. It showed one of the many gruesome photographs of Lucy Collins. Maggie handed the investigator the remote, inviting him to use the laser pointer in conjunction with his testimony.

"Each of the strands were collected from the victim's right shoulder area." Bond circled the area with the small red dot. "A few were under the collar of the victim's blouse. Here, I believe."

"What about the other two?"

He moved the dot over a few inches on the screen. "The other two were located near the upper right arm."

Maggie thanked him and took the remote back.

"So, is your theory that there was a struggle between Ms. Acker and Mrs. Collins? A confrontation?"

"No, ma'am. Based on the grouping of the bullet casings found at the scene, we believe it was probably an ambush."

Maggie pointed the red dot on the victim's hands. "No hair was found in between her fingers, right?"

"No."

"Nothing got hung up on the buttons on the victim's shirt, right?"

"We didn't find any."

"The hair was just lying on top of Mrs. Collins's shoulder?"

"And tucked under the collar of the blouse."

Maggie turned and walked along the edge of the jury box. She wanted the response to hang in the air for another few seconds.

"In all your years as an investigator," Maggie said, propping up the adverse witness. "Have you seen strands of hair just conveniently lying on a victim's body?" She knew he would say that he had, but she wanted the jury to see him explain his answer. "Not caught on anything or stuck to any substance, I'll add."

Hart stood and objected the question. A reaction that was even better than a bad answer from the candidate for sheriff.

"Sustained," Judge Balk grumbled. "Move along."

"Can we take a short break, Your Honor?"

The judge liked to be the one to propose the breaks, but she knew it was close to stretch time for the old jurist.

"Very well, let's recess for fifteen minutes."

Maggie could smell the cigarette smoke on the investigator as she neared the witness stand. As she handed over a bag that was already in evidence, she thought of Sheriff Charlie Clay. The health nut probably made his smokers take their puff breaks on the other side of town. She assumed it was just one of the long-time investigator's many reasons for going after Clay's job.

"You mentioned the grouping of the bullet casings earlier?"

He nodded. "Yes, ma'am. They were all found close to one another."

"Why is that important with your ambush theory?"

Bond coughed into a hand. "Well, for one, they weren't in a line moving away from the victim. If there is an altercation and gunfire is exchanged, usually you'll see a line of casings moving away from the victim, indicating retreat."

"So, your theory is that Ms. Acker ran over from her home and ambushed Mrs. Collins outside the main house on Kelley Hill Plantation?"

"Yes, ma'am."

Maggie pointed to the evidence bag. "Those are the casings you found at the scene?"

"Uh-huh."

"Can you explain to the jury what those are?" Maggie asked, a question more commonly asked by a prosecutor tossing softballs.

Bond smiled as he looked over at the twelve. They were South Georgia people just like him. He knew they weren't felons because they were serving on a jury, so they probably each had a gun somewhere at home.

"The casing of a cartridge is basically the container that holds the primer, the gunpowder, and the bullet."

"And these would be fired from what kind of firearm?"

"A nine millimeter," he said, his answers growing shorter.

Maggie smiled at the witness. She recognized the look of a witness that had just realized they were swimming in a shark tank. "Now, you didn't locate a firearm in this investigation?"

"Well," he said slowly. "That wasn't because we weren't looking. We believe the defendant probably disposed of it."

"That's one guess."

"We searched the woods, drug the river, inventoried her family's home."

"Which home?"

He started to rattle off the Ackers' address. "I believe it is 8580 Feather—"

"We know you searched Ms. Acker's home and didn't find anything. Did you inventory the home of the victim?"

Bond shook his head. "No, ma'am. The interviews we conducted all suggested Ms. Acker didn't have access to the victim's home."

"Right, but other people did. People you interviewed during your investigation."

"Okay," the investigator said, slowly looking over at Hart.

The prosecutor stood and objected, based on relevance. A lame objection meant as more of a grievance to the courtroom's umpire.

"I'll move along," Maggie said, stepping closer to the witness stand to pick up the evidence bag. "Now, you found Ms. Acker's fingerprints on these casings?"

"On two of them."

Maggie jostled the evidence bag as she walked along the rail of the jury box. The metal clinked together as the casings bounced about. She knew every juror had their eyes on her.

"Wouldn't you agree that this fingerprint discovery was rather unusual, Investigator Bond?"

She had her back to the witness, but she sensed he was treading water. She'd wait for his response as long as she had to.

"Maybe a little bit," he finally said. "It's not unheard of, though."

She turned with an eyebrow raised. "Latent prints on a spent shell casing?"

"I'd say that—"

"How many times have you seen it?"

Hart stood and objected, based on a weak complaint around relevance, again.

"I'll allow it," the judge said. "Overruled."

"Can you repeat the question?"

"Sure," she said, glancing over at the jury to make sure they were with her. "How many times have you seen latent prints on a spent casing in your career as an investigator?"

"I've never seen it."

"And these fingerprints," Maggie said in a loud voice. She raised the evidence bag above her head. "These are about perfect, right?"

"I don't know if 'perfect' is the word I'd use to—"

"Then what would you use?"

"They are usable," he replied. "Very usable."

Maggie placed the bag back on the witness stand. She squared up to the witness, arms crossed.

"Your theory is, then, that Ms. Acker ran over to Kelley Hill Plantation—

a distance of about six miles as the crow flies—with a 9mm tucked in her running shorts, and when she got there, she ambushed Mrs. Collins in her front yard."

"That's right," Bond replied, his arms crossed now.

"Then, after she shoots Mrs. Collins, she picks up a couple of the spent casings with her bare fingers?"

"That would be one way—"

"She sets the casings back down and drops a few perfect strands of hair on the body."

"It's not that she—"

"Then she runs off with the gun to go hide it somewhere!"

Hart stood. "Objection, Your Honor. Counsel is testifying and—"

"Sustained."

Maggie didn't respond as she walked back toward the defense table. She was about to sit when Charlotte leaned over and whispered in her ear.

"Investigator Bond," Maggie said, her voice still clear for everyone to hear. "Did you ever, at any point, consider looking at another suspect?"

"There wasn't any reason to, ma'am."

"Did you ever consider the possibility that Ms. Acker was framed?"

43

Maggie arrived home after dark. She found Tim's car in the driveway. Lawton's on the street. She cut the engine and sat for a moment, listening to the sound of the radio as it played an alt-favorite of hers from the early aughts. She nodded along as she remembered the lyrics, words that were so poignant at that time in her life. Music had the power to trigger strong memories. Ones that had long since been forgotten. She listened to the fading sounds of her high school days, humming along until she stepped out of the vehicle. She heard laughter from inside the house as she started toward the brick steps of their front porch. The plan was in effect.

"Hey, Mags!" Tim yelled from the direction of the living room. "I was thinking that might be you!"

His voice was loud in an effort to overpower the music playing from the kitchen. He winked at her as he came over to give her a hug. She looked toward the noise from the kitchen. The sound of reggae, pots and pans clanging together, a faucet running. Lawton's head appeared in the doorway.

"Lawton's making us dinner," Tim exclaimed before leaning in for a kiss. She tasted the whiskey on his lips and scrunched her nose. "He claims his chicken marsala is unrivaled."

She pulled her heels off and tossed them by the door. "Is that so, Lawton?" Maggie asked, offering a smile to the DC lawyer. "Unrivaled?"

He had a beer tucked between his index and middle fingers, an aw-shucks grin on his face. "I thought it might be a nice celebration for us all. Since we just finished up half of the trial."

She chuckled at Lawton's use of the word "we" as he disappeared into the kitchen, soon returning with a glass of red wine.

"This is the Cab you mentioned last month," he said. "Had it shipped in from Oregon."

"Nice," she replied. "Thanks, Lawt-man."

"I love it!" he yelled, clearly feeling it that evening. "You two sit, relax. Let the Lawt-man do his thing in the kitchen. We'll eat in about twenty."

The music in the kitchen changed from a Bob Marley hit to an old jam-track, something released by Dave Matthews in the nineties. The crack of a beer top punctuated the brief transition between songs.

"So?" Maggie said, nudging in close to her husband on the couch. "Are we going to have the talk with our chef in there?"

Tim laughed as he reached for another sip from his glass. "I'm doing my part to stay in character."

"I'll still need you for court in the morning, big guy."

"Don't worry, Mags. I'll drag my ass in there."

"Good, because I—"

Tim snapped his fingers as he leaned forward on the couch. "That reminds me," he said, suddenly excited. "I need you to take a look at something." He stood from the couch and went over to pick up his laptop on the other side of the room. Flipping it open with one hand, he balanced it in the other as he walked back toward the couch. "I went through that discovery that Jack Husto sent over."

Maggie's brain was fried from the day in court, and she hadn't thought about Husto since their conversation the week before. She wasn't sure she'd be able to absorb any more information, so she just sipped her wine, listening.

"The supplemental responses that BTF Freight—the trucking company —sent over for the Jones case. You sent me an email last week and told me to go through it."

"That doesn't sound like me," she said with a smile, leaning over to look at the screen. "I don't think I would *tell*—"

"Yeah, yeah," he said, pushing the laptop closer to her. "Check out these receipts they provided us."

Lawton popped back through the doorway of the kitchen. "How about an aperitif?"

"I'm good," Maggie said, scrolling through the PDF on the screen. She patted Tim's knee with her free hand. "I bet Tim would like to join you, though."

Tim squeezed her leg as he stood to head in the direction of the kitchen. She listened as Lawton started to describe the specifics of his recipe for a boozy Italian aperitif. On the screen in front of her were all the shipping receipts for the items in Jimmy Benson's truck the day he ran into the Joneses' vehicle. She scrolled through it until she found the batch of paperwork that appeared to correspond to Borroka S.A.—the Spanish weapons manufacturer.

Sifting through the orders, she skipped over the names of different types of metals that she assumed would be used in their manufacturing process. Every document produced in the discovery included the item being shipped, the name of the sender, the party receiving the shipment, and the name of the person that placed the order. All items destined for Borroka S.A. had been ordered by the same individual, A. Baez. All except for one shipment of rare ammunition. Maggie stared at the document on the screen. *Product description—1 Case (250 x 320) 9MM – 115GR – S&B.*

"Hey, Mags!" Tim called from inside the kitchen. "You about ready for dinner?"

She scrolled down to the next page to find the name of the person that placed the order. *Customer contact—J. Deese.*

Charlotte sat alone in her cell, working away on her laptop. After the long day sitting in trial, she felt tight. She'd asked for the opportunity to go for a run that evening, but the sheriff nixed the idea due to the large media presence in town. The decision disappointed her, but she understood his concerns. Every regional network had a story on the developments in *State v. Acker*, and a few of the national outfits had limited coverage of the proceedings. With elections happening all over the country, though, there were more important matters to write about.

Charlotte heard a quiet knock on the metal door to her cell. "Come on in, Mr. Monroe."

The door opened slowly, and she saw the face of the night manager. Charlotte grinned at the old man from her seat on the bed. For a jailer, he'd been beyond courteous, treating her with a level of respect that she felt she didn't deserve.

"There's a call for you out here in the booking area," he said. "You want to take it?"

She looked at the time on her laptop. It was after eleven. "Who is it?"

"It's the senator's office," he said. "A Mr. Dell."

As Charlotte thought for a moment, her email account dinged. She lifted a hand up. "One second, Mr. Monroe."

The email read: *Charlotte, Please see attached shipping receipts. Deese ordered bullets used in murder. Let's get it tomorrow. – Maggie*

"Should I tell Mr. Dell anything?" Elroy asked, still waiting in the doorway.

"Yes, sir," she replied. "Tell him we'll see Bill in court tomorrow."

44

Charlotte sat in the courtroom, alone at the defense table. The lawyers were all in a meeting in chambers, discussing the proceedings ahead. Charlotte turned to look at the two places reserved behind her table. Her mother and Cliff still hadn't arrived. Along the back row, Charlotte noticed more cameras had found their way into the room. She knew that with her team's plan to put Bill on the stand today, there'd be added interest from the national news bureaus. She knew that to accuse a man of being involved in the murder of his own wife was beyond the pale. *What would he say?* she thought. *He will deny it, of course, but how?*

The cloakroom door from beside the judge's bench opened, and the lawyers poured out one by one. Charlotte noticed that Maggie and Hart both wore strained expressions. There'd been an argument of some kind in chambers.

"What's going on?" Charlotte asked as Maggie arrived at the table. "Everything okay?"

"We'll see," she said, speaking in a low voice. She looked over at Hart for a moment, watching him as he readied his table for battle. She turned back to Charlotte. "There have been some developments."

"Okay."

"The State is going to rest, so we're going to be up." Maggie sighed. "There's a problem, though."

Charlotte took a quick stab at a guess. "Deese is on the run, isn't he?"

Maggie nodded. "He hasn't officially evaded appearing at trial, but Sheriff Clay went out there to check on him this morning, and Deese was gone. Both numbers we have listed for him are cut off. No one knows where to find him."

"Shit," Charlotte murmured. "I bet Bill can hide him anywhere. At least long enough for this to blow over."

"I told the judge the same thing, but he's not inclined to delay the trial. In fact, he's a little upset with me now."

"It would have been unfair for him to be on our side the whole trial," Charlotte replied with a grim smile. "Is Bill in town to testify?"

"He is," Maggie replied. "But we're missing our link now. Lazkano links us to Deese. Deese gets us to the senator."

Charlotte was silent, thinking as she scanned the courtroom. The deputy assigned to watch her stood nearby, flirting with the clerks. The bailiffs drank coffee and talked football at the corner of the jury box. Chatter from the spectators in the gallery blended behind her in an indecipherable hum. Everything looked to be in order, except for her table.

Maggie placed a hand on her shoulder. "I'm thinking we call the senator first, then Lazkano. After that, you can decide whether to testify."

"I'm testifying, Maggie."

"We need our link in the evidence to make your defense work."

"It's not just a defense," Charlotte said, a little louder than she intended. "It's the truth."

Maggie started to say something but stopped when she saw Tim pushing through the gate. Charlotte considered him as he sat down next to her.

"Looking rough," she said, hoping her comment would ease the tension. "I know you weren't out jogging last night?"

Tim rubbed his eyes. "Yeah, I feel like hell."

"Tim and Lawton had a little heart-to-heart last night, but it didn't go as planned."

"Yeah, that punk denied everything," Tim said, looking around to make sure he wasn't overheard by the DC lawyer. He made a second pass over the courtroom. "Wait, where is Lawton?"

Maggie stopped writing on her legal pad. "He was still at home when I left for the meeting this morning. Didn't he come over with you?"

"No, Mags," Tim replied slowly. "He was gone when I left the house. I figured he was up here with you for the meeting with the judge."

The door behind the bench opened, and Judge Balk strode through it. The deputy sounded the standard introduction as the judge took his seat. Charlotte could tell from the expression on His Honor's face that he'd not calmed down from the morning meeting. He barked his commands to the parties.

"Is the State ready?"

"Yes, Your Honor."

The judge swung his gaze over to the defense. He eyed the empty seat between Charlotte and Tim.

"Is the defense?"

"I believe we are, Your Honor."

He squinted his eyes at the open chair, looking for a fight. "Where is Mr. Crane?"

Maggie took a deep breath in, considering her response.

"Counsel," the judge added sharply. "I asked you a question."

Maggie glanced over her shoulder toward the main door to the courtroom before she stood. She knew the coward wasn't coming back.

"Honestly, Your Honor, I'm not sure."

45

Maggie believed that if her opponent were to be honest, he'd express to Maggie his disappointment with the way in which he was forced to present his case in *State v. Acker*. He was a career prosecutor. A man that relished the opportunity to go head-to-head with talented criminal defense attorneys. Black hats that made the good guys fight to get every single piece of evidence in front of the jury. Maggie knew that those were the kinds of trials that made a prosecutor better. The courtroom brawls that asked a government lawyer to reflect on whether they were a true believer in the system. Maggie hadn't given her opponent that kind of trial, though. She'd allowed him to prove his case, but she cut his legs out from under him in the process. In doing so, Michael Hart left the jury with a case that was compelling—but not memorable.

"We have no other evidence to present at this time," Hart said from his position at the lectern. "The State rests, Your Honor."

"Very well," Judge Balk said, his tone even. He turned to the jury box. "Ladies and gentlemen of the jury, as the State has closed its presentation of evidence, I'm going to have you exit to allow the parties to handle a few matters that will have to take place outside your presence."

The twelve had only been seated for about five minutes, so the news that they would be returning to the jury room was met with some muted disappointment. They'd be forced to engage in awkward conversation with the strangers seated next to them. A task that wasn't difficult for a Southerner in a small town, but it was still one that they'd prefer to engage in on their own time.

"The bailiff will retrieve you from the jury room when we are ready."

With that, the parties stood to watch the jury leave.

With the close of the State's case, Maggie stood to announce the filing of several motions. Criminal defendants can request that the court render a decision at the end of the prosecution's case in chief. Judges are often reluctant to take a case out of the hands of the jury, but there are situations where such a decision is warranted. Maggie had a formal motion in writing prepared, laying out her arguments.

"I have a motion, Your Honor," she said, holding up a packet for the judge to see. "I'd like to file it with the clerk now and argue the points on the record."

"I'm going to deny the motion," Judge Balk said without input from Hart's table. "The State has offered evidence as to each element of the offense of murder."

Maggie figured that with a courtroom full of spectators and journalists, now wasn't the time to test the legal theories in her briefs. She walked over to the clerk and handed over her motions. The judge wouldn't even look down at her as she waited near the bench. Maggie returned to her place at the defense table and waited to be acknowledged again.

"Does the defense intend to present any evidence?"

"Yes, Your Honor."

"Okay," he said. "Would you like a brief recess to get organized?"

"I'd very much appreciate that."

"Anything else that needs to be taken up?"

Hart stood. "Nothing from the State, Your Honor."

Maggie waited to respond until the judge looked in her direction. "How about the defense?"

"There is one other matter," Maggie said, looking over at Tim. He handed her a slim printout. "I'd like the court to consider issuing a bench warrant for a couple of potential witnesses."

"The defense hasn't attempted to call a witness yet."

Maggie nodded slowly. "You're correct, Your Honor. However, we believe that these potential witnesses are quickly fleeing the jurisdiction of the court. In the interest of justice, we'd like to prevent that from occurring."

"The names of the witnesses?"

"The first is John Deese, Your Honor."

The judge nodded. "The second?"

"Lawton Crane."

46

When Fernando Lazkano entered the courtroom, most of the spectators in the gallery turned their heads for a glimpse of the defense's first witness. The Spaniard acknowledged the stares from those seated in the pews with the nod of a gentleman. He appeared unhurried as he confidently pushed through the low gate that divided the gallery from the well of the courtroom. Dark hair, dark features, and standing well above six feet, he looked supremely comfortable in his camel-hair blazer and olive slacks.

"Good morning, Mr. Lazkano," Maggie said as the witness assumed his position on the stand. He sat tall in the chair, shoulders back. "You can pull that microphone closer to your mouth if you need to."

He smiled, nothing more.

"Mr. Lazkano, how do you know Charlotte Acker?"

One of the challenges for a defendant that needs to present a true defense, through evidence of their own, is the fact that much of that defense must come in through the direct examination of witnesses. While the ability to capably employ the technique of cross-examination is considered a measuring stick for trial lawyers, the right approach to the direct examination of witnesses is just as important. The cross-examination phase allows for pointed questions to a witness, often meant to direct the person testifying to a desired answer. The direct examination phase, however, requires the use of open-ended questions, meant to allow the witness to expand on the evidence for the jury. Maggie preferred to cross-examine.

"I met her when she was working with the senator's office."

The answer highlighted a fact that had not been drawn out in the State's case. Several whispers in the gallery could be heard. The early stages of theories that would soon turn into full-fledged gossip.

"Did that meeting occur this summer?"

"During the month of June," Lazkano said. "We met in one of your government's buildings in Washington."

"Well, I'm sure there are quite a few there," Maggie said, offering some comic relief to her twelve jurors. She suspected a few harbored some wayward feelings about the business of Washington. "Was that your only meeting?"

Maggie and Charlotte had discussed this specific question in depth, as it would preview a fact to the jury that was almost never discussed in a criminal trial. The fact that she was being held in jail without bond.

"We met here in Blake County," he said, looking over at Charlotte as he spoke. "I visited her at the jail."

Hart stood and requested another bench conference. The judge lifted a hand and looked over at Maggie.

"Did you mean to elicit this information from the witness?"

She nodded. Though it was information readily available to the public, the fact that her client was being held at the county jail was typically a detail that could result in unfair prejudice, and any reference to it in the courtroom—especially in the presence of the jury—was off-limits without the accused's consent. In Charlotte's case, she wanted the jury to know that their golden girl was serving time for a crime she didn't commit.

Judge Balk nodded. "You may proceed, then."

Hart returned to his seat, frustrated. Maggie ignored him as she moved on. She quickly collected the evidence bag that contained the 9mm casings found at the scene of the murder and walked the bag to the witness stand.

"I'm handing you some cartridge casings that have been admitted into evidence."

Lazkano held the bag in his hand for a moment, then lifted it up above his head to look at the casings in a different light. Maggie took her time, allowing the jury to watch as he evaluated the evidence in the bag.

"Do you know what those are?"

"They are the casings from nine-millimeter cartridges."

"Have you seen them before?"

"Not *these*, specifically," he replied, carefully choosing his words. "This is Czech ammunition, though. It has been bought and sold in Europe for a long time."

"Would your family have purchased it?"

Lazkano turned to the jury and explained to them the brief history of his family's company. He'd grown up around the weapons manufacturing industry, so of course his family had purchased products from the same manufacturer.

"Does your family have a facility here in Blake County?"

"We do," he replied. "My brother and I lead the US operations for the company. That is how I met the victim, Mrs. Lucy Collins."

"And the senator, too?"

Lazkano paused as he appeared to consider the question. "I've never personally met the senator. I spent plenty of time with members of his team."

Maggie took a step closer. "And who would that be?"

"Mr. Deese," Lazkano said. "I've spent lots of time with John. He explained to me that he has worked for the senator for his entire career."

"Who else?"

"Mrs. Collins," he said after another careful pause. "She and the senator were married. She told me that the senator was very much in our corner."

"No one else?"

Lazkano shrugged in a demonstrative way. "Others, yes. I just don't remember their names."

Maggie pointed to the evidence bag that still sat on the witness stand. "Where could someone buy those rounds?"

"These specifically?"

She liked this witness. He wasn't one to bullshit on the generalities of things.

"These are very old," he said, lifting the bag up again to look at the stamps on the jackets. "It would have to be a vintage dealer."

"Would your company have those relationships?"

He smiled like a man that had nothing to hide. "Of course."

Maggie walked over to the defense table. Although Lawton had served as nothing more useful than a potted plant during the trial, his absence made the table look empty, disadvantaged. Charlotte handed her the copies of the shipping receipts. Maggie handed one to Hart as she made her way toward the witness stand.

"Mr. Lazkano, I'm going to show you what I've marked as Exhibit—"

Hart stood. "Your Honor, I've just been provided a document that wasn't made available to my office during discovery."

Maggie carefully placed the document on the edge of the witness stand before the judge looked in her direction. It was placed just close enough for the witness to read it.

"Is that true?" the judge asked.

"It is," she replied, knowing the jury sat right behind her. "This document was provided just recently, though, through discovery in a civil matter."

"Was it available to you before the trial started?"

Maggie considered anew the line that divided gamesmanship and misrepresentation. A gray and oscillating line, in her opinion. Still, to not disclose to the court that the discovery had been sent to her last week would be misrepresenting the facts, even if it resulted in an unfair outcome for her client.

"It was provided to me last week, Your Honor. However, it is material to the case. I'm asking that you take it under advisement."

Judge Balk shook his head. "I'm going to sustain the objection."

Maggie knew that begging wouldn't help her case with the judge, nor would it benefit her in the eyes of the jury. She started to walk back to the defense table.

"Did you have another question?" Lazkano said.

Maggie turned and caught the last glimpse of an unspoken exchange between Charlotte and Fernando.

"Why did you go see Charlotte Acker in jail?"

"To tell her she was being framed by the senator."

"By Bill Collins?"

He nodded as Hart stood to object. Whispers started throughout the gallery.

"That is what I believed," Lazkano said, pushing on before Hart elaborated on his objection. "I don't anymore, though."

Hart returned to his seat, pleased with the answer, one that torpedoed the defense's theory. More whispers and murmurs continued between those seated as spectators in the courtroom.

Lazkano turned to the jury. "It was John Deese, people. It had to be."

Hart sprang to his feet as Judge Balk started to hammer his gavel.

Lazkano picked up the evidence bag. "These casings were ordered by John Deese. Charlotte's lawyer has the proof. I'm telling you it was—"

A deputy was on the witness stand before Lazkano could move. On Judge Balk's orders, they restrained him and hauled him out of the courtroom.

"They know the truth!" Lazkano shouted as the deputies pulled at his arms. "I'm telling you, she's innocent!"

"You'll disregard what that man just said," Judge Balk said, angered by the commotion in his courtroom. "I'll deal with his contempt at the end of the day."

Maggie returned to her spot at the defense table and leaned close to her client. "There's some reasonable doubt for you, kid."

47

Lawton pulled up alongside the Blake County Courthouse. He parked his rental car on a portion of the downtown sidewalk, tossing the keys onto the front seat before slamming the door. His suit jacket was off, tie loose around his collar. As he meandered through the people milling around the front steps of the courthouse, he listened to their casual discussions with one another about the wild incident that had just taken place during the trial.

"They straight up arrested a dude," one guy said, describing the incident in colorful terms. "They slammed cuffs on him and paraded him right out the door. Right in front of everybody!"

"You think she, you know, did it?

"Nah, not if people are willing to get booked for speaking the truth."

The DC lawyer smiled at the sounds of the accents around him as they continued to discuss the trial. In the weeks Lawton had spent living in Blake County, he'd come to enjoy the smooth South Georgia drawl. It would always remind him of this place, of the senator—and especially Charlotte.

Once inside the courthouse, Lawton jogged up the steps to the main courtroom. The tall wooden doors were closed with a deputy standing guard. A hearing of some sort was in progress. As he neared the doors, the deputy lifted a hand.

"It's a closed hearing in there," he said. "Only the lawyers and the defendant are allowed."

Lawton smiled as he straightened the knot on his tie. "I'm one of the lawyers."

"You the Lawton Crane guy?" the deputy asked, offering a grin of his own. "You know they have a bench warrant out for you?"

The news didn't necessarily surprise Lawton. He'd heard stories about small-town judges issuing bench warrants for lawyers that willfully evaded court.

"I better get in there, then."

Maggie didn't hear the courtroom doors open. She was too focused on looking up the caselaw she needed to argue her position to the judge. The parties were engaged in a fiery debate around the issue of a mistrial. The State wanted one. Maggie, for her client's sake, did not.

"A mistrial is warranted," Hart said loudly. He pounded the lectern as he spoke. "I can't have a jury believing what that man said about—"

"Mr. Crane?" the judge said, interrupting the prosecutor's fit. "We've been looking for you."

Maggie turned as the DC lawyer started striding down the center aisle of the courtroom. His clothes were wrinkled, his dark hair unkempt. After one look at him, she decided to stop researching for her argument. Lawton's timing and appearance had sealed the deal.

"Judge, I apologize for being late, *and* for my appearance. I normally look better than I do this afternoon."

"I signed a bench warrant for you this morning," the judge responded tersely. "I've only done that to a lawyer one other time in my career. It's embarrassing to our profession and to our—"

Lawton cocked his head to the side, holding up two fingers as he pushed through the low gate. "I'll take number two, Your Honor."

One of the clerks seated at the foot of the bench started to laugh at the bizarre comment. She quickly covered her mouth.

"We're discussing a mistrial, Mr. Crane. I can assure you that your unorthodox approach to these proceedings hasn't helped your client one bit with her argument that this—"

"Wait!" Lawton said, walking to the lectern. "I'd like to be heard."

He looked over at Maggie, then at Charlotte. Maggie knew he was prepared to make the situation worse.

"I'd like to testify at trial, Your Honor. I've not been completely truthful about my involvement and—"

Judge Balk waved a hand dismissively. "I shouldn't have to remind you that a lawyer can't act as both a witness and advocate in the same matter. A moot point given the fact that I'm inclined to declare a mistrial based on the—"

"Then let me testify with respect to the matter of contempt, Your Honor. Am I not entitled to a hearing?"

The judge considered this as he rubbed his chin. His eyes went to the back of the room as another visitor entered the courtroom. Maggie turned and saw the senator leaning against the back wall, Sheriff Clay on his right.

Judge Balk nodded. "We'll take a short recess, then I'll hear from you, Mr. Crane, on the matter of contempt of court."

When the judge returned to the bench, he found that no one new had joined his courtroom. He scanned the back wall for members of the media. Seeing none, he instructed the deputies at the main entrance to the courtroom to lock the doors. No one would be allowed back into his courtroom until he expressly authorized it.

"Now," he said, looking down at the parties. "I see it appears we have everyone here."

Maggie and Tim sat with Charlotte at the defense table. On the opposite aisle, Michael Hart sat alone. The judge informed both parties that the hearing would be transcribed, but that the transcript would be placed under seal. As he said this, Bill Collins rose from his seat in the front row of the gallery to address the court.

"Judge Balk," the senator said, pushing through the low gate into the well of the courtroom. "I'd like to be heard in this matter as well."

"This hearing will be in connection with a contempt matter, Senator Collins. I'm not opposed to you observing, but I don't believe you'll be able to add anything that is relevant."

Bill nodded. "We'll just have to see, Your Honor."

The judge looked over in the direction of the jury box. Lawton sat with his feet propped up. He had his head back, eyes closed.

"Mr. Crane, let's go ahead and proceed with your hearing."

Lawton walked to the lectern and raised his right hand to be sworn. The judge advised the out-of-state lawyer as to the potential penalties for his offensive conduct to the court. He assured Lawton that he would be allowed to obtain counsel if he so desired.

"I understand my right to have counsel present," Lawton said. "I'd like to move forward with the hearing, though."

"Very well," the judge said. "I'll allow you to offer your own evidence, then I'll permit limited questioning from representatives for both parties involved in this trial. Is that agreeable?"

The parties all nodded their agreement.

"You have the floor, Mr. Crane."

Lawton began in a calm, lawyerly tone. "I want to first say, Your Honor, that I'm sorry for the harm that this testimony is going to cause to our profession. I understand that these proceedings are going to be placed under seal, but I believe people are going to want to hear what I have to say. I've been a lawyer for a little over fifteen years. It has been an honor to practice in courtrooms across this country, and to represent the interests of others."

Judge Balk nodded, listening.

"By all accounts, I've had a successful career. I've made three mistakes, though."

Lawton held his index finger up in the air.

"The first mistake I made was by taking the money."

Lawton shook his head as he walked around the lectern. He pointed that same index finger over in the direction of the senator and held it for a moment.

"I took the damn money," he said. "Money from people that I should have never even been in the same room with. People that traded on the bodies of others. That funded the trafficking of lives."

The senator's face didn't change as he listened to the testimony.

"The second mistake I made was not telling anyone that I'd messed up. Not telling anyone that I'd made the wrong choice. That I'd done a bad thing and wanted to fix it."

Judge Balk chimed in. "Mr. Crane, can we focus on the contempt matter?"

"Yes, Your Honor, I'm getting there."

Lawton held up three fingers.

"The third mistake, though." He shook his head as he looked over at Charlotte. "That might be the worst of them all."

"What did you do, Lawton?" Charlotte asked, standing from her chair.

Lawton stared at her for a long moment.

"Tell me. Tell me the truth."

"I helped them frame you," he replied. He slowly lowered his hand and pointed it in the direction of the senator. "I helped him—"

"I don't believe you."

"He sent John Deese," Lawton stammered. "He sent him over to help me, and in return, I told them I would help frame you."

The senator spoke up now. "Charlotte, I'm telling you that is *not* true. I promise you that I would never do something like that. I've never spoken to this man about anything remotely close to—"

Judge Balk was invested now. "Mr. Crane, what did this Deese person ask of you?"

Lawton shrugged. "He told me to get close to Charlotte. To get to know her. To earn her trust."

"Then what?" Charlotte shouted. "Sleep with me? Lie to me as my attorney? Sit quietly as I went away to prison?"

Judge Balk raised a hand to calm the room down. "Was the senator involved, Mr. Crane?"

"I wasn't involved!" Bill shouted before Crane could answer. The senator slammed a fist on the wooden bar that ran along the front of the courtroom. "I swear it, Judge."

"I never heard it from the senator," Crane said in a low voice. "Deese told me it was on his orders, though."

"A lie is what he told you!" Bill barked.

"How'd you do it?" Charlotte said, ignoring the senator's plea of innocence.

"I sent Deese the hair samples from your apartment," Lawton said. "I helped him get the right pair of running shoes. I—"

"What about the prints?" she asked. She was moving toward him now. "How'd you manage that?"

"The candles," he said quietly. "We played with the candles at your place. I pulled a soft print out of the candle and sent it to Deese."

Judge Balk looked over at the prosecutor. Hart already had a cell phone out.

"I believe this is a good place to stop," Judge Balk said, pointing to the deputy in the courtroom. "I'm sure Mr. Hart here is going to want to interview you, Mr. Crane, along with members of the BCSO."

"What about him?" Lawton shouted as a deputy approached. He turned to look at the senator. "He was involved, too. I just told you that everything was at his direction. Find John Deese. He'll tell you everything that I—"

"Mr. Crane, we're already looking for Mr. Deese," the judge said. "When he is brought into custody, I'm sure Mr. Hart will be able to evaluate what level of involvement you've had in this awful incident. I'm sure he'll ask about Mr. Collins's involvement as well."

"You don't need to ask him!" Crane shouted. "I'm telling you—"

Maggie whispered in the direction of the DC lawyer. "Don't say anything else, Lawton. Not until your lawyer is present."

"I assure you, Your Honor," the senator began. "I've had nothing to do with what this man is accusing me of."

The judge offered a knowing nod.

Maggie stood. "And my client, Your Honor?"

Judge Balk looked over at Michael Hart. "I hope to see a dismissal of this indictment against Ms. Acker filed today."

"That it will, Your Honor. As far as the State is concerned, Charlotte Acker should be free to go."

THE WIREGRASS WITNESS

Who knows what dark secrets hide in the southern wiregrass...

After seven long years in prison, Colt Hudson is finally returning to Blake County, Georgia. But in his hometown, he's treated like just another criminal—with good reason. The scion of a tight-knit southern clan, Colt's family is deeply involved in one of the most dangerous meth operations in Georgia. An organized drug ring that authorities have worked for years to break up.

Colt's early release from prison comes with strings attached—a deal with narcotics squad commander Tim Dawson, who wants information that could help bust the family business. But when the drug agent who put Colt away seven years ago turns up dead, a dangerous conspiracy begins to unravel.

Tenacious lawyer Maggie Reynolds finds herself drawn into the case as she uncovers a shocking cover-up by the Sheriff's office. As she navigates a labyrinth of deceit and corruption, Maggie must fight to uncover the truth...even if it means putting her own life on the line.

Get your copy today at
severnriverbooks.com/series/blake-county-legal-thrillers

ABOUT THE AUTHOR

Joe lives in Thomasville, Georgia. When he is not writing in the early morning hours, he devotes his attention to his family and law practice. The love he has for travel, sports, and the practice of law play a large part in shaping his stories. If the sun is shining, you may find him holding tight to his Triumph's handlebars.

Sign up for Joe Cargile's newsletter at
severnriverbooks.com/authors/joe-cargile

A DECADES-LONG FAMILY FEUD CULMINATES IN
MURDER, AND A SMALL-TOWN LAWYER MUST UNCOVER
THE TRUTH...BEFORE MORE LIVES ARE RUINED.

The national exposure of the Lee Acker case put the trial skills of Maggie
Reynolds on full display. Now she is intent on pursuing more profitable
victories in the courtroom. Leaving behind her work as a criminal defense
lawyer, Maggie is hot on the tail of her highest-profile job yet: a personal
injury case with the potential for an incredible paycheck. Maggie hopes
that a win will give her the recognition—and the bank account—that she
deserves. Even if it means contending with shady lawyers who are willing
to cut corners and backstab anyone for easy money.

But when Blake County native Charlotte Acker is accused of murdering
Lucy Kelley Collins, the wife of a Georgia senator, Maggie is pulled back
into the world of criminal defense...and immersed in a local drama,
generations in the making.
Charlotte's guilt seems undeniable. Her hatred of the victim is
well-known; a product of bitter and longstanding tensions between the
Acker and Collins families. In a case that appears to be open-and-shut,
Maggie must unravel the complicated history between the two families in
order to clear Charlotte's name...all against the ticking clock of a
senatorial election.

Torn between the lucrative payout of a personal injury case and the
satisfaction of a career-defining murder trial, Maggie must reconcile her
ambitions with her calling.

SEVERN RIVER
PUBLISHING

severnriverbooks.com